LEAVING THE STATION

Also by Jake Maia Arlow

How to Excavate a Heart

Leaving the Station

JAKE MAIA ARLOW

STORYTIDE

An Imprint of HarperCollinsPublishers

CONTENT WARNINGS: discussion of religious trauma, internalized transphobia

HarperCollins Children's Books,
a division of HarperCollins Publishers,
195 Broadway, New York, NY 10007

HarperCollins Publishers, Macken House,
39/40 Mayor Street Upper, Dublin 1, D01 C9W8, Ireland

Storytide is an imprint of HarperCollins Publishers.

Leaving the Station
Copyright © 2025 by Jake Maia Arlow
All rights reserved. Manufactured in Harrisonburg, VA, United States of America. No part of this book may be used or reproduced in any manner whatsoever without written permission except in the case of brief quotations embodied in critical articles and reviews. Without limiting the exclusive rights of any author, contributor, or the publisher of this publication, any unauthorized use of this publication to train generative artificial intelligence (AI) technologies is expressly prohibited. HarperCollins also exercises their rights under Article 4(3) of the Digital Single Market Directive 2019/790 and expressly reserves this publication from the text and data mining exception.
harpercollins.com

Library of Congress Cataloging-in-Publication Data
Names: Arlow, Jake Maia, author.
Title: Leaving the station / Jake Maia Arlow.
Description: First edition. | New York : Storytide, 2025. | Audience term: Teenagers | Audience: Ages 14 up. | Audience: Grades 10-12. | Summary: "Zoe takes a cross-country train over the fall break to sort out their falling out with friends, come to terms with their gender identity, and more while making new friends and connections"-- Provided by publisher.
Identifiers: LCCN 2024040719 | ISBN 9780063078772 (hardcover)
Subjects: CYAC: Railroad travel--Fiction. | Gender identity--Fiction. | Lesbians--Fiction. | Friendship--Fiction. | Romance stories. | LCGFT: Queer fiction. | Romance fiction. | Novels.
Classification: LCC PZ7.1.A7475 Le 2025 | DDC [Fic]--dc23
LC record available at https://lccn.loc.gov/2024040719
Typography by Chris Kwon
25 26 27 28 29 LBC 5 4 3 2 1
First Edition

For my uncle Lee,
from whom I get my passion for learning about
religion and who introduced me to the TV show
that made me want to be a writer.
You are deeply missed.

LEAVING THE STATION

One

Monday, 6:45 a.m., just outside Manhattan, New York

"You're going all the way?"

"Excuse me?" I ask the man seated across the aisle from me.

He's burly, with leathery white skin and sport sunglasses resting on the back of his head like some kind of off-brand Guy Fieri.

"To Seattle?" He leans over and points to the ticket on my phone. I pull it away. "You're going all the way out there?"

"Oh. Yeah."

"Ah, a long-hauler." He grins at this, and it's a grotesque thing that makes him look less like Guy and more like Pennywise. "I'm getting off at Chicago."

I laugh, but it comes out forced, the way it always does when an adult man is talking to me and I don't want him to be. I turn and heave my suitcase onto the rack above my seat, hoping this will put an end to the conversation.

"What do you have in there, bricks?" he asks, not getting the message.

"Textbooks," I mutter.

"Same difference."

I rummage through my bag for the book I bought at the Hudson News in Penn Station. The cover is a sepia-toned image of a woman facing backward as she runs through the war-torn streets of 1940s Berlin.

I don't plan on reading it, but having a book in hand on the train is mysterious movie-extra behavior, and that's the energy I'm trying to bring to this cross-country journey.

I'm happy to fade into the background, to not be perceived except vaguely in people's peripheral vision, filling out the scene.

I hold up the book and wave. "See you around."

"You *sure* will."

On that ominous note, I sling my backpack over my shoulder and head to the front of the car, pushing the button that opens the air-lock door to the next one with a satisfying *whoosh*. There are more rows of coach seats with people milling about in the aisles, preparing for a long day on the train.

They whip out playing cards, chess sets, coloring books, crossword puzzles—idle things to occupy their hands. Some people are on their phones, but most aren't. Maybe it's because train travel feels so fancy, so Victorian. No one would bat an eye at a woman in a petticoat.

It's the Monday before Thanksgiving, so the train's completely full, but there isn't the frantic atmosphere of an airport during the holidays. The people on the train aren't trying to get anywhere quickly—they're just trying to get there.

"Excuse me," I say brusquely to a woman who's blocking my path forward, only to see that she's carrying a baby so small that it must've been born on the train.

She gives me a dirty look but lets me pass, and I whisper, "Sorry," no less than ten times.

"Gooood morning. This is your conductor speaking," a voice booms from the loudspeaker. "We are at capacity. If there's no one sitting next to you now, there will be in a stop or two. Your backpack doesn't need its own seat. I repeat, your backpack doesn't need—"

The loudspeaker crackles, and there's a moment of dead air before a second voice comes on, cheerier than the last.

"Helloooooooo, folks, Snack Conductor Edward coming to you live from the café car. Come on down anytime, my lovely train people. We've got coffee, candy, wine, beer, and so much more. Next stop, snacks!"

The loudspeaker cuts out again and the first voice comes back on. "No, actually, the next stop is Croton-Harmon."

The conductor reminds us again that riders will be boarding the train at each stop. After a minute of this, his voice fades into the background and everyone resumes what they were doing: puzzles, sleeping, breastfeeding, etc.

The sun hadn't risen when we left Penn Station, and it's only now cresting the horizon. It's going to be another hazy late-fall morning, cloudy and gray.

I rarely saw this time of day at school. When I did, it was during the first few weeks of the semester, when I could bring myself to care about assignments enough to try to finish them at the last minute.

Being awake at this time on the train is different. Before boarding, I was so anxious that my whole body was shaking—which isn't unusual, though this specific instance may have been caused by chugging a giant train-station iced coffee on an empty stomach—but now that we're on the move, I feel lighter.

Because I made it out.

College hasn't exactly been "great." I would struggle to characterize it as "fine." "Steaming pile of dog shit" is about right, though not entirely accurate, seeing as dog shit can be cleaned up.

No one on the train knows about my first months of college, though. They don't know what I've done.

On the train, I'm not Zoe Tauber, fuckup to end all fuckups.

I'm just a passing nuisance who bumps into infants and makes unpleasant conversation with strangers.

I'm free.

Day Two of College

"Oh my god, he's even creepier in person."

"I thought we didn't *have* a mascot."

"His face makes me want to puke."

Everyone clapped half-heartedly as our school's mascot appeared out of nowhere. He was an ungodly, bearlike creature who looked more like taxidermy that had escaped a natural history museum than a proper mascot.

He stumbled onstage and raised his hands like he was ready to party; no one else was.

I turned to the three people next to me, who I'd been seated with by virtue of our alphabetical adjacency.

"What happened to the costume? I remember the bear from the brochure being . . . cuter. At the very least his eyes were pointing in the same direction."

They all stared at me, and I was worried I'd said the wrong thing until they started laughing.

"You're so right," the person farthest from me said as they extended a hand. "I'm Rex, they/them, undeclared but thinking of majoring in Feminist, Gender, and Sexuality Studies or French."

I held my hand out and we shook, which would've felt overly formal if Rex wasn't wearing a blazer.

The three of them arrived at this event together, laughing and moving with ease as if they'd known each other all their lives. Maybe the hours it had taken me to work up the courage to leave my dorm and come down to today's orientation activities were crucial friendship-making time that I would never get back.

Next to Rex was Autumn ("she/they, Architecture"), and Shelly ("he/him, Fiber Science").

When it was my turn, I didn't know what to say. They all seemed so sure of themselves, and I was not. Nearly all the introductions I'd made since arriving the day before had involved pronouns and majors, and I didn't feel confident in my choice of either.

"Zoe," I told them finally while the haggard bear did a poorly choreographed dance to "Low" by Flo Rida. "She/her. Biology."

They were all satisfied with that answer, so, for the time being, I was too.

The previous day, when my dad had left me on my own in my freshly unpacked dorm, I'd felt almost *too* free.

We'd just left a premed reception, where he was on his worst behavior.

"You should talk to the professors," he'd told me through a mouthful of sharp cheddar. "The other kids will mingle among themselves, and then you'll have a leg up when it comes time for med school recs."

My parents had always had high expectations for me, and those expectations increased tenfold when college was involved.

It wasn't that I didn't want to be premed or go to med school or be a doctor. I wanted those things desperately. Or maybe, more accurately, I *wanted* to want them.

My brain naturally worked in the way someone's needed to in order to be good at science. I didn't have to try all that hard, and for that, I was rewarded with constant positive external validation: high test scores, Science Olympiad trophies, acceptances into my choices of premed programs.

But from the second I'd set foot on Cornell's campus, the forward momentum that had propelled me from competition to competition, test to test, application to application, had vanished.

I'd been planning my grand entrance into college life for a while. The academics didn't matter, but the aesthetics did. Leaving for Cornell meant I'd get a chance to present more masc, to figure out what being a lesbian *meant* to me, when it had previously been put on the back burner.

I was across the country from home; there was anonymity here. But I couldn't bring myself to do it. I was wearing a dress that day—a cute one and a go-to of mine in high school. It didn't even feel wrong; it was stretchy and comfortable, perfectly molded to my body.

So maybe it was fate that I was seated next to these three queer people and not some random premeds with something to prove. It was the universe telling me that I could do what I wanted to do, wear what I wanted to wear. That the plans I had weren't for nothing.

When the mascot finished dancing and the dean finished speaking, everyone funneled out into the lobby for "light refreshments."

"Wanna go to a diner instead?" Rex asked. "I have a car."

I nodded a bit too aggressively.

The four of us piled into Rex's ancient Toyota Corolla and drove across town to a run-down Greek diner. We took videos of each other trying to fit as many fries as possible in our mouths. Autumn won with thirty and insisted she could've kept going if we hadn't made her laugh.

I was amazed and proud of myself for how quickly I had found a group of friends. I imagined a future with them in it: living together post-college, going to each other's weddings in ten years.

I may have been a tad overeager.

MONDAY, 7:15 A.M., APPROACHING CROTON-HARMON, NY

Most people have settled into the ride by now. This leg of the journey runs along the Hudson, whose waters are dully reflecting the cloudy sky. I grab a seat in a booth in the nearly empty café car and turn to face the river, open my book to a random page where the main character is fighting her primal lust for a soldier, and promptly ignore it.

It's the first calm moment I've had since I bought my ticket. Other than walking (which I considered), the train is the slowest way to get back to the West Coast for Thanksgiving break. That's why I chose it.

I'll go all the way across this terrible country, from sea to shining sea, by rail. I could've left from the Syracuse stop, which is much closer to Ithaca, but I figured if I was going to be on the train for days anyway, I might as well be completist about it, so I took the bus down from Cornell in the middle of the night.

The longest train ride I've been on before was from Seattle to Portland, which is just over three hours. All I knew about this route when I booked the ticket was that I couldn't be in Ithaca for one second longer, but I also didn't want to be in Seattle right away. I needed a liminal space to think through the life choices that brought me here.

Now I've bought myself four days of time, which isn't much, but it's enough to try to figure out what I'm going to do once I get home.

The journey will be so slow that I'll barely make it home for Thanksgiving dinner, which is great because then I won't need to fight with my parents about how it's a holiday celebrating genocide or how I'll never live up to their expectations and we can all avoid each other until we descend to the kitchen for cold, greasy leftovers on Friday morning.

Not only that, but the Amtrak website warned that, for the most part, there's very little cell service.

That was what really sealed the deal.

I stare out the window again. That's all there is to do, all that's expected of me.

It's almost pleasant, until my phone lights up on my lap.

I swipe the notification away before I can read who it's from, then turn my phone off for good measure. I don't want to know what anyone is trying to say to me.

What I want is to be an entirely different person, one who made at least one correct choice at some point in the past. But even on the train, I'm still myself. I'm the one person I can never escape.

A small child scoots into the booth across from me. I wave and smile. She stares.

She's long and gangly, though I can tell she's younger than she looks. When I was a little kid people thought I was years older than I was because of my height. It's her face that gives it away, the same way mine did. She has round cheeks that aren't stretched out like the rest of her.

She's silent for a long time, staring. It's unnerving.

Finally, she speaks: "Did you know that former President Richard M. Nixon created Amtrak?"

Two

Monday, 7:30 a.m., Still near Croton-Harmon, NY, Just a Bit Closer than Before

"What?" I ask the long child.

"You know, Richard Nixon?"

I hold up two peace signs and lower my eyebrows, reluctantly remembering the US history class where I learned about him. "This guy?"

"Um, maybe?" she says. "Like, the old president who sucked or whatever." She rolls her eyes and I try not to laugh as she continues. "So, he signed this law, and then the government got to own the railways."

"How old are you?"

She crosses her arms. "Why do people always ask me that?"

"Would it help if I told you how old I am?"

She nods.

"I'm eighteen."

"I'm nine," she says.

"That's half my age."

"Duh."

"I'm Zoe," I tell her.

"That's a good name," she says approvingly. "I'm Aya."

"It's nice to meet you, Aya," I say. "That's a good name too."

"Thanks, it's Japanese," she tells me. "That's where my great-grandparents are from. Did you know that Japan was the first country to have rail lines that were made just for high-speed travel?"

"I didn't."

"It's true! The first-ever bullet train was the Tōkaidō Shinkansen. But 'bullet train' isn't its *official* name; it's just what they call them in English. The old slow trains from before the Shinkansen that went from Tokyo to Osaka took six hours and forty minutes. But guess how long the Shinkansen took?"

I know from previous experience speaking to children that I should highball the number. I don't want to upset this child who has deemed me worthy of her train facts.

"Five hours?" I guess.

"Four!" she says, her face lighting up.

"That's so cool."

She goes on to tell me about how, in 1997, the Shinkansen was only delayed on average eighteen seconds from schedule, when a tall woman walks into the café car with a worried look on her face. The look eases slightly when she spots Aya.

"There you are," she says, smoothing Aya's hair, which is shaped into a classic childhood bowl cut. "What did I say about wandering off?"

"To not do it," Aya mumbles.

"Or at least tell me where you're going." She glances at me, and her eyes are bloodshot. "Sorry about her."

"No no, not at all." Aya has been the first person on this train that I've actually *liked* talking to, and I tell her as much.

Her mom leads her in the opposite direction then, toward the sleeper car, and as the door slides open, Aya turns around and waves to me. I wave back.

Clearly, I'm not the only one trying to avoid my parents.

I ease back into my seat and let my eyes unfocus. In this first hour of the trip, I've had more conversations with strangers than I've had since the first week of college. But maybe this is what's meant to happen on a long train ride. We're going to be sharing this small space for at least a few hours, possibly days. We need to build some train solidarity.

And I don't mind the conversations like I usually would, because the people I've been speaking to don't know anything about who I am off the train. To them, I'm a way to pass the time. They're not my college friends, who I've done a fabulous job of disappointing.

And they're certainly not my parents, who've pushed me my whole life to be the person they want me to be.

It was a constant, from when they had me quit dance in third grade to "focus on my studies," all the way up to the day my dad dropped me off at college.

I did everything right, from kindergarten to senior year, but recently something broke inside me. All I can do is stare at my phone and play Tetris. I don't know what happened, but being alive feels a thousand times harder than it did last year.

I went to college to be a doctor, and now, less than four months later, I have no idea who I am or what I'm going to be.

But my parents are contributing what they can to my college fund so that I can be Dr. Tauber.

They should use that money to buy a condo in Florida or whatever it is old Jews with disappointing children do.

Day Four of College

It was the third time in as many years that I had been forced to learn about the electron transport chain.

I had a hard time figuring out why I needed to know this. I didn't think that doctors gave this much thought to basic biological processes. It couldn't have been relevant to them as they were saving lives or shaving bunions or what have you. Electrons moved, our cells made energy, and none of it mattered.

Once I came to the realization that *nothing* we were learning in Intro Bio would be of any use to me in the future, I stopped paying attention.

It was the second day of class.

The girl next to me bounced her leg under her desk as she carefully transcribed the professor's every word. Instead of listening to the lecture, I studied her leg. When she was anxious, it bounced faster. When she was focused it was slower. Sometimes, it barely bounced at all.

I recorded my observations in the margins of my notebook. I figured I was *doing* science, and that had to count for something.

I didn't have a control group or consistency or government funding, but neither did Darwin.

Or maybe he did. I didn't know.

When the professor dismissed us, I shoved my pen into my backpack and ran out of the classroom. I was going to meet Rex and Autumn and Shelly at Jansen's Dining for dinner.

I felt decently good about my chance of having real friends. We even had a group chat, called "Tees Have More Fun," since all of our last names began with T.

Rex: freaking out . . .
they've got tomato bisque here
Autumn: sending out a news alert rn
Shelly: more like a bisque alert

I smiled down at my phone as I ran out of the classroom.

Zoe: be there in a sec !!!!

Due to an unfortunate asbestos-related incident, my biology lecture was temporarily being held in the student union, nicknamed "the Straight," (after a dead investment banker, not a sexual orientation, which thankfully I googled before asking anyone) so in order to get outside I had to walk through crowds of people ordering large quantities of coffee or handing out flyers for hyper-specific clubs.

The crowds didn't matter too much in the end, though; I never made it to dinner that evening.

Because there, in the lobby, was the most interesting person I'd ever seen.

I know that sounds like a nice way of saying he was unattractive or weird to look at, but that wasn't true at all. This kid was objectively good-looking—even a lesbian could think that about a boy, and I was. Thinking that about him, that is.

And a lesbian.

He was wearing a brown crewneck sweater that matched the color of his hair, which was bouncy and dynamic. He smiled widely at his own jokes in a way that was ridiculously charming, and while he didn't have a dimple, he had a birthmark on his cheek that changed shape when he grinned.

But it was more than his appearance; there was something intangibly magnetic about him.

I should've been on my way to dinner with my new friends, who were bantering about bisque. I really *did* want to go, but I physically couldn't pull myself away from this boy.

He was standing in front of a group of people strewn over chairs and couches, commanding the crowd with the expertise of a televangelist.

"So, Dickens, right?" he said to the group, his hair bouncing with each syllable.

He was doing some sort of presentation, and everyone gathered there was eating it up. I wasn't listening to what he was saying. I watched his hands as he gestured, watched his mouth as he grinned goofily.

I don't know what possessed me to do it, but when he was

done practicing his presentation—for a class, it must've been—I approached the group, squatting next to someone who was sitting at the edge of the crowd on a large worn armchair.

"Who is that?" I asked the Armchair-Person.

"That's Alden," they said. "He lives in my building. He's actually so funny."

"Cool," I said, not taking my eyes off Alden as he sank into the couch in front of the TV to allow someone else to practice their presentation.

I sat there for two hours and learned about everything from nuclear fission to stoicism. When the group dispersed, Alden stood from the couch and stretched.

We were the only two people left, and I wasn't sure if he'd even noticed me. It was too late to go to dinner now—I had about fifty messages asking where I was and if I was okay—but for some reason I couldn't let this boy go. I needed him to know I'd been here the whole time, waiting.

So I twirled my long thick ponytail around my palm and took a deep breath. "Cool presentation," I said, then wished I hadn't.

Cool presentation?

It was a terrible opening line, and he knew it as well as I did.

Not that it *was* an opening line.

When he smiled, it didn't look like he was humoring me. He seemed genuinely happy. "Thanks." He sat back down on the couch, which emitted a cloud of dust. "It's for my Victorian Novel class."

"That sounds tedious," I said, then quickly added, "Sorry, no, it's—"

"I like it." He shrugged, and I was relieved that he'd put an end to my fumbling. "I don't know if I'm for sure going to major in English, but the professor told us we could have class outside when it's nice. What are you studying?"

"Mostly bio."

"Sounds tedious," he said.

I laughed. "I'm Zoe."

"Alden."

I sat on the couch then, with a full cushion between us. As we spoke, he pressed his legs to his chest, and I did the same, his mirror.

He told me more about his first days at school, and I told him about the girl in my bio class. He laughed at that, which felt remarkable.

I'd never experienced this before: talking to someone where it felt like everything I said was interesting and right and true.

It was miraculous.

When I finally checked the time, it was one in the morning.

"Oh my god, it's so late." I turned my phone around so he could see my lock screen.

"Or maybe early?" He stood from the couch. "There's somewhere else that should be open. Well, *open* as in they sometimes forget to lock it. Care to join?"

I nodded. Even then, I knew I would go wherever he asked.

The *somewhere* Alden had mentioned turned out to be the clock tower, the giant obelisk at the center of campus that marked the hours with kitschy songs played on clanging chimes.

"Are we allowed in here?" I whispered as he pulled the doors open and we began our ascent.

"Probably not," he told me. "But we won't get in trouble. I promise."

For some reason, I believed him.

We were both breathing heavily as we climbed the spiral staircase to the top of the tower.

There wasn't much to see at the lookout except for the chain-link fence enclosure, but the strong upstate wind blew in our faces, and the lights of campus shone below. When I turned to Alden, he was smiling, his birthmark hidden in his cheek.

"I used to be afraid of heights."

It wasn't what I thought he'd say.

I stuck my fingers into the empty spaces of the chain-link fence. "What changed?"

He joined me, our bodies pressed against the fence, and our gazes focused only on each other.

"I realized I didn't want to miss out on anything."

"That's a good reason."

And that's when footsteps echoed from below. Alden froze.

"We have to go," he whispered.

"You said we were allowed to be here!" I whisper-yelled back.

He didn't respond, just took my hand and pulled me down the stairs. Somehow, no one caught the two of us sprinting out of the base of the tower, barely able to catch our breaths as we fell into the grass nearby.

For once, my life felt like a scene from a movie. *Alden* made me feel like that.

When I snuck back into my dorm, the sun was rising, and I felt invincible.

"Where were you last night?" Rex asked the morning after my unintentional all-nighter.

I was struggling not to fall asleep into my dining hall pancakes.

"What?" I shook my head, forcing myself to look into Rex's eyes. "Nowhere."

After almost getting busted in the clock tower, I was exhausted, but I also couldn't stop thinking about Alden.

Autumn grinned. "Did you meet someone?"

"Oooooh," Shelly said, leaning forward. "I bet she did."

"So," Autumn said. "Who is she?"

I had told them I was a lesbian when we all went to the diner. It had felt nice to come right out and say it. I hadn't told anyone in high school, not because I couldn't, but because there wasn't anyone to tell. I had friends, but none I hung out with outside of extracurricular activities.

"It's no one," I told Autumn, but as I said it, heat rose in my cheeks.

And Alden really was "no one." I hadn't thought of him as someone I wanted to date. Just someone I wanted to know better.

If anyone at Cornell was my type, it was Autumn—they had long curly hair that they tied back with a bandanna and a seemingly endless supply of floral dresses that were designed for frolicking in meadows of wildflowers.

But Autumn wasn't the person I'd spent the whole night talking to.

19

"Oh, she *definitely* met someone," Rex said. "Do tell. We all want to live vicariously through your dating escapades."

"Speak for yourself," Shelly said, gently shoving Rex.

I could've told them about Alden then and there. I could've said I spent all night talking to this guy and that we got along and I could see us being friends, and none of that would've been a lie.

It wasn't anything yet, between me and Alden. It was an . . . interest, in an interesting person.

"Seriously, it's nothing," I said instead. Then, to move the conversation along, I asked, "How was dinner? Was the bisque everything you dreamt of?"

"And more!" Rex said, and we all laughed.

"Speaking of bisque—" Autumn began, but Rex interrupted her. "I always am."

Autumn threw a balled-up napkin at them. "*Speaking of*," they continued. "I got a job through Cornell dining."

"And they haven't even said the best part," Shelly tells me.

So Shelly already knew what Autumn was about to say. I felt yet again like I'd missed out, or maybe more like *I* was missing something, a crucial piece of machinery.

But that was silly to think, because they were making an effort to include me, and we'd barely hung out as a group three times.

Autumn smiled and put a palm to her cheek. "You're looking at the newest dining hall brand ambassador."

I told her that it sounded like the perfect job for her, and after that, we all searched the campus employment website for opportunities as good as the one Autumn had found.

"This one could be good for Zoe," Rex said as they scrolled through their phone. "It's for bio majors: Greenhouse attendant."

"Wait, I love that," Autumn said as she leaned her head on Rex's shoulder to get a better view.

Seeing as the other potential jobs all involved calling alumni and begging for money, I agreed that it *was* perfect.

I applied, and I had my interview later that day.

"Why do you want to work in the greenhouse?" the manager, Randall, a man who could've been anywhere from fifty to one hundred years old, asked when I arrived in his humid, damp office.

The greenhouse was across campus from my dorm, and even though it was open to the public, I'd never been before, except if you counted the virtual tour my parents had forced me to take after I'd been accepted. The person who'd been running the tour had shaky hands, so everything had been a green blur.

I thought about how to respond to Randall's question, then decided to answer honestly. "I won't have to interact with people."

He laughed and combed his fingers through his coarse beard. "Do you know anything about plants?"

"I mean, I like them."

He smiled. "Do you know how to *care* for them, that is?"

Not a single helpful or intelligent plant fact came to me, so what I said was, "They need water and light."

He laughed again. "How do you feel about sweeping?"

"Great," I said quickly. "I feel great about sweeping."

He told me I could start the next day.

"Would you like a tour?"

I nodded, and he led me around the greenhouse, explaining which plants needed special care and which had been the toughest to acquire. It was nice to pretend I was in a jungle, to be smothered by greenery. It was raining lightly outside, and the glass ceilings fogged as the drops *pinged* pleasantly.

I loved it—I felt safe there, like I was outside of my body looking in. Through the greenhouse window, I could've been anyone, my figure obscured by the humid air.

"And this," Randall said finally, "is my pride and joy."

He pointed to a large empty pot.

"What is it?" I asked him.

"That, my friend, is an *Amorphophallus titanum*." He smiled at me. "Do you speak any Latin?"

I shook my head.

"Look it up when you get back to your dorm." He patted the side of the pot. "It's also known as the corpse plant, and it only flowers once in a blue moon. But when it does, it's a sight to behold." He grinned at the plant and his face came alive. "It's the largest flowering plant in the world, and it smells like a rotting corpse. Hence its nickname."

I didn't want to sound unenthused about this shit-smelling plant that didn't currently exist, so I just nodded.

When I got back to my dorm, I did as he told me and looked up the definition of *Amorphophallus titanum*.

It means giant misshapen penis.

Monday, 11 a.m., near Rensselaer, NY

The first morning of the trip speeds by. I should be bored, staring at the overgrown shrubbery lining the tracks, but instead, it's almost meditative.

"We'll be pulling into Albany in about an hour here, folks," the conductor says over the loudspeaker sometime around eleven. "If Albany's your final destination, take a second to gather your belongings. We'll have a bit of a stopover there—you'll have one hour to stretch, grab some lunch, and explore New York's beautiful capital."

The train, as it turns out, does not stop directly in Albany, but in Rensselaer, a town situated across the river from "New York's beautiful capital." Rensselaer might not be the seat of the state's government, but it *is* home to a large construction debris landfill, which I overheard someone in the café car tell their partner.

After this stop, the train will veer off, eventually leaving New York behind, the place where I've spent nearly four of the longest months of my life.

I thought when I escaped to the opposite side of the country I would be able to change how people saw me, how I saw *myself*, but it only made me more confused.

When the train stops, I run to a nearby store called Daughter of Egg to grab a snack, and wind up with four family-sized bags of pretzels. When I make it back to the station, the conductor is shouting, "All aboard," which I thought only happened in movies.

The train is now double the length it was when we pulled into Albany, because this is where the cars that originated in New York

City and the ones that originated in Boston merge. Which also means there will be twice as many people on the train as there were before.

I drop three bags of pretzels off at my assigned seat.

"Hungry girl," not–Guy Fieri says.

The sheer skeeviness of the comment nearly melts the flesh off my bones. "It would appear so."

I don't tell him I'll see him around this time as I walk through coach to the café car with the fourth family-sized bag of pretzels in hand.

The conductor gives his spiel to the new people who've joined us, then adds, "Lunch in the dining car will begin shortly. We've got a great menu here, folks. Nothing quite like a meal on the train."

I hadn't considered eating in the dining car, but it's something to do. So, as the attendant passes by, I flag him down.

"I'd like to make a reservation."

He nods and smiles at me like I've given him a precious gift. "Are you in a sleeper car?"

"No."

"That's quite all right," he says. "Only asking because meals come free with a sleeper ticket."

"I'm in coach."

"And that's gorgeous," he says. He looks down at his notepad. "How does one thirty sound?"

I check my phone—which is on but in airplane mode—as if I have anywhere else to be. "One thirty sounds great."

He grins. "Wonderful."

An hour and many pretzels later, the conductor announces that they're seating 1:30 reservations. When I arrive in the dining car, an attendant tells me I'll be at table four. "Have fun," she says.

"Thanks," I tell her.

I walk past her to find tables similar to the booths in the café car, except these are covered in smooth white tablecloths. I locate table four but stop before I get too close.

There are already three people sitting in the booth. There's an elderly couple facing me, and they smile as I approach. "Table four?" the woman asks.

"Yeah, sorry," I say, turning around. "They must've given me the wrong number."

"No no," the man, broad and frowning, says. "This is how it works on the train."

"We all sit together," the woman adds.

I look around, and the rest of the tables are full of people from all different walks of life talking animatedly.

"Um, okay." I step closer.

The third person sitting at the table is facing away from me, so all I can see is shiny blond hair pulled up in a high ponytail.

"I'm Virginia," the woman says.

"Clint," the man tells me.

"Zoe."

"Zoe!" Virginia echoes. She points across the table. "And our new friend here is Oakley."

Blond Ponytail—Oakley—looks up and flashes me a smile.

25

Her teeth are perfect—neatly aligned, bright white.

She's wearing a light pink cable-knit sweater and a gold necklace, and she's the kind of hot that would've intimidated me in high school, the kind of hot that would grant her automatic popularity regardless of her personality.

"Hi," she says.

"Hi," I say.

I sit down in the booth next to her.

Oakley is the exact type of person I'm trying to avoid on the train—someone around my age, someone hot and cool who probably has specific expectations of me based on how I look. Maybe it's the only child in me, but I've always been more comfortable with adults than people my own age.

At least I have Clint and Virginia.

I take a deep breath and tell myself that it's just lunch on a train with people I've never met. That it'll all be okay.

Maybe if I keep telling myself this, it'll be the truth.

Three

Monday, 1:30 p.m., outside Albany (Rensselaer), NY

"Who knew we'd be seated with not one but *two* charming young ladies?" Virginia asks. She nudges Clint's shoulder. "Can you believe it, sweetheart?"

Clint clears his throat and rolls up one of his shirtsleeves. I'm sure he'd rather not say one way or the other how he feels about us, just like I'd rather not break it to Virginia that something about the phrase "charming young lady" makes my skin crawl.

I glance at Oakley, and she's staring out the window.

She's intimidatingly hot, sure, yes, fine. But maybe that doesn't matter here. Much like me, Virginia, and Clint, she's just trying to have lunch.

The waiter comes by with a menu. The options are short ribs, veggie noodles, chicken, salmon and shrimp (combined, for some reason), and baked ziti.

I'm wondering what kind of person orders short ribs on a train when Clint says, "I *always* get the ribs." He looks up from the menu. "It's all reheated, but even microwaved food tastes better on the train."

"Have you done this before?" I ask. "Taken this trip?"

Virginia and Clint burst out laughing.

"Oh, hon, *have* we?"

"We take the train across this great country of ours at least once a year," Clint tells me. "More now that we're both fully retired."

"Cool," I say, but what I'm thinking is, *How could you bear to do the same thing over and over?*

I would get fed up with myself.

"This is my first time," Oakley says.

She's still facing the window.

"You know what they say about the cross-country train?" Virginia asks. I stare at her blankly, so she adds, "Once you've ridden it once, you'll never want to stop."

"Is that the official slogan?" I ask, and Oakley snorts, which turns into a cough as Clint stares her down.

"So," Virginia says in a chipper voice, "we have to play our little game."

"Not before the meal," Clint says. "At least let them eat first."

"No no, it's better when they're cranky." Virginia clasps her hands together. "Makes them more honest."

"Let's hear it," Oakley says. "What's the game?" She turns from the window then, and her face is even more striking in profile.

She has the kind of turned-up nose that I coveted as a child, probably because of some powerful internalized antisemitism.

"Okay," Virginia says. "Here's the question: Do your parents approve of the life you're living?" Clint crosses his arms over his stomach as Virginia continues. "I mean to say, are they proud of you?"

"You two don't have to answer that," Clint says. "This isn't even a game. It's Virginia's twisted idea of fun."

Virginia slaps Clint's hand. "Stop it, of course they have to answer."

"Mine aren't," Oakley says casually.

I shift my eyes to get a better look at her, to see if she's serious. She is.

I want to know why this beautiful blond girl's parents don't approve of her. Maybe this is ignorant, but it's hard for me to imagine a blond person not having their parents' approval. I can't help but picture her childhood in a big house with a big dog and a blond sibling and two sturdy parents (also blond, of course).

Okay, scratch that, it's *definitely* ignorant. But it's what I'm thinking.

Instead of voicing these thoughts, all I say is, "Neither are mine."

I'm not sure why I admit it, but it's true—or it will be soon.

"I knew it," Virginia says triumphantly. "No one who takes the train across the country is living a life their parents approve of. That's my theory, and it's yet to be proven wrong."

"There was that guy from that movie," Clint says.

Virginia makes a *psh* sound. "He doesn't count," she says. "And I don't believe that any actor's parents are truly proud of them."

"All right, let's ask someone else." Clint sticks a leg out into the aisle and twists around. "Hey, Paulie, your parents proud of you?"

he shouts at a guy sitting a few booths back.

"Ha," the man who must be Paulie says. He's wearing a trucker hat and has a face that's more sun-spotted on one side than the other. "Who knows? Probably not."

"Thanks, pal," Clint says, untwisting to face me and Oakley.

"Do you know him?" I ask Clint.

"Met him while I was coming out of the bathroom earlier."

"See, I'm always right," Virginia says. "The theory holds."

"Of course you are," Clint says in a way that makes it clear they've had this conversation countless times.

I'm about to try to steer the discussion back to Oakley, since I desperately want to know why her parents don't approve of her, but before I can, she asks Virginia, "So, do *your* parents approve, then? Of your life?

"Oh, absolutely not," Virginia says. "Didn't stop me from spending most of my adulthood trying to earn their approval, though. They're long dead now, and I don't have anyone left to disappoint." She laughs a little. "So, I take the train back and forth across the country." She leans forward. "Want to know how they spent their retirement? Volunteering at a local food bank." This time she really laughs. "They were saints, God rest their souls. I'm sure they wouldn't approve of this either."

"The train is much more exciting than the food bank anyway," Clint adds.

After this, the waiter makes his way down the aisle, and the conversation dies.

I know my parents were proud of who I was in high school.

But I couldn't continue being that person. When I got to college, it felt like a lie, even though nothing had changed except my surroundings.

Maybe that was why I spent so much time with Alden.

DAY TEN OF COLLEGE

For most of my first week at Cornell, I would return to my dorm at the end of the day and immediately fall asleep on top of my floral twin XL comforter.

In high school, I had a fixed schedule. I knew that by nine every night, I'd be at my desk, doing homework, my lamp shining into my bloodshot eyes.

But that wasn't the case here. I was regularly getting back to my room at midnight or later, having spent most of the day with the Tees.

They took me to improv shows and club meetings (mostly for the free food) and to get plenty of late-night french fries.

And it did feel like that—like *they* were taking *me* places. They made an effort to include me, but I always felt separate from them, however much I wanted to slide comfortably into the group.

Autumn and Shelly were both solidly declared in their respective major, which meant that Autumn was always busy with an architecture studio assignment, and Shelly was taking a yarn analysis laboratory that took up a shocking amount of his time.

Rex didn't know what they were doing, academically speaking, but they were already running to be an officer of the LGBTQ Student Union.

I had none of that certainty or drive.

But there were two evenings a week where I had a purpose: Tuesdays and Thursdays, in the Straight, after my biology lecture.

I'd seen Alden a few times since that first night, but he was always on his way somewhere else. He would wave to me, then smile like we had a shared secret, which I guess we did. We were bonded by our time at the top of the clock tower, by our poor decision-making.

The only reason I went to class at all was because there was a chance I would run into him as I left the temporary lecture hall. Plus, I couldn't give up on my study of the girl's bouncing leg, results pending.

I didn't have Alden's number, so after class, I would not-so-subtly sit on the same couch where I'd found him that first night, hoping that he might join me.

Finally, he did. He sat on the armchair across from me, and I spent another few seconds staring at my notebook, pretending not to notice him.

"Hi, Zoe," he said when I finally looked up—casually, of course—and acted surprised by his presence.

"Hi, Alden."

"I was just thinking about you."

My heart fluttered almost painfully. "You were?"

"Do you know the band Dunk Sonic?"

I shook my head and closed my notebook, giving him my full attention.

"They're *so* cool." He pulled out his phone. "They're from

Seattle—that's where you're from, right? I'm not misremembering?"

"No—I mean yes, yeah." I had the sudden urge to suck on the tip of my ponytail, a bad habit I'd finally broken in middle school. "I'm from Seattle."

"I made a playlist of their music for you, if you wanted to listen." He tossed his phone back and forth between his hands. "I could send it to you."

"Yeah," I said, slightly breathless. "That sounds nice."

We exchanged numbers, and I expected him to leave after that, but he pulled out a deck of cards.

"Wanna play a game?"

"Yes."

There was nothing else I wanted to do. Being with Alden felt like floating in a warm bath—I didn't have any sense of time or place.

He taught me a card game with too many rules and beat me handily each round.

"It's getting late," Alden said quietly, leaning closer to me. He'd moved from the armchair to the couch during the first game.

He was right—it was 1:59 a.m., and the student union was empty and echoey. I'd easily lost track of time with him.

"I guess we should go back to our dorms," I said, not meaning it.

"I guess," he said, but he didn't move. "It's a shame we have to sleep at all."

"Yeah?" I could feel heat traveling to my face, but I didn't hide it from him.

I knew he was saying that he wanted to stay up with me.

I wanted to stay up with him too.

"Yeah," he confirmed.

When I got back to my dorm, I was wired.

I listened to the playlist, but all I heard were Alden's words, over and over: *It's a shame we have to sleep at all.*

He made me feel like someone worth staying up for. Like I was special and important.

He made me feel like a different person entirely.

MONDAY, 2 P.M., NEAR SCHENECTADY, NY

When the waiter takes our order, Clint gets the short ribs, as promised, and Virginia, Oakley, and I all get the veggie noodles.

"Come on, none of you ladies want a little meat on your bones?" Clint asks.

Virginia rolls her eyes. "We're not all brutes."

Oakley puts her forearms on the table. "It's all a gender display anyway," she says, and I freeze. "I was reading this article the other day about how meat is associated with a more masculine identity. You know, the big strong man ripping into a lower animal's flesh, proving he's at the top of the food chain."

"Sounds like Clint," Virginia says, laughing.

As well-meaning as they seem, I hate the way Clint and Virginia talk to each other. The way they fall into precise stereotypes of a straight couple their age.

But Oakley's unphased. "The fact that it's a *display* is what's really important in this situation. There's a theory that gender isn't a stable identity but that it's constructed through social interactions. So Clint orders ribs; the three of us"—she gestures to me and Virginia—"order a vegetable dish, and we've proven something about ourselves to each other. But maybe if we were dining alone the roles would be reversed. Maybe Clint would want noodles and the rest of us would have ribs."

I try to stop myself from staring at Oakley. I've never heard anyone speak this way outside of a classroom, where everyone would compete to try to make the most intelligent comment. She's not competing with any of us, though. She just *said* it.

I want to have some sort of cogent, beautiful, theory-based reply, but I don't know anything about this topic. All I manage to say is, "That's so true." Because it is. Or it seems to be. "Well, not the ribs part. I wouldn't get those if I was by myself—I'm a vegetarian."

Oakley adjusts in the booth slightly so she's facing me. "I could've guessed that."

My cheeks heat. "What's that supposed to mean?"

"Let me guess, you love animals?" She artfully raises one dark blond eyebrow. "And you'd feel bad eating them. You're concerned about factory farming for both environmental and ethical reasons. And look, you're even dressed like a farmer." She doesn't say any of it meanly; she's just stating a series of facts.

To be fair to her, I *am* wearing a ratty white T-shirt under black overalls, with an old flannel shirt to top it off.

"I'm from Seattle," I say, to at least provide an explanation for the dressing-like-a-farmer part.

"That'll do it," she says.

It's been a long time since I've spoken like this to a girl, and—though I could very well be mistaken—it feels kind of flirty. Or at least flirt-adjacent.

The problem is that I'm too out of practice to know for sure. Not that I was ever *in* practice.

"Okay, but was I wrong about the rest of it?" she asks.

"Well, no," I admit. "But it doesn't exactly seem like a hard guess. You got the veggie noodles too. I have to imagine that you care at least a little bit about the environment, or about animals, or *something* that made you order one of the only vegetarian options on the menu."

"I'm not even a vegetarian," she says, running her hand along the chain of her necklace. "I just thought the noodles sounded good. Or maybe it was social pressure after you and Virginia ordered them."

"I didn't know we were sitting at a table with a certified genius," Virginia says, touching Oakley's hand and looking at Clint like, *Can you believe this?*

"So, this is what they're teaching you in those fancy little East Coast colleges, huh?" Clint asks.

"No," Oakley tells him. "I don't go to college."

"Good on you," he says. "You'll learn more in the real world anyway. They brainwash you at those places."

The waiter comes around with a cart and drops off our noodles and ribs. They're glorified TV dinners, but Clint was right: food tastes better on the train.

And it's not just the food. If we weren't on the train, I would politely end this conversation with Clint and Virginia and their wild commentary as fast as possible. Though, if we weren't on the train, I don't think I'd be talking to them at all.

There's a romantic, rose-colored filter on everything: the run-down dining car, the reheated meals, even this elderly conspiracy theorist.

I kind of like him.

We all inhale our food. Another train quirk—it makes you ravenous.

Oakley finishes her noodles before me and announces, "I'm going now, but it's been nice talking to you all." I could be imagining it, but I'm pretty sure she looks at me longer than she does at Clint and Virginia as she says it. "So, um, could you move?" she asks me after a beat. "I need to get out."

Okay, yes, she definitely was meeting my eye longer because I have to scoot out of the booth so she can leave. Perfect. Cool cool cool.

"Bye, hon," Virginia says. "Nice chatting with you."

"You too," Oakley says as I stand from the booth to let her out.

And then a wild impulse strikes me: I want to follow her. If she's leaving the train in Chicago, I might never see her again.

This feels different than the force that drew me to Alden. That was complicated, difficult to name. This is easier: she's smart and cute, and I'm bored.

Or maybe it's not easier at all. Maybe I'll repeat the same pattern of latching on to someone like a leech.

That's a better descriptor of me than farmer: leech, blood-sucker. I take people's life force and try to have it for myself.

But still, the idea of letting her walk off without me is worse than the thought of going with her.

Before I can make a decision, though, she's gone.

"What a bizarre girl," Virginia says. "Don't you think?"

Four

Monday, 3:00 p.m., Somewhere in Upstate NY

We careen through the landscape in the low light of a late-fall afternoon. The café car is fairly empty, and the excitement of the first few hours of the trip has died down. Now there's a lethargic feeling; it's nap time for everyone.

There aren't many sights to see, nor is there much to do, but I can't bring myself to fall asleep. I try to read, but that's not happening either.

As a last resort, I pull out my phone and turn off airplane mode, only to find that there's no service. If there was, I don't know what my notifications would look like. I might have texts from several people asking where I am and why, or there might be nothing.

I'm not sure which would be worse.

We're barreling closer and closer to Ithaca, though the train's path doesn't cross through the city. Even so, my hands dampen at the thought of being back at school.

I'm not there, I remind myself.

So, instead of worrying (which I'm sure I'll do anyway), I play

Tetris until my eyes glaze over. I used to play it so much back in middle school that I would have dreams of the bricks falling into place. I don't play much now, but being on the train makes me want to return to old comforts.

Maybe it's also that there was some part of me that understood who I was in middle school. I might've called myself a responsible student, the way my parents did, or a Tetris player.

I don't know what I would call myself now.

For the time being, I can be a Tetris player again.

I'm about to beat my high score when a voice booms over the loudspeaker.

"Hello, my beautiful train people," the voice says. "It's your Snack Conductor Edward again, reminding you that the snack car is! Still! Open! I'm here for all your snack needs. Chocolate? Check. Nachos? Check. Coffee? Still got it! Come on down. . . . I'm waiting for you." He whispers that last part into the intercom.

I'm technically *in* the snack car, but the area where the self-proclaimed Snack Conductor is selling food is at the opposite end. I figure I'll have to meet this Edward guy at some point, so I might as well get it over with now.

There's a short line, and I stand awkwardly near a trash can so I'm not in the way. Even here, in the snack car, I can't bring myself to take up space.

It's not that I thought I wouldn't feel this way on the train. I knew I would, but living like this is exhausting.

Edward the Snack Guy is stationed behind a bar with a coffee machine, a fridge, a microwave, and, of course, a variety of snacks lining the wall.

"And here's your Diet Dr Pepper," Edward says, overenunciating each word and presenting the soda with a flourish to the person at the front of the line. The guy nods and walks away with his head down.

"Now, what can I get for you?" Edward asks the next person. "Anything your heart desires—so long as I've got it. HA!" He throws his head back and almost knocks over a cardboard container of granola bars.

He's working the crowd, and no one's enjoying it.

"Can I just have a coffee?" I ask Edward when it's my turn to order.

He gasps dramatically. "*Just* a coffee? Not a snack?"

"I'm good."

"You hear that? This kid is good!" he says to the person behind me in line, laughing like it's the funniest thing he's ever heard. "You sure I can't interest you in . . ." He ducks below the counter and pulls out an array of bars and bags. "Snickers? Potato chips? *Kettle* chips?"

I feel bad enough that I agree to the Kettle chips. He grins and hands me a cup of coffee and the bag, and I pass him my debit card.

"You made me proud today." He wipes a fake tear from his eye as he swipes it. "Are you heading to Chicago?"

"To Seattle."

"Even better," he says. "I'm on the next train too, so we'll be seeing a *lot* of each other."

I smile politely—if all the coffee on the train is being held hostage by Edward, I at least have to try to make nice.

I slink back to my booth with the coffee and Kettle chips I didn't want, then stare out the window yet again.

Now the only company I have is myself, who happens to be one of the people I don't particularly want to spend time with.

Day Eleven of College

Randall handed me a broom. "You know what to do with this, yeah?"

"Pretty much." I pantomimed sweeping.

He laughed and patted me on the shoulder, a paternal gesture that stirred unwanted emotions inside me.

Sweeping in the greenhouse was a futile effort; once I dumped a batch of leaves in the compost, a new layer would fall. But it was gratifying for the brief moments in which the floor was clean.

Being in the greenhouse was an escape from everything else in my life. Randall told me on my first day that I was allowed to listen to music, but I never did. I loved hearing how the outside world bumped up against the glass.

When I made it over to the corpse plant, I leaned the broom on a bench and examined the future misshapen penis. The giant pot had a prized spot, one with easy access to the overstory and the sun beyond.

"Hi, little buddy," I said to the empty pot.

Except it wasn't empty.

In the center of the soil, barely visible, was a gnarled ball. It looked almost alive—it was a mostly submerged dark green orb covered in stringy white roots.

But it was there—what could've been the first sign of a bloom. An event so rare that people came from far and wide to see it.

And that's when I started feeling so protective of the plant that it made me almost sick with worry. I wanted to watch it day and night, to nurture it so that it flowered.

But on the flip side, I *never* wanted it to bloom, because I knew that when it did, it would last for less than a week.

It was a corpse plant no matter what it looked like, but there was only one stage of its life during which people traveled to see it.

I loved it like this, alone and underground.

I turned my attention to the other plants then, and wound up by the machine that sprayed mist throughout the room. The mister in the tropical section went off on a timer; it sat next to the vanilla vine and across from the coffee plant.

I closed my eyes and breathed in the warm spray, allowing myself to feel like one of the plants.

"How's it going in here?" Randall asked as he carefully opened the heavy door into the climate-controlled room.

"Great," I told him, clearing my throat and sweeping the area around my feet.

He laughed to himself. "It's all right to take a break. You don't need to be working all the time."

"That's okay," I told him. "I like it in here."

"So do I," he said. "But the plants are hearty. Tea?" He nodded to his office, and I followed him across the hall.

"I like to dry my own leaves." He filled the kettle and set it to boil. "All the teas in here come from the greenhouse."

"That's so cool," I told him, meaning it with every fiber of my being.

He worked methodically, the same way he did with the plants, weighing the dried leaves and then placing them in the strainer. When the tea was ready, he handed me a mug.

"So," he said as he sat at his desk chair with a thermos. "I'm glad you found your way to the greenhouse. You seem to have a real interest in it."

"Yeah," I told him, sipping the tea and letting it sit on my tongue. The flavors were potent and aromatic. "I guess so."

"Good," he said, though I could tell there was more he wanted to say.

I hoped desperately that he wouldn't bring up my future or "career paths" or anything of the sort, because the greenhouse was the one place where I didn't have to think about any of that.

Randall sipped his tea, then stood up. "Well, let's get back to work, shall we?"

I nodded. Maybe he could tell that was what I needed to do, or maybe he had been in my position once, a kid on the precipice of something beyond them, wanting nothing more than to be surrounded by plants.

"Let's end the night with the sounds of the stars," Rex said into the mic at the student radio station. "So sit back, relax, and try not to think about the impending heat death of the universe."

They hit a button on the soundboard, and chill radio static filled the room.

"You're about to give the whole campus an existential crisis," Autumn told them as she spun around in a rolling chair—her curls were glowing under the color-changing LED lights of the studio.

Rex shook their head. "No one actually listens to this shit."

They moved from their position in front of the microphone down onto the floor, where Shelly and I were sitting cross-legged, eating tortilla chips out of a bag that was so large my entire arm fit inside.

I was itching to text Alden, but I didn't want to seem too eager to hang out again.

"We're going to Wegmans after this, right?" Autumn asked as they grabbed a handful of chips.

Everyone else agreed that the late-night diner was a good idea, but I was staring at my phone, willing Alden's name to appear.

"You okay?" Autumn asked.

"Definitely," I told them, putting my phone away.

I tried to push Alden out of my brain, but I couldn't do it. I thought about him all the time. Not about anything in particular, just *him*.

"Wouldn't it be fun if we all lived together next year?" Rex asked as they bit into a chip.

"One of the sophomores in Fabrics lives in Loving House," Shelly began, "the queer res house."

45

"We should apply!"

I wanted to be as excited as them, but the more they talked about it, the more I felt like I was an inconvenience, like I was tagging along on their big plans.

I'd been so sure of my identity as a lesbian in high school. Girls were pretty, and I liked them and wanted to kiss them, but I never had the chance to actually *do* that.

But now, when I thought of kissing someone, the only person who popped into my head was Alden.

It clicked then, in a way it hadn't before: I *liked* Alden. The feeling of wanting to be around him all the time—that was a crush.

A crush on a boy.

Monday, 9:30 p.m., Somewhere in Ohio

"All right, folks, just a reminder that it's lights-out in coach at ten p.m. So get all your rustling and fussing out of the way now."

I haven't been back to my seat since I dropped the pretzels off, partly because I don't want to deal with Guy Fieri, but also because I can roam free in the café car. The coach seats are spacious enough, but I'd rather not annoy my seatmates by getting up to stretch my legs every five minutes.

The sun set hours ago, and now the only view through the large window is my own face reflected back at me.

Before I went through puberty, I liked the way I looked. People would compliment my long straight-ish brown hair, my rosy cheeks, my quiet but polite little-kid demeanor. But then I turned twelve and my hair curled, my cheeks became a breeding ground for angry red pockets of acne, and my mood soured.

It's also when I realized that I liked girls.

I shouldn't have been exposed to the general public while I was going through puberty, growing into my body Hulk-style; I was absolutely miserable.

Not much has changed, except that my hair is cropped and my parents don't know yet.

And, well, a few other things too.

I was such a good little girl—that's what my parents would tell their friends. I spent more time with adults than with anyone my age, and they complimented my maturity and lamented the fact that their own kids acted like, well, kids, rather than whatever I had going on.

I finish the last of my already-stale Kettle chips and stare at my face in the window until the whole is lost to the parts—all I see is my large nose, my dark eyes, my down-turned mouth. My short patchy hair that I should've let a professional cut but chose instead to hack with a pair of fabric scissors in the middle of the night.

And then it's almost lights-out, and I figure I should at least *try* to sleep, so I head back to my coach seat. Luckily, Guy Fieri's already fast asleep under a Chicago Bears blanket.

Most other people have pillows and blankets, but I didn't have the foresight to bring either, so I grab my jacket from my bag and ball it up behind my neck. The seats recline, and there's a little footrest, and it's not horrible. But after tossing and turning for half an hour or so I pull out my phone and open Tetris.

I manage to beat my high score three times, until a woman

with fuzzy socks and a fleece wrapped tightly around her taps on my shoulder.

"Excuse me, miss," she whisper-yells. "Could you turn that screen off, please? It's interrupting my REM."

I quickly put my phone face down on my lap. "Sure, sorry."

She walks away without another word. A few people around us stir, looking dazed. I have to imagine that her shuffling down the aisle and reprimanding me was more disruptive than me silently playing Tetris on my phone, but now I'm too embarrassed to stay here.

So, I grab my book, earbuds, and phone and return to the café car. It's nearly midnight, but there are a few people still sitting in the booths, bleary-eyed and restless.

This time nearly twenty-four hours ago, I was in my dorm, frantically packing my things. That feels like it happened in another lifetime. Yesterday.

Mere hours before that, I was with Alden.

I play Tetris to stop myself from thinking about school; the falling blocks become meditative the longer I watch them. Maybe there are Tetris competitions—I could do that. I'll be a Tetris vagabond, going from tournament to tournament. I make a mental note to look up whether competitive Tetris is a thing once I have service again.

"You have to do a T-spin," a voice behind me says.

I turn around, startled.

There, peering over my shoulder, is Oakley.

Five

Monday, 11 p.m., outside of Cleveland, OH

"Oh, hey," I say, trying to sound casual. I slide my phone into the front pocket of my overalls, suddenly self-conscious about my Tetris abilities.

"You have to do a T-spin," Oakley repeats.

"A what?" My heart is racing.

"A T-spin," she says, leaning forward. "You know the T-shaped block?"

I nod, unsure whether or not I'm dreaming.

"You create a slot for it then spin it into place. Here, I'll show you." She holds out her hand. When I continue sitting like an absolute lump she points to my pocket and says, "Your phone."

I give it to her.

"You can't get a *really* high score without a T-spin," she says as she moves to my side of the booth so we can both see the screen. She has me type in my password, then navigates to the Tetris app and proceeds to intricately set up the pieces so that there's a perfect space for the T-shaped block. Then she rotates it 90 degrees and it

49

falls into place with a flash, clearing two rows. "A double T-spin is worth more than a Tetris." She hands the phone back to me.

"How did you know that?"

"I know a lot of things."

She's changed her clothes since lunch and is now wearing pajamas—a pink silk set with matching slippers.

"Did you get dressed in one of the bathrooms?"

I need to get out of my overalls and into sweatpants, but I don't want to do it in the cramped bathroom stalls. If my overalls fell into the Amtrak toilet, I would have to abandon them there.

She shakes her head. "I'm in a sleeper car."

"By yourself?" I ask, then I realize how that sounds so I add, "I thought they were usually for families."

"They're for anyone who wants to sleep in an actual bed."

Or anyone with $1,000 to spare.

A coach seat on this train cost me around $150 for both parts of the trip. A lot of money, but not horrible. The cheapest room in a sleeper car costs over $350, and that's only for the Lakeshore Limited route, which is the New York to Chicago leg.

I have so many questions about Oakley: How could she afford a sleeper car? How does she know so much about hyperspecific Tetris plays?

But I start with the most pressing one: "Why are you here?" I ask. "In the café car, I mean."

She gets up and moves back to the other side of the booth so that we're facing each other.

"Couldn't sleep."

"Me neither."

I stare at her reflection in the train window. She stares back at mine.

"Virginia and Clint were kind of wild," I say after a minute, trying to make small talk. I look away from Oakley's reflection and over to the corporeal version of her that's sitting across from me.

"Yeah, kind of," she says. "But I know tons of men who are exactly like Clint, down to the 'college will brainwash you' part." She sighs then. "And they're all oppressively heterosexual."

There's an obvious next question: Is *she* heterosexual? I wouldn't usually be brave enough to ask, but it's the middle of the night on a cross-country train and I'm talking to a hot girl who I may never see again. All bets are off.

"Does that mean you're not?" I ask. "Heterosexual?"

She tilts her head. "What do you think?"

"That you're not," I say. Then quickly clarify: "As in, I don't think you're straight."

"That would be correct," she says. "And I don't think you are either."

"No shit," I say, gesturing to my whole deal—the DIY haircut, the ripped overalls.

"You're the one who used 'being from Seattle' as an excuse for your outfit."

"Both can be true," I say. "I can be queer *and* from Seattle. Plus, I didn't want to say anything in front of Clint and Virginia."

"Fair," she says. "I don't think they'd quite understand the nuances of a soft butch aesthetic."

My face heats as I pull on a strap of my overalls. "Is that what you think this outfit is?"

"Well, yeah," she says. "And I would say I lean more toward the femme side of things, though I don't think those terms have much use beyond their historical definitions."

Once again Oakley's speaking like she's teaching a college-level course on gender and sexuality. The Tees would have discussions like this sometimes, but when they did, I felt like an outside observer. Here, though, with all of Oakley's attention focused on me, I have an answer, or at least an opinion, even if it isn't as eloquent as hers.

"I don't think that's true at all," I say. "Having a label you can identify with, it helps a lot of people, and it's rude to say that they don't have use." My leg is bouncing. "Maybe rude's the wrong word, but it's narrow-minded. Not that *you're* narrow-minded."

"No, yeah," she says, sounding excited. "That makes sense, but I also think we shouldn't have to fit into those stereotypes at all."

"I'm not the one who gave some random person they just met a label."

It comes out harsher than I mean to, but I don't even know what I'd call *myself* and definitely don't want to be defined by an aesthetic, queer or otherwise.

Like I said, labels can be helpful. But only if you know how to label yourself.

"Okay, I'm glad I found you here," Oakley says, eyes wide. "This is the kind of thing I've been wanting to talk about for months."

"What? Queer labels?"

"Not specifically," she says, wired now. "This is just what I thought I'd be talking about all the time when I moved to New York."

"But you didn't get to?"

She shrugs and turns away. After a moment, she asks, "Where are you heading?"

It doesn't escape me that she ignored my question. But asking someone on the train where they're heading is the equivalent of asking someone at college what their major is, so I knew it was coming.

"Back to Seattle," I say. "To my parents' house."

"I'm going back to Washington to see my parents too," she says. "They live in Ritzville."

I frown. "That's not a real place."

She rolls her eyes. "Yes, it is," she says. "It's in Eastern Washington, about an hour outside of Spokane."

I make half-hearted jazz hands as I say, "Ritzville," like it's the title of a vaudeville show.

But then I take in what she said: Oakley isn't getting off the train in Chicago. She's going to Washington.

She's going to be with me for the next three days.

"I've literally never heard of Ritzville," I say when she doesn't add anything else.

"That doesn't mean it doesn't exist." She hugs her knees to her chest. "People from Seattle have blinders on. You have no idea what's happening in the rest of the state."

53

"That's not fair."

"You didn't even know that my town existed."

"How am I supposed to know every town in Eastern Washington?"

"You're not," she says. "But you have to at least acknowledge that there are places you don't know. Places where other people live and work and pray."

"Exactly—they're praying at church. I'd bet you money there's not a single Jew living there," I say, ignoring her comment in favor of being contrarian. "Or at least that there's not a synagogue."

"No, yeah, there *definitely* isn't," she says.

"What's that supposed to mean?"

"Just that there isn't a synagogue," she says plainly.

"Why'd you say 'definitely' like that, then?" I don't know why I'm getting defensive, but if I'm talking to someone who has some weird thing about Jews I'd rather know now. "I'm Jewish—and look, no horns." I scrape through my short thick hair like I'm doing a lice test.

I'm being a piece of shit—at least that hasn't changed.

She rolls the sleeves of her silk pajamas, then unrolls them. "My Sunday school teacher would always say that people think Mormons have horns too."

"Wait, what?" I ask, confused by the subject change. "That can't be right."

"Why are you so convinced everything you say is right and everything I say is wrong?"

"I'm not," I tell her, and it's true. Based on the limited interactions we've had, I'm pretty sure Oakley is much smarter than me.

Sure, I take tests well, but that's the extent of it.

Oakley, on the other hand, *knows* things, and she's good at expressing her ideas. But frankly, the things she knows are bizarre.

She leans back in her chair. "I don't think the horns thing was ever true, though. Mormons just love imagined persecution."

I narrow my eyes at her. "What are you talking about?"

"What would you say if I told you I was a member of the Church of Jesus Christ of Latter-day Saints?" she asks, not answering my question.

"I'd say that's a mouthful."

"I mean, what would you say if I told you I was Mormon?" she asks with no hint of an answer either way.

I laugh, an automatic response to being slightly unnerved. "I don't know," I say. "Are you?"

She unfolds her legs and leans forward. "I was."

I laugh nervously again, but her face doesn't change. "Wait, seriously?"

"Are you going to ask me to prove it?"

"No," I tell her. "It's just that this sounds like a setup for a joke," I say, shaking my head. "A Jew and a Mormon walk onto a train."

"It's not a very funny joke," she says. "And I'm not a Mormon anymore."

"Well, that's the setup. The funny part is the punch line."

"Yes," she says, pulling her hair out of her ponytail and braiding it over her shoulder. "I know how jokes work."

"Right, of course," I say. "Because you know everything."

"If the shoe fits."

"Can I ask you something?" I say, trying to get back on solid ground. "About Mormonism?"

"All right," she says. "But if it's about underwear or planets I'm leaving."

"It's not," I tell her, though it might've been. "No, here's what I want to know: Did you believe it? I mean, did you *really* think that all of it was true?"

"That's a big question."

"You agreed."

She raises her hands, like I caught her in a lie. "Yes, I believed it." She fidgets with one of her earrings, her pointer finger and thumb squeezing her earlobe. "I believed that Jesus Christ was my savior, that He lived a perfect life, that I got to be a part of His restored church on Earth—the *one* true church." She flinches as she says this. "I liked that there were rules, and that if I followed them, I would be rewarded."

"But did you *believe* it?" I repeat. It's the genuine belief part of religion that I've always been stuck on.

I wish I could believe wholeheartedly in a greater power, in a life beyond. Then, maybe, I wouldn't be so panicked about figuring out who I'm supposed to be right now, in this life.

"Yes, of course," she says. "I really did. I read my scriptures; I prayed every day, on my knees, listening for the Spirit. Even when I started asking questions, I prayed then too."

"What kinds of questions?"

"No no, you asked your one thing," she says. "Now I get to ask mine."

"'What kinds of questions' hardly counts. It's more of a follow-up."

"You can't change the rules."

"Fine." I need to know what questions led her to stop believing in an entire religion; they must've been pretty powerful.

But fair is fair.

She shifts in her seat. "Do you believe in God?"

I frown. "That's what I asked you."

"No, you asked me if I believed in Mormonism," she says slowly. "I'm asking you if you believe in God."

I dig under my fingernail. "Another super chill question."

"I answered yours."

There are a few people who've fallen asleep sitting up in booths, but other than that, the train is quiet. There's nothing happening except for this conversation. So I answer her question.

"No," I say. "I don't."

She doesn't respond; she's braiding her hair, watching me.

"Is this your strategy? Get me to keep talking so that you don't have to ask another question?"

She doesn't say anything.

"I don't think it matters that I don't believe in God," I tell her. "Because that's not what I like about Judaism. The parts that are God-heavy have always freaked me out. I don't like reading the English translations of the prayers we say at services, 'Blessed be our God, ruler of the Universe,' and all of that stuff."

Oakley's watching me carefully now, her back straight.

"I think what I really believe in are people," I say. "Maybe that's cliché, but . . . I don't know. When I'm at synagogue and everyone's singing together and the candles are lit and the ark is open, it feels *bigger*." My idea solidifies as I say it. "There's something holy about being with other people. About the fact that I can say I'm Jewish and it connects me to my ancestors going back thousands of years."

Oakley stills. "That's not the answer I thought you'd give."

"What did you think I'd say?"

"Nothing serious," she tells me.

"I could say something wild to cancel it out."

"Like what?"

"Like that I believe squirrels are government spies."

She laughs. "No, you don't."

I smile. "No, I don't."

We talk for a bit longer; about hikes we've been on in Washington and the people we've spoken to on the train.

The conductor announces that we've arrived in Cleveland, and that, "If this is your stop you'd better wake up," and then we make a few brief stops in towns in Ohio that I've never heard of, though I don't say that to Oakley.

When I flip my phone over to check the time, it's five in the morning.

Oakley and I were talking for most of the night.

Some of the people sleeping in coach have wandered into the café car, and there's the faintest hint of blue in the previously black sky.

Oakley yawns. "I should probably try to sleep."

"Yeah."

"Are you going to try too?"

The thought of going back to my seat next to Guy Fieri as everyone's waking up is the worst thing in the world. "Maybe. I don't know."

"You should try," she says. "It was nice talking to you, Zoe."

"Was it?"

She gives me a weird look. "Obviously, yes." She turns to go, but before she does, she says, "If it wasn't, I wouldn't have looked for you here."

THREE WEEKS INTO COLLEGE

I debated not answering my dad's call. It would've been so much easier.

But with every ring, my Jewish guilt spiked. So I picked up.

"Hello?"

"Hi, kid," his disembodied voice said in my ear. "How's my future doctor?"

"Good," I told him. It was an automatic response; anything else would've led to more questions. It would've required me to tell the truth, that I wasn't a future doctor. I wasn't a future *anything*.

The idea of a successful, productive life in the future tense was hard to imagine, because I couldn't picture myself any different than I was now.

It was easier to tell my dad, "Good," and leave it at that.

He told me about fall in Seattle, and I mentioned the foliage on the East Coast, about autumn in a city where the trees weren't evergreen, where things *changed*. He told me how the Mariners were doing and whether they would make it to the playoffs (almost certainly not). He told me about my grandma's physical therapy and how she wished I would call more.

I didn't tell him about my job at the greenhouse or the Tees. I *especially* didn't tell him about Alden.

We didn't talk about anything of significance at all.

"My classes are going well," I assured him once again. "And actually, I'm meeting up with my bio study group, so I should go."

"Good for you," he said, and sounded like he meant it. "Study hard, but don't go overboard."

"I won't."

It was the first honest thing I'd said.

I went to Rex's dorm after that, where we were having a "Tees Night In."

Autumn brought sheet masks, Shelly brought weed, and I arrived empty-handed, feeling foolish.

When our faces were covered with bologna-like masks, Autumn took a selfie, then put her head in my lap.

"Is this okay?" they asked.

"Of course," I said, surprised.

We were talking about our first queer crushes, and when the conversation turned to me, I was suddenly hyperaware of my body, of the part of my thigh Autumn's head was touching.

"I haven't really . . . ," I began.

There was no good way to finish that sentence.

I *hadn't* really had a queer crush. There were girls in high school who I thought were cute, and there were TV shows I watched more for the actresses than the plot.

But there wasn't a name I could give, because the only one that came to mind was Alden.

"That's so valid," Shelly said, and the conversation moved on.

They were all so nice to me, so considerate. And yet I felt like an impostor in their presence.

So when I got a text from Alden asking if I wanted to meet at the Straight, I jumped at the opportunity.

"I'm not feeling so well," I lied, excusing myself from Rex's dorm room.

The Tees told me to feel better, and I *did* as I stepped outside into the late-night air.

Alden was sitting on what I'd begun to think of as *our* couch, shuffling a deck of cards.

"Hey," he said, grinning when he saw me.

"What's up?"

"You ever been to the bowling alley?" he asked.

"I thought that was just a place they bragged about on tours," I said. "No one actually *goes* there, right?"

"We could!" He sat forward, like an excited puppy.

"Doesn't it close at ten?" It was nearly midnight then.

"Not if you know the custodian."

I raised an eyebrow. "Do *you* know the custodian?"

"I do." He pulled out his phone. "He's my uncle."

"And why haven't you mentioned this before?"

He shrugged. "Didn't seem relevant."

61

"You mean like when we snuck into the clock tower and your uncle could've busted us?"

"But he wouldn't have," Alden said. "He's a cool uncle. I call him Big Paul."

"How come?"

"Because my cousin is Little Paul," he said as if it were the most obvious thing in the world.

He pressed his uncle's contact after that and put him on speaker. He said we could go into the bowling alley for fifteen minutes while he was waxing the basketball court upstairs, but after that we had to get out.

"And don't fucking touch anything," Big Paul added.

"You got it, boss," Alden said.

We ran from one side of campus to the other, with Alden in the lead. He moved through the world with such ease, and when I was with him, I could too.

I was finally able to admit to myself that what I felt toward him was a crush, but that word was so amorphous.

"Crush" could mean anything.

But whatever it was, I liked it.

Alden was opening a bizarre, underground world to me. He was like a character in a movie, a manic pixie dream boy, and I didn't mind.

"I need bumpers," I told him as we opened the door to the darkened basement bowling alley.

He laughed as he turned on the lights and the large room powered up. "No, you don't."

62

"I'm telling you, I do. Or I'll get gutter balls."

He reached out to grab my hand, and I let him take it. "Well, good thing we're not bowling."

With that, he pulled me across the cavernous space until we were standing in front of the middle lane.

"Now take off your shoes," he said, turning toward me.

"Absolutely not."

He didn't respond to that, just pulled his sneakers off.

"Ta-da," he said, arms spread wide. He was wearing crisp white athletic socks that stopped halfway up his calves. I cursed myself for not throwing away my ratty socks before college. I was wearing a pair that I had won from a DJ at a friend's bat mitzvah and hadn't had the heart to get rid of all these years later.

"You don't have to take your shoes off," he said finally. "But if you do . . ."

He walked back a few steps, then ran forward, sliding down the lane.

I rolled my eyes but reached for my shoes. There'd been so many times that I'd missed out on parties or friendships or *life* because it wasn't what was expected of me, because my parents wouldn't have approved.

But my parents were across the country.

"Let's gooooo," Alden shouted from the end of the lane, jumping up and down and sliding in the process. "On my count."

When he reached three, I took off, my body tilting backward and my feet gliding along the lane.

I wanted so badly to impress him.

"I'M GONNA FALL INTO THE BALL RETURN!" I shouted as I careened toward Alden and, ultimately, my doom.

But before I could get sucked into the void, he caught me and pulled me toward him, hands around my waist.

"Don't worry," he whispered. "I got you."

It felt like a promise.

TUESDAY, 6 A.M., OUTSIDE TOLEDO, OH

It's dreary yet again as the sun tries its best to rise, but there's the promise of a bright morning here somewhere.

It doesn't feel quite like déjà vu, though, entering a new day after staying up late talking to Oakley—we're on the train, and there's nothing better to do. It's not like it was at Cornell, where I was forgoing responsibilities to stay up with Alden. There are no classes on the train, no tests, no jobs, no life.

The early hour, however, cannot subdue Edward's snack-based excitement. He announced ten minutes ago that, "The conductor is back and reporting for duty," and his volume was dialed to an eleven. If anything, the fact that it's barely dawn seems to be *energizing* him.

"Back for more already I see," Edward says as I roll up to his section of the café car.

"Just need some coffee."

"I get that," he says too loudly for the hour. "Though I don't drink it myself."

I'm about to ask if he snorts cocaine instead when he adds, "I sleep so well on the train. It's like I was *meant* to work here."

I can't imagine that anyone's higher calling is "snack conductor," but Edward clearly derives joy from serving snacks and coffee.

I wish I felt that way about anything. I get glimpses of it sometimes, of who I'm meant to be, but the feeling never lasts long enough for me to bottle up and store it.

I felt it briefly that night with Alden in the bowling alley, when I was running behind him, following his lead, the wind rushing through my thick ponytail.

I never felt that way about being a doctor, that's for sure. Maybe I felt it a bit in the greenhouse, but that wasn't a career. That was a part-time student job where I went to escape the rest of my life.

When I'm back in my trusty booth, I can barely keep my eyes open as I sip my coffee. I'm in the fuzzy space between sleep and wakefulness, and I let my mind drift. I think about spending last night with Oakley. I love that when I was talking to her, I didn't back down on my beliefs. I wasn't compromising any part of myself.

I let the train lull me into this sleep-adjacent state until someone shouts, "ZOE!" near my face.

It's Aya, kneeling on the booth across from me. She crawls to the window and presses her face against the glass, fogging it up with her little-kid breath. She writes, "AYA," in precise letters with her index finger.

"Where's your mom?" I ask, not wanting her to be reprimanded for running into the café car by herself.

"Oh, it's fine," she says. "She knows I'm here. I told her I saw you."

"Right."

Her mom must be desperate for a moment alone if she's letting her daughter hang out with a random person she met in the café car.

Aya talks at me about trains for an indeterminate period of time, and I sip my coffee and try not to fall asleep. When she's in the middle of telling me about how the Grand Canyon Railway steam trains run on vegetable oil, the conductor gets on the loudspeaker to make an announcement.

"All right, folks, we're approaching our final stop: Chicago's Union Station. If you're joining us on the Empire Builder heading out west, you'll have a four-hour layover to explore the beautiful Windy City before boarding."

"Are you going on the Empire Builder?" Aya asks.

I nod. "Are you?"

"Yup, my mom and I have to go to Seattle to visit my aunt. We were going to fly, but I wanted to take the train and since it was just my ninth birthday my mom said we could do it. Like, for my last year before I'm double digits. Well, she didn't say that exactly, but that's pretty much what it is."

"That's really cool," I tell her.

"I know."

Aya runs to the sleeper car to meet up with her mom, and I head to my seat to grab my backpack.

"Hey, you getting off at Chicago?"

I look up, and there's Guy Fieri.

"Pretty sure we have to." I heave my suitcase off the rack, trying to end a conversation before it begins.

But when I disembark, he's there.

"I'm going to get lunch," he tells me. "You should come with."

"I'm okay," I say, walking down the platform.

"My apartment isn't far at all," he adds.

And then, an oasis in the desert: Oakley, struggling with a large pink suitcase a few train cars ahead.

I point to her. "I'm getting lunch with my friend."

I take off, not quite running, but moving as quickly as my wobbly train legs will allow.

Oakley must see the look on my face as I approach, because she says, "What's wrong?" just as I whisper, "Play along."

When I turn around, sure enough, Guy Fieri is approaching.

"This is my friend," I tell him awkwardly. "The one I'm getting lunch with."

Oakley gives me a slight nod before she steps between me and Guy and says, "Reservations soon, don't want to be late."

Oakley holds his gaze for longer than I'd be able to, and finally, he spits on the ground and walks away, muttering a word that sounds an awful lot like "dykes" as he does.

Oakley must've heard it too, because she shouts, "REALLY OBSERVANT!" after him.

When he's gone, I can breathe.

Oakley turns to me. "You okay?"

Half of me feels like I got doused in slime, but the other half is grateful for her protection.

"Come on," she says, waving me over to her luggage and handing me a granola bar. "Follow me."

I roll my eyes, but it's more perfunctory than anything else.

After her performance, I'll follow her without question down the platform, toward Chicago.

Toward a new world.

Six

Tuesday, 10 a.m., Chicago, IL

Oakley walks briskly next to me, rolling her giant pink suitcase behind her down the platform, the air outside the train cold and fresh.

"That's a pretty big suitcase for someone who's just going home for Thanksgiving," I say, struggling to keep up with her and her sleek, blond ponytail.

She nods at my suitcase in turn, which is roughly the size of a large eight-year-old. "What's that saying about the pot calling the kettle black?"

"Touché."

At the end of the platform there's an archway that separates the tunnel from the station proper; it's decorated with hand-traced turkeys and vulgar graffiti.

But when we make it to the other side, I stop short.

"Shit," I remark as I get my first glimpse of Union Station's main hall. It's giant, with a domed ceiling that's at least three stories high. Marble columns line the periphery. "This is so beautiful."

Oakley huffs, and I frown, my eyes ready to roll at a moment's notice. "What?"

"It's just that everyone in the US is weirdly obsessed with classical architecture."

"You don't think this is cool?" I gesture to the giant gilded hall.

"Haven't you noticed that every important building in the country looks like a bad imitation of ancient Greek architecture?"

"What, because of the columns?"

"Well, yes, that's part of it, but also the scale of the building. The architects wanted to give America some semblance of legitimacy. They were trying to situate it in an extended historic timeline that it's not a part of."

"But . . ." I gesture around the room again, as if my waving arms will help Oakley see its majesty. "Look how big it is! That has to count for something."

"Isn't that sort of a smooth-brain way of thinking? Like, 'ooh room's big, so it must be important.'"

"Are you calling my brain smooth?"

"Not yours specifically. I'm just saying that the size of a room shouldn't be a measure of its architectural significance."

"Excuse you, I'll have you know my brain has many folds," I tell her, which might be true anatomically, but it's not how I've been feeling lately.

Oakley's brain, on the other hand, must be made entirely of folds. Deeply annoying, too-smart-for-her-own-good folds but folds nonetheless.

"So," Oakley begins, turning to me but not quite meeting my eyes. "What are we doing for lunch?"

She sounds nervous, and I try to hide the smile that creeps onto my face. She wants to hang out with me. She wasn't just saying it to get rid of Guy Fieri's evil twin.

"We could eat in the station?" I suggest. "I don't want to lug my suitcase around."

"I'm sure there's a place where we can drop off our bags."

"So if we find a place to put our bags, you want me to walk around with you and have lunch? Outside?"

"Do you have a better way to waste four hours?"

I have plenty of ways to waste four hours. I'm an expert at it.

But I find, as I think about it, that I want to waste this time with her.

"Yeah, I do," I say, taking a breath. "But sure. Let's go waste four hours."

I've never been to Chicago before—it's freezing, and I'm underdressed.

"Why didn't you bring gloves?" Oakley's bundled in a peacoat, topped with a white cable-knit hat with a matching scarf and gloves.

She looks polished and preppy. Meanwhile, I'm wearing a light shell over my day-old overalls and flannel.

"I don't know. I didn't think I'd be walking around Chicago!" I shiver, and Oakley burrows farther into her jacket.

"Did you not look at the itinerary?" she asks.

"No, not really." I booked the train so last-minute that I only checked to make sure it would get me to Seattle. I didn't focus much on what would happen in between.

She eyes me suspiciously. "So you're taking a cross-country train ride and you don't even know where it's stopping?"

"I know where it's stopping, just not for how long," I admit.

I don't want her asking too many questions about the logistics of my trip, because if she does then she might want to know the reason I'm taking the train in the first place.

And I can't have that.

I *like* that Oakley doesn't know me or why I'm riding the train. The expectations she has of me are only based on how I look and what we've talked about, and both my outfit and our topics of conversation have been very queer, so it feels right. She knows a part of me that I've been stifling for months.

"Where are you taking me?"

When we left Union Station, Oakley said she had a place in mind, so I let her lead the way, which may or may not have been a mistake. She's been guiding us for half an hour or more, with no sign of stopping.

"You'll see."

We're silent again for a few minutes as we walk and Oakley checks the directions on her phone.

And then she pauses in front of a church.

"It's here," she says, pointing at the large beige, brick building.

"You wanted to see . . . a church?" I jump in place, trying to warm myself up.

"No," she says, pointing to a second-story window. "I wanted to see a ghost."

I'm beginning to think that Oakley took me here to murder me and/or engage in some sort of occult ritual, but then I examine the window more closely. Or rather, the space where a window should be.

"It's a ghost church," she tells me, walking down the street and turning the corner. I run to catch up. "Look."

We're standing facing where the side of the building should be, but all that's there are exposed steel beams and overgrown grass.

I shiver, though I'm not sure if it's from the cold this time. It's a skeleton of a church, like a set piece from a Hollywood lot that was only meant to be filmed from the front.

There's nothing inside, just a crumbling brick foundation and a badly burned crucifix nailed to the inside of the one remaining wall.

"This is unbelievably creepy," I say, turning to Oakley, but she's already walking toward the church, through a gate that should probably be locked. I follow reluctantly.

It's almost too quiet within the church grounds, as if even the sounds of the city are scared to pass through the hollow shell of a building.

"I shouldn't be here," I say. It's one thing to trespass into an old, definitely haunted church. It's another to trespass into an old, definitely haunted church when you're a Jew.

It's ominous, like I might be smote if I take another step.

"If you shouldn't be here then I *definitely* shouldn't be," Oakley says, bending down to pick up a chunk of stone that must've fallen off the building.

"At least you were a Christian at some point."

"You know you're allowed to go inside of churches. You're not going to burst into flames because you're Jewish."

"Maybe not, but it kind of feels like I might." I've been inside a church a couple of times, once for an old teacher's wedding and once for an interfaith event that the church was doing with my synagogue, but both times I felt deeply uncomfortable.

"Okay, but here's the thing," Oakley says. "I don't think the religious power of a church is in the building. Like, this"—she points to the hollow interior of the former church—"isn't a religious space anymore." She rubs a hand on the exposed brick of the inside wall, and I look around to make sure no one's about to arrest us and/or condemn us to eternal damnation. "The English word for church is a rough translation of the ancient Greek word ecclesia, which basically means an assembly of people."

"I feel like you'd do well on *Jeopardy!*," I say, trailing anxiously behind Oakley as she explores the grounds. "You know too much."

"Oh, I *know* I'd do well," she says casually. "But anyway, that's all it means, ecclesia, assembly. It doesn't matter that we're here, walking around the grounds of this church, because it's nothing. It's not a spiritual place anymore; it's only a building. And it's barely even that."

"But that's not true," I insist, and it feels good to push back. "Like, for Jews, we still have a fast commemorating a temple that was destroyed thousands of years ago." I look up and try to figure out how to explain what I'm feeling. "I don't know if I believe in God, like I told you, but I believe in tradition. I like being a part of a ceremony that people have done for thousands of years. And that includes being in a physical space—a synagogue, a temple, what have you."

"Wow, okay, brag," Oakley says. "Not everyone comes from a religion as old as yours."

I roll my eyes and point to the charred crucifix. "I stand by what I said, though. It's deeply creepy."

She shakes her head. "Feel how you want."

"Fine."

"Fine."

I reluctantly smile at her.

She smiles back. "You want to know what churches are good for?"

"Not particularly, but I'm pretty sure you're going to tell me anyway."

"Free food and well-maintained public bathrooms," she says, and when I look over at her, her face is more serious than it was before.

"I'll never say no to a public bathroom."

"Exactly."

I like talking to Oakley like this. Half of what I've been saying aren't even thoughts I've had before. But being with her opens all these faucets in my brain, and ideas come flowing out: ideas about the nature of religious spaces and buildings. About tradition and ceremony.

I didn't have this at Cornell.

All I had, after a while, was Alden.

NEARLY A MONTH INTO COLLEGE

If I didn't kiss him, it wasn't real.

That's what I told myself, even though Alden and I spent every day together, talking and flirting and hanging out. At a certain point I knew we would have to break the seal. To do *something* to signify once and for all that we were both into each other and wanted to date.

I was seeing the Tees less and less and him more and more, but I still made excuses when I couldn't hang out with them. I didn't come right out and say, "I'm spending time with a boy I have a crush on," because that would invite questions about my sexuality, which I wasn't prepared to answer.

Then Alden broached the topic himself.

"Remember that night in the clock tower?" he asked. "When we first hung out?"

"Of course," I told him.

"Well, I've been thinking a lot about it. About the tower and about, like, time." It was late and we were in our usual spots in the student union, on opposite sides of our couch.

"Oh yeah?" I didn't know where he was going with this, but he sounded serious.

"So, it's like this: without marking time, we're just floating through life." He was speaking quietly, and I leaned forward so I didn't miss a word. "But the tower ringing every hour lets us know that time is moving forward, that it's actually progressing. It lets us assess our life and how we're spending our days—you know?"

"Okay, Mr. English Major," I joked, but his face was serious.

"I'm trying to tell you something."

I stilled. "Okay?"

"I feel like I'm, well, *time*," he said. "And that night we spent together? I don't know, I haven't been able to stop thinking about you since. You're the clock tower, Zoe. You mark my days; you give them meaning and structure. You *are* my time."

I could tell it was a line. I would've cringed at it in a movie, but somehow it worked when he said it. I wanted to believe that I was his clock tower, that I mattered to him. That there was a reason I was here, in this student union, not studying to become a doctor.

"I wanted to kiss you that night," he said. "But I've been waiting because I didn't want to rush you."

"I wanted to kiss you too," I whispered.

Because even if I didn't know it at the time, it was true.

I *liked* him.

But there was more in that *like* that I didn't quite know how to name.

Maybe it was because I could see myself in him, a more masculine side of me. We were the same height, we had the same build. Even our hair color was the same.

But the *like* was there above it all, coursing through me as he held my hand.

Then, because I needed to know what he would say: "What have we been doing, Alden?"

"I thought we were kind of . . . dating?" He looked so hesitant, so boyish. "You're not seeing anyone else, are you?"

"No," I said quickly.

"Me neither."

"Cool."

"Cool."

We both let our gazes drift to the rest of the Straight; at this point everyone was gone for the night except for some kid passed out on their laptop.

An eternity later: "Can I kiss you now?"

I nodded. I had stopped breathing.

"Okay."

He stood up. I followed. "Let's make this a no-judgment kiss, all right? It can be practice."

I nodded again.

Then he stuck his tongue down my throat. It was warmer and thicker than I'd imagined a tongue could be. Like a large worm or a small snake.

It wasn't bad *or* good, just a new sensation.

He held my hips, and I wrapped my arms around his neck, the way I'd seen girls do in movies. We kissed for a while, and it got better the longer it went on.

With that, the seal had been broken; we were well past due for this kiss.

Afterward, we stayed up all night talking and kissing. It was nearly six in the morning when I got back to my dorm.

I collapsed onto my bed, wired. I ran a hand through my hair, which was coming loose from its ponytail.

That was my first kiss.

TUESDAY, 1 P.M., CHICAGO, IL

Once Oakley's had her fill of the ghost church, she shepherds me to a place where we can order take-out deep-dish pizza for lunch.

"There's this spot right by Union Station," she says, and once again leads the way.

The restaurant's packed, and when we make it to the front of the line, we each order an individual six-inch, deep-dish pizza and get out as quickly as possible.

"Oh my god, why is this so heavy?" I ask, doing a biceps curl to adjust the bag in my hand.

"Maybe you're just weak," Oakley says as she holds her bag with ease.

"Excuse you, I'm very buff."

"Yeah, you're practically a bodybuilder." She points to my noodle arms and I swing my too-dense pie into her leg in response.

"Careful with that thing; you'll knock me out."

We make it back to Union Station before they've announced our track, so we pick up our suitcases and camp out in the center of the Great Hall.

There are a bunch of people milling around who were on the first train with us. I spot Aya in the distance, doing laps, getting out her little-kid energy. And there are Clint and Virginia, napping next to each other.

"This is not pizza," I say once I've opened the container and taken a bite. "This is casserole."

"You're from Seattle; you can't talk," Oakley says, sawing at her slice with the plastic fork and knife from the bag.

"It's not like there's good pizza in Eastern Washington either."

"Yeah—I mean no, there's not," she admits. "But I just spent four months in New York City eating pizza by myself every day, so I'm something of an expert."

I turn to Oakley, the bite I took burning the roof of my mouth. "By yourself?"

She shrugs. "At least I got good pizza out of it."

She's trying to sound nonchalant, but it's not working.

"What did you do all day?" I ask, not wanting to let this go. "If you were by yourself?"

"I told you." She says this in a harsher voice than I've heard from her. "I ate pizza."

"Right, but now you see my predicament," I tell her, trying to ease the tension. "I'm thinking eating a pizza takes maybe five, ten minutes, max. So what did you do for the other twenty-three hours and fifty minutes of the day?"

"I walked around. Read a lot of weird things." She stabs her plastic fork into the mass of cheese. "Did you know that there was a poet in Victorian England named Michael Field who was actually two lesbians?"

"No." She's being obtuse, and she knows it.

I try to shake the image of her eating pizza alone out of my head, but it's stuck there. I need to know more about Oakley's time in New York.

But then again, if I keep digging, she'd be within her right to direct questions back at me.

"Well," I say, pointing to my lunch to distract from the awkward pause. "I wasn't saying that this isn't good. It's buttery and cheesy and shit, so obviously it tastes great. But it's simply not pizza."

"Don't say that too loudly or they'll come for you," Oakley says.

"Who?"

"*They*," she repeats.

"Ominous."

"As it should be."

We chat and eat for a few more minutes as the deep-dish "pizza" sinks to the bottom of my stomach like a brick.

Aya waves to me from across the hall, then sprints over at breakneck speed. She runs up behind my chair and grabs my shoulders, using them to spring into the air.

"Ow," I say automatically, rubbing my back where her little viselike hands had taken hold.

"Very buff," Oakley murmurs under her breath, leaning into me.

"Hi, Zoe!" Aya says, walking around the chairs so we're facing each other.

"Hi, Aya!" I point to Oakley. "This is Oakley."

Aya waves, but she looks suspicious. "Are you two girlfriends?"

Oakley laughs so loudly that it echoes around the room, which turns into choking as she coughs up a chunk of cheese.

"Ew," Aya says, backing away from the cheese chunk. She looks between us again. "So, are you?"

Oakley's still coughing, and my heart is beating too fast.

"No," I tell her quickly. "We're *definitely* not."

I turn to Oakley for backup, but she's staring down at her lunch.

"Oh, okay," Aya says. "It would be cool if you were. I only asked because my best friend, Cayden, has two moms."

"Nice," I say, my voice approximately three octaves higher than normal.

"See you on the train!" And with that, Aya's gone, back to running in circles, leaving only destruction in her wake.

"Sorry about her," I tell Oakley.

"Don't apologize," she says. "That kid is iconic."

"Agreed, but I mean about what she said about us being girlfriends."

"So?" Oakley shrugs.

"It doesn't bother you?"

"Nope," she says, standing up. "We're not girlfriends; we just met. She can think what she wants."

"I guess that's true," I say, and the "I guess" is doing the heavy lifting there.

She plays with the chain of her necklace. "But we *could* hang out more, you know? On the next leg of the journey."

"You actually want to hang out with me?"

"Unless there's someone hotter than you," she says, not quite meeting my eye. "Then I'll ditch you for them."

I nearly choke on my own saliva until Oakley adds, "Kidding, kidding."

After a long moment I say, "Sure, Oakley. Let's . . . hang out."

She nods, and it's settled. My train companion: a mouthy, blond ex-Mormon with too much information stored in her huge head.

Let's see how this goes.

Seven

Tuesday, 2 p.m., Leaving Chicago, IL

It's a completely different feeling, boarding this second train; there's an air of excitement that wasn't there yesterday. The train to Chicago was one night, but this leg of the journey is two nights and three days, and we're crossing a part of the country that I've only ever flown over.

"I'm gonna drop my stuff off at my seat," I tell Oakley. "I'll see you around?"

"Sounds good," she says. But she doesn't move. "*Or* you could drop your stuff off in my sleeper car. If you wanted."

"It's fine," I tell her. "I can just—"

"Do you want someone to steal your stuff?"

"They can't," I tell her. "Train law."

She rolls her eyes and walks away, giving me no choice but to follow. We head through coach, through the dining car, then into a space we didn't have on the last train: an observation car.

It's already popular, with people claiming seats that look out onto the landscape. The windows go from the floor all the way up to the roof of the train.

Finally, we make our way to the first of the elusive sleeper cars.

"It's this one," she says, as she opens the door to her bedroom.

"This is it?" The room isn't how I expected, especially since there's no bed. There's a sink, a sofa, and a chair. It's tiny, with barely enough room for me and Oakley to stand.

"Oh, this is way nicer than the room on the last train." She shrugs off her backpack and throws it onto the sofa. There's a chair facing it, where I put my own bag.

"Where's the bed?" I ask, examining the small plastic door labeled "closet" that couldn't fit a single jacket.

"There are two, actually," Oakley says. "They fold down." She points to the sofa. "That one's a double bed, and then there's a single up top."

I nod, feeling awkward now. I'm in a girl's bedroom.

Well, a girl's bedroom on a train, but still.

Before I can contemplate this further, the conductor comes on over the loudspeaker, a different voice than the last one. "Folks, folks, folks, folks, folks. We've got a full train, so say hi to your neighbors because we're going to be getting cozy. The time now is approximately"—she pauses—"2:08 p.m., so we're starting our journey out west about as on time as can be expected. Our first stop will be Glenview, Illinois, in half an hour."

Then, of course, Edward breaks in. "Well, no, Camila, I'd say that our first stop will be SNACKS. Folks, for those of you who are new here, I'm your snack conductor—"

"Edward, I'm not doing this today," the conductor—Camila—says, cutting him off.

I bark out a laugh, and Oakley looks at me.

85

"Did you buy a snack on the last train?" I ask her.

"Nope."

"Then you haven't had the absolute pleasure of meeting Edward."

"Not yet," she says. "I did everything I could to avoid him."

"Smart."

That's all I say because I know what it's like to do everything in your power to avoid someone.

I watch Oakley watch the shimmering gray expanse of Lake Michigan. She's probably the most beautiful person I've ever seen—and she's certainly the smartest.

Maybe it'll be nice spending more time with her. It's only three days, and my plan had initially been to stare out the window and be miserable for those seventy-two hours. This could be better.

This could be *something*.

ONE MONTH INTO COLLEGE

After our kiss, I thought everything would feel easier. And it did, in that I wasn't constantly thinking about what it would be like if we kissed or if we should kiss or if Alden wanted to kiss me or if I wanted to kiss him.

This was a definitive answer: we were dating, and that was that. It was better than the undefined half-relationship we'd had before.

The only issue was that Alden didn't want to see me during the daylight hours. Or, at least, that's what it felt like.

But after dark, he was all mine. I became nocturnal, sleeping until three or four in the afternoon, skipping classes, and dragging myself out of bed only to rendezvous with him, work a shift at the greenhouse, or occasionally eat a meal with the Tees.

I wanted the Tees to tell me to fuck off. I was being a shitty friend, and I still hadn't told them about Alden.

But somehow, they didn't.

"I have something to show you," Alden said one night, grinning.

I smiled back; he was always happy to see me. "All right."

Alden put his hand on the small of my back and pushed me forward. I could feel the heat and the sweat and the energy of it long after he took his hand away.

When we were touching like this, I was acutely aware that we were the same height, that our bodies matched up, his shoulders level with mine, his fingertips brushing the same spots on his thighs.

I'd never cared about his height before, but now that we were dating, it felt wrong, or at least significant.

I knew I was feeding into problematic ideals, but I couldn't stop fixating on it.

Sometimes, looking at him was like looking in a fun house mirror.

"Where are we going?" I asked as he reached out for me.

"Have you ever been to the rare-manuscript library?"

He liked to go places no one else went, to take advantage of everything the school had to offer. He behaved as if the world had swung its doors wide open for him, and really, it had.

I shook my head. "Isn't it closed?"

He pulled a key chain out of his backpack. "I know a guy."

"You always know a guy."

"It's always the same guy."

This time, to get to yet another place we weren't meant to be, we walked through the main library and beneath an archway, then down a dark set of stairs past foreboding signs claiming that trespassers would be caught on camera and persecuted to the full extent of the law.

"There are no cameras," Alden assured me. "They just say it to scare you."

It was working; I wanted to turn back.

But I kept my feet firmly planted as Alden fumbled with the key, then pushed open the door.

"Voilà," he said as if he had built the room just for me.

I took in the scene: the walls were lined with giant leather-bound tomes, and there was an overpowering mildewy stench.

He wandered the room, rubbing his hands against the spines of the books. "Look at this one," he said. "It's old herbaria pressings."

Alden pulled it off the shelf—he wasn't wearing gloves, which felt wrong. There had to be a fixed protocol for handling a book that delicate. It was part of a collection labeled "Nineteenth-Century Friendship Albums."

"I thought you'd like it," he said. "Since you work in the greenhouse."

I nodded as I carefully flipped through the pages, silently apologizing to the people of the past who had created these notes and ephemera, as well as the current librarians who would kill Alden if they knew.

"I *do* like it," I whispered. "Thank you."

I read the finding guide of the collection, which said that the flowers held within were pressed by a woman named Henrietta to give to her "friend" Jane. But the letters Henrietta had written to Jane were far from "friendly."

These were lesbian flowers, and once I figured that out, my heart was beating out of my chest.

Because, of course, I assumed that the next thing Alden would say was, "*I* also *thought you'd like it because you're a lesbian.*"

I glanced up at him, but I had to look away before he could see in my eyes the lie on which our relationship was based. But it *wasn't* a lie, I reminded myself, because I *did* like him. So that made me something other than a lesbian.

He was too *good*, and I was too *wrong*.

After I made him try to put the pressings away exactly as he'd found them, I pulled out my phone—I had a number of texts waiting for me in the Tees group chat.

Rex: COME THROUGH
UNDERWEAR PARTY IN DONLON
EVERYONES A LIL NAKEY

They sent a video to go along with the messages: Rex, Autumn, and Shelly were dancing in one of the auditoriums, surrounded by people in varying states of undress.

I had vaguely remembered hearing about the party from them earlier in the week: some queer senior was having a clothing-optional dance party, which was my worst nightmare.

Me: ah i totally forgot!!
i have a ton of hw to do but have so much fun!!!!

Autumn thumbs-upped the message, and I turned back to Alden, the presumably straight boy who'd dragged me to the library to see pressed flowers.

I almost laughed at the irony of it: a boy showing me a book with historical lesbian love notes when he didn't even know I was queer.

"Those flowers are beautiful," I told him finally.

He turned to me. "You are too."

I shivered. "That's not what we were talking about."

I was deflecting, but the thought that he saw me as someone who *could* be beautiful made my cheeks warm.

We received a school-wide message the next day that there had been a break-in in the rare-manuscript library. That a page of a herbaria had fallen to the floor.

Alden sent me a screenshot of the email.

ALDEN: worth it

TUESDAY, 4 P.M., NEAR MILWAUKEE, WI

"So," Oakley claps her hands together, "what should we do to pass the time?"

We're already behind schedule, which is a small miracle.

"I was thinking about singing that song that's like 'Ninety-nine Bottles of Beer on the Wall' until you wanted to murder me in cold blood."

"You wouldn't even be able to get to 'ninety-eight bottles' before I threw you out the train window."

"Violence is never the answer," I tell her, placing a hand to my chest, mock-offended.

She snorts. "I was thinking something more *active*, you know, to get the blood pumping."

"I'm not doing push-ups."

She looks me up and down. "Of course you're not."

"Excuse you," I say. "I might be scrawny, but I can do at least ten push-ups."

Oakley raises her hands in surrender, and some part of myself needs to prove to her that I can, in fact, do this. So I roll the sleeves of my flannel up to my elbows and find a spot on the ground of her sleeper car.

"It's so gross down there," she says, but I'm not listening.

"Count for me."

I can't see her as I'm staring at my scrawny arms and the stained carpet, but I can practically hear her eyes rolling as she says, "One," and I do my first push-up.

Which is also my last, because, as it turns out, I am extremely weak.

Oakley laughs, quietly at first before it turns into hysterics.

"Okay, okay," I say, but I can't help but smile too. At least if I'm making a fool of myself, it's for Oakley's entertainment.

Once she calms down, she says, "So obviously not push-ups. I was thinking a mini scavenger hunt." She's sitting with one of her legs up on the seat in a half-butterfly, holding on to her ankle, lovely and sun-drenched in the afternoon light.

"What kind of scavenger hunt?" I ask, knocking myself out of that thought.

She pulls out her backpack, rips a piece of paper out of a notebook, and quickly scribbles a note.

"There," she says after a few seconds of writing.

OAKLEY AND ZOE'S TRAIN SCAVENGER HUNT:
FIND SOMEONE WHO'S FROM ANOTHER COUNTRY
FIND SOMEONE WHO'S NEVER RIDDEN THE TRAIN
FIND THE OLDEST PERSON ON THE TRAIN (OAKLEY)
FIND THE YOUNGEST PERSON ON THE TRAIN (ZOE)

"That's not much of a scavenger hunt," I tell her, looking at the list.

"Sounds like loser mentality to me."

"Fine," I tell her, not backing down from the challenge. "I'm in."

"All right, should we say . . . thirty minutes?" Oakley pulls up the clock app on her phone and hands me a piece of paper and a pen.

"You're on."

She counts down from ten, and as she says one, we push past each other and sprint out of her sleeper compartment. The first place I go is the nearest coach car, hoping that the woman with the fresh baby came on this train too.

Luckily, she's there, breastfeeding while watching a movie on her laptop.

"Excuse me?" I whisper, not wanting to bother her, but she doesn't hear me, so I say it louder.

At that, the baby turns with their big eyes to look at me, but the mom doesn't react.

"She sleeps with her eyes open," the person across the aisle says. "Thought she was dead at first, but she's fine."

The man looks like a stretched-out piece of taffy. Even his mouth is long, and he's using it to smile at me.

"I know this is going to sound weird," I start, then check the note Oakley wrote for me. "But are you from another country and/or is this your first time taking this train?"

"You're in luck." He's grinning now. "I'm from Canada."

I smile back at him and write his name—Mike—on the piece of paper. We talk for a minute, and I tell him that I've only ever been to British Columbia, but that I'd like to visit more of Canada.

"Try the Canadian National Railway," he says. "I took a cross-country train trip with them a few years ago, so I figured I'd try the US next."

I tell him that if I ever have a reason to take a four-day train trip again, he'll be the first person I call.

Then I turn to the woman with the fresh baby, and she snores loudly.

The sound wakes her up, and though her eyes were already open, the life jumps back into them.

"Hi," I say carefully. "I wanted to make sure you were okay."

It's not the entire truth, but it's not a lie either.

She purses her lips, and her baby stretches their balled fists in the air. "I'm fine, thanks."

Then the baby starts screaming.

Everyone around us looks over, clearly done with this infant and their many loud noises.

"Shh, shh," the mom coos, bouncing the baby over her shoulder while staring daggers at me.

But then the baby looks me dead in the eyes and immediately stops crying. They have the most perfect face I've ever seen, even though it's splotchy with tears.

The mom's eyes are nearly as wide as her child's as she turns to me. "Can you take him?" she whispers.

"I don't know if that's a great—"

But my protestations don't stop her from shoving the small thing into my arms. I cradle him like he's made of glass. I've never held a baby before, but this one's warm and wriggly, and I immediately know I'd do anything to protect him.

"Thank you," the mom whispers. "That's Alberto. Or Bert. I'm still trying to figure out which to call him. And I'm Elaine."

Alberto/Bert squeezes his eyes shut as if he's planning on crying, but I bounce him a little and he stops.

"You have the magic touch," Elaine tells me.

"I don't think so," I say quietly as I stare at him. He's so small and . . . human.

And then Elaine starts crying too.

"I'm so sorry," she mutters through tears.

I don't know how to comfort her, so I bounce her son and make gentle shushing noises in the hopes that what works for him will help her as well.

"I can't do this on my own," she whispers, and it's unclear if she's telling me or just admitting it aloud.

Now I *really* don't know how to comfort her. I don't have anywhere close to the same level of responsibility that she has, and even so, I've dropped the ball.

But when *I* dropped the ball, it was only me who suffered. My grades slipped; my life felt like it wasn't mine anymore. Still, I wasn't hurting anyone but myself.

Elaine can't drop the ball, even if she wants to. She's got this small helpless person who relies on her for everything.

But maybe I can relieve some of that pressure.

"Do you want me to take him for a little while?" I ask, and she nods gratefully through hiccups.

When Oakley arrives back in the observation car, the sight that greets her is me sitting with an infant strapped to my chest in a BabyBjörn.

"I hesitate to ask," she begins.

"Shhhh," I tell her, then mouth, *Baby sleeping*.

It's mostly a joke, because Alberto/Bert can apparently sleep through anything. The train bumps and clangs over the tracks, and he keeps snoozing.

"How did you acquire a baby?" Oakley asks as she slides into the seat next to mine.

"You said, 'Find the youngest person on the train.'"

"I didn't mean *kidnap* him."

When I explain the truth of the matter, Oakley is only slightly less concerned.

"So, where's the oldest passenger on the train?" I ask to fill the silence.

"I tried to strap her to my chest, but she didn't quite fit."

"Ha, ha." I roll my eyes.

"Her name is Nellie and she's one hundred and two."

"How do you know she's the oldest person on the train?" I ask while hiding my surprise that someone that old is taking a journey this long.

"The same way you know your baby is the youngest one."

"Fair enough," I admit, and as if in response, Alberto/Bert wraps his miniscule hand around my pinkie finger.

Oakley leans back in her seat. "Nellie was telling me about how train travel used to be luxurious."

I point around the stained, beat-up observation car. "More luxurious than *this*?"

"Velvet-seat luxurious," Oakley says. "Caviar-in-the-dining-car luxurious. And get this: she was wearing her *travel hat*. She had a box for it and everything and wouldn't stop adjusting it on her head. She is *deeply* mother."

"Sounds like it," I say. "Why haven't I seen her?"

"She slipped one of the attendants a hundo to bring everything to her sleeper car."

"I love her," I say as Alberto/Bert fusses. I bounce and he calms down.

"And he seems to love you," Oakley says. "Would you ever have kids? You're good with him." She asks it so casually that I'm taken aback. It's not a casual question.

"I don't know," I say honestly. "What about you?"

"Someday, probably," she says. "Maybe one."

"Don't have one," I tell her emphatically. "Being an only child is terrible. I grew up with my parents laser-focused on every little thing I did."

"I'm sure being an only child is better than being the last of six."

"*What?*" I ask. "Six?"

"You can't be that surprised," she says. "I thought that was the first thing everyone knew about Mormons, that they have a lot of kids."

"Yeah, but *five* siblings?"

"'*And God blessed them,*'" Oakley begins. "'*And God said unto them, "Be fruitful, and multiply, and replenish the earth."*'"

"Okay, but that's, like, Old Testament shit," I say. "That's not unique to Mormonism."

"You're not wrong," she says. "But I was also taught that there was a set number of spirit children in a premortal existence who were waiting in line for bodies, and it would benefit them to be born 'in the covenant.'" She says all of this with a blank expression. "That's why my parents had so many children—if the spirits are born into a Mormon family, they'll have a leg up for the Second Coming."

After a moment of surprise, I clear my throat. "So, one kid?" I say as lightly as I can, trying to bring the conversation back to the more surface-level place it had been before.

I like having fun with Oakley, but the more I learn—about her upbringing, her religion, her beliefs—the more I want to know.

And the more I begin to care.

Eight

Tuesday, 5 p.m., near Columbus, WI

"Edward, I'm baaaack," I call, as if we're an old married couple and I'm returning home after a long day at work. "And this is Oakley."

I dragged her down here after returning Alberto/Bert to Elaine.

The café is located in a different spot on this train than the last: on the lower level of the observation car, down a steep staircase.

Edward gasps and points to Oakley. "Did you just board?"

She seems taken aback. "No? I've been traveling since New York."

"And you haven't come to see me?" He shakes his head "I'm glad Zoe helped you come to your senses."

I don't remember telling him my name, but I don't question it. Chalk it up to train magic.

"I'm glad too," Oakley says, grinning at me.

And I can't help but smile back.

"You two are so cute." Edward claps. "You know, I've officiated a number of train weddings."

"We're not dating," I say as Oakley says, "Train weddings?"

Edward gestures between us. "Okay, loving this vibe." He sighs as he pours me a cup of coffee without taking my order. "I was in love once, but he didn't understand that my one true love was the train. He couldn't handle playing second fiddle to this magnificent beast." He tenderly pats the wall of the snack car. "But this is where I belong."

"That's beautiful," Oakley says. I don't know why she's so on board with Edward's chaotic energy, but the two of them seem to be hitting it off.

"And we're not dating," I say again for good measure.

It's the second time someone has mistaken us for a couple, which is bizarre. Often, even if lesbians are making out, people will coo about how they're such "good friends."

Not that Oakley and I are a couple. And not that I have any experience being with a girl.

Edward hands me the coffee in exchange for my debit card, and I mumble out a thanks.

"Coffee for you, hon?" he asks Oakley.

"I'm all good, thanks."

He winks. "My pleasure."

"You're not tired?" I ask as I open a wobbly packet of cream and three sugars at once.

"I am," she says, " but I don't drink coffee."

"How come?"

"Fear of becoming a heathen, mostly."

I turn around. "What's that now?"

"Mormons don't drink coffee."

A beat. "You're not a Mormon."

"Old habits die hard I guess."

We walk up the narrow staircase back to the observation car, and when we get there, Aya's in one of the seats nearby, reading a thick book.

"Whatcha reading?" I ask her as Oakley and I take the seats nearby.

"Percy Jackson," she tells me.

"What, you're not reading about trains?"

"I like other things too, you know," she says with a sigh, closing the book to show me the cover. "I'm on the third one."

"The fourth is the best," Oakley says.

Both Aya and I stare at her.

"What? It is."

Everything that comes out of Oakley's mouth surprises me. She has theories on religion, gender expression, and, of course, a favorite Percy Jackson book.

"I brought that one on the train too!" Aya says excitedly. "I'll let you know when I get up to it."

"Please do," Oakley says earnestly.

Aya goes back to reading, and a few minutes later her mom comes to grab her, looking as frazzled as ever.

"Why didn't you tell Edward we weren't dating?" I ask Oakley once they're gone.

I shouldn't care so much, but she didn't shut down Aya either back in the train station. She just let it happen.

"I don't know." She shrugs. "I guess I'm just happy to be read as queer. Obviously we're not dating, but the idea that someone thinks we *could* be, that I could be queer enough to date someone like you. That's kind of nice."

"Oh," I say, but my mind is focused on the "queer enough to date someone like you" part. I know what she means in the abstract—on the outside, it's hard not to read me as queer. Not that being read as queer makes you queerer than someone else.

Except she doesn't know that just weeks ago I was read almost exclusively as straight. That I was *trying* to be read that way in public.

Oakley nudges me gently, and when I turn to her, she has a sly smile on her face. "Though of course if he knew that I have my entire birth chart memorized, he'd probably have figured it out already."

I snort-laugh at that. Oakley's good at knocking the bad thoughts out of my head. "What's the part of your chart that makes you such a know-it-all?"

"My Virgo moon," she says without a hint of sarcasm.

"I'm a Pisces," I tell her. "I don't know my moon sign, though."

"So *that's* why the baby loves you so much," she says. "My sun sign is Cancer."

"What does that mean?" I know enough about astrology to tell people my sign but not enough to be able to understand anyone else's.

"It means I'm protective of myself."

"Oh yeah?" I ask. "What are you protecting?" I try to sound flirty, but it comes out serious.

Oakley glances down at her seat.

"You don't have to tell me," I say quietly.

"No." She shakes her head. "It's okay." I wait for her to continue, and eventually, she does. "I only left the Church last year. I knew I would, one day, but I thought maybe—" She takes a deep breath, then looks me right in the eye. "I wanted to travel the world. I wanted to fall in love."

I'm taken aback by her directness. "Why couldn't you do that while still being part of the Church?"

"Why do you think?" She gestures to herself, then sighs. "I would've done it. I would've gotten married to a man and had an eternal family. I might've become a Mormon family vlogger—"

"You would've been good at that," I say. "You have the right aesthetic."

"I know." The corner of her mouth turns up. "But the problem is, it would've been a lie. There are plenty of lesbians married to men in the Church, some are even married to *gay* men, but I didn't want that. I care about love. About loving someone."

I let her words hang in the air between us, unsure what to do with them.

"So, you're a hopeless romantic?" I ask eventually. "And that's why you moved to New York?"

"Partially, yes." She shrugs. "I thought it would be easier to find other queer people there. To befriend them and date them and actually have a *community*, you know?"

I *do* know. More than I can say. Because, at the beginning, that's what I wanted too. Until I found Alden, and I tried to make two different parts of my life fit together when they had no business doing anything of the sort.

One Month and a Few Days into College

I knew I needed to be better about hanging out with the Tees if I wanted to maintain that friendship, but they always made plans at night, and that time was reserved exclusively for Alden.

So I came up with a solution: we'd all hang out together. I organized the whole thing, but when the time came, we were running late because I had no idea what to wear. I couldn't decide between something obviously queer—whatever that meant—or something I usually wore around Alden. Maybe it was a false dichotomy. Maybe I could've worn the more masculine clothes I'd brought to college in front of him, but I couldn't bring myself to do it.

I felt like I did when I had to dress up for my cousins' b'nai mitzvahs. I would wear an old cardigan and a skirt and I would want to tear my skin off when we took family photos.

But this was different. This was a dinner in the dining hall with my friends and my boyfriend.

Boyfriend.

It was weird even to think that word. I'd been certain I'd never have a boyfriend in my life, yet here I was, just over a month into college, with one of my very own.

"Do you think they'll like me?" Alden asked as we walked over to the table in the dining hall the Tees had grabbed. He was wearing khaki pants and a black button-up shirt, and every part of me wanted to run.

"Of course," I told him, even though I wasn't entirely convinced that the Tees liked *me*, let alone if they would like him.

I didn't know how this dinner would go, but I needed it to work, to ensure that all the parts of myself that felt so disparate could somehow mix.

I had told the Tees over text the day before that this guy was "someone I was kind of seeing." They had all given the message a thumbs-up but hadn't responded beyond that. I knew, therefore, that they were all sprinting to the group chat they had without me to gossip about this shocking turn of events.

"Heyyyyyy," Shelly said as we walked over to the table, stretching out the word in a way that made him sound guilty, like he hadn't stopped talking about me and my heterosexual boyfriend since last night.

"Did someone die?" Rex asked, making room for me and Alden at the table.

I turned to them as I dropped my backpack on the food-scrap-covered floor. "What?"

"You two look like you're dressed for a funeral."

I was wearing a black dress that I'd had since ninth grade and used to wear to Science Olympiad competitions.

And of course, Rex called me out on this right away. They always wore bright colors and jumpsuits and generally looked like a queer clown in the best way, so they were never *not* going to notice my clothing choices.

"Just coming from the greenhouse," I lied, as if I'd wear an outfit this formal to muck about in the soil and humidity.

"It's nice to meet you, Alden," Autumn said, changing the subject. She was resting a hand against her cheek, and she looked so cute sitting like that that it made me wonder, not for the first time, what these past few weeks would've been like if I'd dated her instead of Alden.

"Thanks," he said, clearing his throat. "It's nice to meet you too."

"We've heard so much about you," Rex said, and I tried to silently thank them for so boldly lying.

Alden smiled awkwardly, and I could tell we were both thinking the same thing: Alden had not heard much about the Tees. Or anything at all.

"So, what's your major?" Shelly asked.

"Ah," Alden said, crossing his ankle over his knee, "the classic question."

I was suddenly hyperaware of him being a cis man. Of him taking up space, wearing khakis, being slightly obnoxious in the way he spoke and answered simple questions.

I found this charming when we were alone, but around my queer friends it was different. I knew it was wrong, but I wanted him to change, if only for this dinner, so that he could better meet their expectations.

But he was who he was, and I liked him that way.

"English," Alden said finally. "I'm majoring in English."

Everyone nodded, and the conversation petered out.

"Should we get food?" Shelly suggested, already standing up from the table.

The other Tees agreed, and off they went.

Leaving me behind with Alden.

"I feel like I failed a test," Alden said as he opened the door to his room. I'd gone back to my dorm to change out of my so-called funeral clothes, and now we were both wearing pajamas.

I was so relieved to be alone with him that I nearly collapsed.

"It was fine," I said, though we both knew that was a lie.

If he'd failed a test, then I had too. The Tees had no reason to continue being my friend.

I'd always felt slightly out of place with them, but with Alden I could be . . . someone different. Not fully myself—I didn't know who that was—but I could at least bask in his easy nature.

We played cards and listened to the playlist he'd made for me. It was nice.

I couldn't manage everyone's expectations, so I would manage only his. He was easy enough to understand. He didn't need me to be the perfect future doctor, or someone who knew everything about themselves.

He was simple when nothing else was.

"Do you want to make out a little?" he asked after a few too many rounds of a card game I didn't fully understand.

I appreciated him asking. He always did—he never rushed me or leaned in without my go-ahead.

"Sure," I told him, scooting closer.

He put his hand on my waist, and I let him do most of the work. Kissing, I'd learned, was kind of nice. It was better than losing at a card game.

I leaned into him and put my hand on his stubbly cheek, imagining having stubble of my own.

That thought stopped me short, and I pulled back.

"Are you good?"

"Yeah," I told him, blinking hard, willing the thought that had popped into my head to leave.

It would not.

"Just kind of tired."

"Oh."

I could tell I'd disappointed him, and I had to fix that. He was the last person on earth—other than Randall—who wasn't even a little disappointed in me.

I knew how to make it up to him. "Would it be okay if I stayed over tonight?"

His face was close to mine, and when I said it, he smiled wider than I'd ever seen.

Like me, Alden had a single room, so neither of us had to worry about roommates. We could've been having sleepovers this whole time, but I hadn't floated the idea, and he hadn't brought it up.

"You seriously want to?" he asked, but before I could say yes, he was already pulling a box out from under his bed and grabbing a toothbrush. "My mom packed me like one hundred extra—she's really concerned about dental hygiene. This one could be yours when you're here, if you want."

Here was this boy, with his floppy bangs, his skinny arms, and his tilted head, holding a bright yellow toothbrush out to me with all the hope in the world.

"Thank you," I told him. "Seriously."

Once we'd brushed our teeth, we both stood in front of his bed.

"We don't have to do anything," he said quickly. "Just, like, sleep."

I nodded, grateful. "That'd be nice."

He was the first to jump onto his raised bed, and I crawled in next to him. We were a few inches apart, and he closed the distance between us by turning on his side and wrapping an arm around my waist.

I let him hold me, and there was something comforting about having another living, breathing person in bed with me.

It was the best night's sleep I'd had since I left for school.

Tuesday, 7 p.m., La Crosse, WI

We arrive at the Mississippi River crossing in total darkness. That doesn't stop Aya from nearly bouncing out of her seat with excitement. Her mom seems to have all but surrendered her to me and Oakley, and I'm not mad about it.

"This is the greatest bridge of all time," Aya says, knees folded on her seat.

"Oh yeah?" I ask. "Why's that?"

I love that she's a child with a favorite bridge.

"It's a swing bridge, and before it existed you needed a ferry to get across the Mississippi River." She jumps up from her seat. "But that was in the way olden days."

"What's a swing bridge?" I try to sound interested, but the longer Aya speaks about bridges, the more I wish I could talk to Oakley alone about her time in New York.

But Oakley had quickly moved on from that conversation, and maybe that's for the best. I don't need to know about her life before this train trip. She's just the blond girl I met in the dining car.

If I keep thinking that, maybe I'll convince myself it's true.

"I think you can figure out what a swing bridge is," Oakley says in response to my question. She sticks out her hand and pivots it at her wrist joint. "It's a bridge that swings."

"Exactly," Aya adds, sounding smug.

"Love that you two are ganging up on me now."

"We're not ganging up on you," Oakley tells me.

"My dad always tells me and my mom that we're ganging up on him," Aya says. "Like, girls ganging up on boys."

Based on how Aya's saying it, I'm not sure if her dad says this as a joke or because he's an asshole, but either way, don't love that.

Then Aya adds, "And my friend Cayden—you know, the one I was telling you about who has two moms—he says that when people do that kind of stuff, like they're annoying you or whatever, it means they have a crush on you." She finally inhales, but she's not done speaking. "And he says that when someone's kind of mean to you, that's how they tell you they like you. Like how my dad does with my mom sometimes. That's what Cayden said."

It's official: I want to punch Aya's dad.

Still, I couldn't help but smile at her monologue, and I try to hide my expression behind my hand as Oakley's face turns serious. "And do you believe Cayden?"

"Well, yes." Aya shrugs. "He's pretty smart."

"Listen." Oakley leans forward, and Aya does too, so their heads are close together. "When you love someone, you don't have to pretend to be mean. You can tell them you love them every single day. You can compliment their outfit or their hair or whatever else you like about them."

"Um, okay," Aya says, leaning away. "I'll try to remember that for when I'm, like, forty."

"Please do." When Oakley sits back, her posture loosens and the urgency from the previous moment is gone as quickly as it arrived.

Oakley and Aya talk about their favorite Percy Jackson characters and if they would join Artemis's hunt (yes for both of them). I have to admit that it's cute, but I'm thinking about Oakley's serious tone, about the way she tried to impart this information to Aya like it was the last thing she'd ever do.

After we cross the bridge, Aya gets bored of the observation deck and runs down to the snack car to bother Edward.

"All right," I say when Aya's gone. "Are we gonna talk about that? Also, we're on the same page about Aya's dad, right? He needs to get a knuckle sandwich."

I hoped Oakley would laugh at my use of the phrase "knuckle sandwich," but her serious expression returns.

"You know how I told you I have five siblings?" Oakley asks.

I frown. "What does that have to do with Aya?"

111

"I have five older *sisters*," Oakley says again. "And all of them are married. I watched them find their husbands. They would come home one day and say they'd met some righteous returned missionary, and weeks later they were talking about marriage. I watched my sisters become subservient; I watched them be belittled by men they'd sealed themselves to for all of eternity." She shakes her head. "I don't want that for anyone I care about. I don't want Aya to think that's what love has to be."

I've never met someone who holds love in such high regard, like it's a basic human right, next to food and water, to have people who love you unconditionally and who you love in the same way.

I nod, unsure of what to say, but after a while of staring out the dark window, I do what I do best: I deflect. "I know this is going to sound like another smooth-brain thought, but I wish I could turn off nighttime for the train ride," I tell Oakley. "There's so much I want to see that I'll never be able to because of the schedule. Aya didn't even get to see the swing bridge in daylight!"

"No, that makes sense," Oakley says. "I want to see everything too."

I nod, wondering if she means off the train as well as on it.

"It's nice in the observation car, though," I say, looking around. "The curved glass roof reminds me a little of the greenhouse I worked in."

I hadn't meant to tell Oakley that, but it came out anyway.

"You worked in a greenhouse?" she asks. "How come you didn't mention it?"

"Sorry, I didn't realize I was supposed to print out my resume and hand it to you at the start of the trip."

I'm deflecting again.

When Oakley doesn't respond, I continue. "There's this plant there; it's called a corpse plant. Well, really, it's called an *Amorphophallus titanum*, which means 'giant misshapen penis.'" I look over at her. "But you probably already have all the Latin names of plants and their translations memorized for when you're on *Jeopardy!*."

"I don't," she says. "I guess I still have a few categories to work on."

"I guess," I say, staring at the floor.

When I look back up, her eyes are wide and curious. "Can you tell me about it?"

So I explain that my corpse plant came from seeds genetically identical to corpse plants all over the country, and that sometimes, if the conditions are right, they all bloom at the same time. I tell her that it's the largest flowering plant in the world, that it looks almost alien when it comes alive.

"That's amazing," she says, and she's looking at me like I've given her a gift.

I'm watching her file away new knowledge in real time. I gave her trivia that she can use on someone else.

"Let me show you a picture of the greenhouse," I tell her instead of letting my brain follow that train of thought.

I turn on my phone for the first time in hours, then navigate through my photos, purposefully scrolling past ones I know will hurt me.

I wasn't expecting to have service, but I do.

And a notification pops up at the top of my screen, with a name that stops me cold: Alden.

Six Weeks into College

The *Amorphophallus* wasn't growing much at all. It was stuck in the same tight ball of roots and soil that it had been for weeks.

Still, I tended to it like a helicopter parent, constantly checking to make sure it had enough water and light, that its growing conditions were perfect.

"You're doing everything right," Randall assured me. "We just have to wait and see whether this will be the year she decides to flower."

As much as I loved hearing the words *you're doing everything right* from an adult authority figure, it didn't make me any less anxious.

In the meantime, I busied myself with the other plants in the greenhouse. I would brush my hand against the *Mimosa pudica*, the sensitive plant that closed in on itself whenever anyone touched it. I'd futz with the pitcher plants and check in on what kind of bugs they'd trapped that day.

There were a few other student workers who came and went, but we didn't talk much. They would drop their bags off in Randall's office, sweep leaves, water plants without care, and leave.

I couldn't imagine doing that. The fact that I had some impact on these living things was enough to motivate me to arrive early to my shift and stay late. I couldn't do those tasks for myself—I couldn't even make it to class—but I could show up for the plants.

Randall made sure I was paid for the extra hours, but I would've worked them for free. When I stayed overtime, he would choose a plant at random and tell me more about it, and I soaked up the information like a sponge.

"Would you ever think about majoring in botany?" he asked me one evening in the greenhouse.

I was taken aback by the question. I couldn't major in botany—I was going to be a doctor, and doctors didn't need to know about plants.

So I gave a noncommittal answer and left the greenhouse quickly after that. When I checked my phone in the chilly evening air, there was a text from the Tees inviting me to a party.

To everyone's surprise, including my own, I said yes. It was at someone's place off-campus, a junior who was in the architecture program with Autumn.

"What should I wear?" I asked Alden an hour or so later as I opened and closed my drawers over and over, throwing outfit options onto my bed.

The calendar had only just flipped to October, yet the themed parties had already started. This one was "beach chic," whatever that meant.

Alden was lying with his back to the wall, one leg bent and the other hanging over the bed, writing an essay.

"You look good in anything," he said, running his hands through his hair as he stared at his laptop. He said it so mindlessly, so sweetly.

As I went through my underwear drawer, I accidentally pulled out an item I hadn't thought of in weeks: my binder.

I'd bought it over the summer, when I'd thought I might experiment more with how I presented in college. When it arrived at my home in Seattle in discreet packaging, I'd run up to my bedroom and tried it on with the door bolted shut. I couldn't stop staring at my flat chest, how it made a loose T-shirt look entirely different on my body. I took pictures of myself from the neck down, and moved them to a private album on my phone.

I hadn't looked at those pictures in a while, but they were there, hiding in wait.

I pulled the binder out when Alden wasn't looking and shoved it under the shirt I'd laid on my bed. It was a loose floral button-up with cuffed sleeves that looked passably beachy.

There was a part of my brain that couldn't stop replaying the moment when we were kissing and I'd thought about having stubble. It was ridiculous, but it had taken root in my head and wouldn't let go.

"I'm going over to the Tees to pregame," I told him, shoving my whole outfit into a tote bag. "You can stay here if you want."

The Tees had extended their invitation to Alden, though I knew it wasn't sincere, and he was too stressed about meeting his deadline to go out anyway.

I hated that I didn't mind.

Because really, I *did* want to spend as much time with him as possible, but not in combination with the Tees. And not right now, when I was having confusing thoughts about him—or maybe about me, but he made me feel those things.

The pregame was happening in Rex's dorm, and by the time I got there, Shelly was using a half-empty bottle of wine as a microphone with which to belt ABBA songs.

"Come be a dancing queen!" Shelly shouted as I walked in, without any trace of awkwardness.

"In a minute," I told him, laughing.

Rex handed me a red plastic cup. "Put anything you want in there. We've got apple juice, wine, and vodka."

I nodded and filled it with apple juice, and even though it was entirely nonalcoholic, I felt floaty after a few songs.

"I brought something kind of beachy," I told the three of them. "I'm gonna change."

"YESSSS!" Shelly shouted. "BEACH FIT! BEACH FIT!"

He was drunk, and I was giggly.

The only bathroom on Rex's floor was a gender-neutral one, so I slipped inside with my tote bag. I changed slowly, then carefully folded the clothes I'd worn to the greenhouse and tucked them away.

The lighting was terrible and the mirror was dirty, but even so, when I stepped out of the stall, I knew I looked good.

I turned to the side and pressed my palm over my chest: there was nothing there, and I couldn't stop smiling.

The only problem was my hair, which was long and unruly. I fixed it as much as I could by putting it up in a loose bun.

"You look HOT!" Shelly said, stumbling forward and grabbing my arm as I reentered Rex's room.

117

Autumn nodded in agreement, and even Rex seemed to approve of the fit.

As the four of us headed over to the party, I walked with my shoulders back. Even though Alden wasn't there, I could still feel his presence.

I *always* felt his presence.

Without him there, though, I could do something I hadn't before: I could act like him. I tried to channel his mannerisms, his ease.

It made me feel powerful and exposed at the same time.

When we arrived at the house, it was so full that people were spilling outside. I wasn't quite ready to go in, so I grabbed a beer from the cooler on the porch for something to do with my hands.

"Need a bottle opener?" a girl standing nearby offered.

"I was just going to hold it," I told her honestly.

She must've thought I was joking, and laughed loudly.

"I'm Mischa," she said.

"Zoe."

She was flirting with me, and the closer I looked at her, the more honored I was.

Mischa was short and curvy, and she was deeply on-theme, wearing a triangle bikini top and a floral wrap skirt in spite of the temperature.

"I like your outfit," I told her. "Kind of weird that the host went with a beach theme in October, though."

"It makes sense to me." Mischa lifted her chin. "It's a reminder of summer."

As she said this, a kid stumbled out of the house and reached out to give Mischa a high five. "Nice party, Meesh!"

I blanched as Mischa thanked the boy.

"This is your party?" I asked.

"Alas, it is," she said, stepping closer. "I'm the one who came up with the 'kind of weird' theme."

"I didn't mean—"

"You did." She put a hand on my arm. "But all will be forgiven if you dance with me."

I told myself her flirting was harmless, because of how nice it felt. It was different than with Alden; it tickled the part of my brain that was more lizard than human.

Girl hot. Say yes to dance, my lizard brain told me.

So I did.

Whoever was controlling the playlist was also on theme, because as Carly Rae Jepsen's bright, summery voice blasted across the crowded first floor of Mischa's house, everyone ran to the center of the room.

I hoped that to the casual observer Mischa and I looked almost cinematic as we danced a little too close, because that's how I felt. I caught Autumn's eye from across the room, and she shot me a questioning-but-not-necessarily-disapproving glance.

A few minutes later, Carly abruptly cut out, and a mellower song came on. Dancing to a fast song with room to spare for Jesus or Moses or whoever was fine but dancing to a slow song with this girl would be crossing a line and I knew it.

I took a step back, and Mischa followed. There were mostly

couples in the center of the room now, swaying slowly and hanging on to each other.

Some danced hesitantly, like it was their first go at it, but one couple was illuminated by a light from upstairs, as if some higher power—other than the recessed lighting—had chosen them.

The two girls held on to each other tightly, swaying to the soft music. The shorter one put her chin on the taller one's shoulder, and they fit together perfectly.

"That's my housemate, May," Mischa said, pointing to the shorter girl when she caught me staring. "And her girlfriend, Shani."

As she pointed to them, the taller one, Shani, waved goofily at Mischa, and May shook her head, but she was laughing.

"It's kind of gross, right?" Mischa whispered.

I nodded, but it wasn't gross at all. It was beautiful.

When the song ended, May dragged Shani over to where Mischa and I were standing, and I took a step back without meaning to.

"I don't bite," May said as she looked me up and down.

"She does," Shani stage whispered, and they both laughed.

May wrapped her arm around Shani's waist, and Shani fixed May's hair. Their movements were seamless.

They spoke to Mischa for a few minutes, but I wasn't paying attention. One thought overwhelmed my mind: *This is what my life could be.*

Maybe it could've been like that with Mischa or Autumn or someone else, anyone else.

120

Yet for some reason, I had chosen a boy.

And I *liked* that boy.

But maybe I hadn't chosen him just because—maybe there was something *more*.

I felt like I was standing on the edge of a cliff: one wrong move and my life would've been irrevocably changed.

Rather than investigating this thought, I pulled Mischa back onto the dance floor.

At the end of the night, we reconvened in Rex's room. I wasn't drunk—I hadn't even had a sip of alcohol—but I *was* dazed.

"It looked like you were having fun with the host," Rex said, raising their eyebrows.

"She was cool," I admitted.

Mischa and I had exchanged numbers, but that was that. I didn't do anything that could've been considered cheating—I'd barely even danced with her—but I still felt like I needed a shower.

We were lying on Rex's blue shag carpet and listening to a vibey playlist that Autumn had chosen. For the second time that night, I was struck with a what-if.

What if I *had* chosen the Tees over Alden?

It hadn't been that long; I could choose them now. I could choose parties with hot queer people, dancing together and ending our nights by grabbing ice cream or fries or whatever we wanted.

I could choose this, being tangled together listening to boygenius and giggling for no reason.

"You should hang with us more often," Autumn said to me after a while.

I nodded. I should've.

Rex sat up and leaned forward so that they were looking right at me. "Yeah, you were actually being fun tonight."

I sat up then too. "What does that mean?"

The three Tees exchanged a look, and I hugged my legs to my chest.

Autumn was the most diplomatic of them, so she spoke first. "Just that you seem a little . . . different around your boyfriend."

They were right, but it still stung. And if they'd left it at that, it would've been fine.

But then Shelly said, "He makes you boring." I froze, and Shelly must've taken that as an indication to continue sticking his foot in his mouth. "You should hang out more with Mischa; she's great."

"Alden doesn't make me boring," I muttered.

I debated telling them about the thoughts I'd had earlier. That maybe it wasn't that I *liked* him so much but more that I liked how he made me feel. Or that maybe I was *like* him in some way that I didn't know how to articulate.

But because I didn't know how to articulate it, I didn't say anything at all.

"I think what Shelly meant," Autumn began, "was that he takes up a lot of your time."

"He's my *boyfriend*," I said. "Of course, he takes up a lot of my time."

"But you never hang out with us anymore," Rex added.

That comment shouldn't have set me off, but it did.

"You were my orientation friends," I said, standing up to leave and hating myself. "The kind you make before you find someone better."

They all stared at me with so much hurt in their eyes. I knew there was no coming back from this, but I couldn't stop. I was furious; I had to defend Alden's honor. Or maybe I was just *done*.

"It's not like you've made any effort to hang out with me either." I grabbed my tote bag from where it was sitting by the door. "You all clearly like each other more than you like me, so go have fun with your 'real queer' friends and leave me the fuck alone."

I flung Rex's door open and slammed it shut. It felt good to say all that, but when I was done, I immediately wanted to apologize.

When I returned to my dorm, Alden was still on my bed, typing out his essay. I crawled next to him and put my head in his lap, and he closed his computer and held me, his arms around my stomach.

In the comfort of my room, with the pressure of Alden's body against mine, it felt safe to dive back into the thoughts I'd been having.

So I replayed the moments early in our relationship: running up the clock tower, sliding in socked feet down a bowling lane with him waiting at the end of it.

Before our relationship became anything physical, there was a *want*.

And I know now what that want was: I wanted to be like him.

I wanted to move through the world in the way he did, the way he was allowed to.

That thought was too much, though, so instead of continuing to think it, I burrowed farther into him.

That night was the last time I hung out with the Tees.

Nine

TUESDAY, 9 P.M., NEAR RED WING, MN

A conductor comes around telling us that there was a mechanical issue in the kitchen, and apologizing for the late dinner hour.

"It's European!" he keeps repeating while dabbing at his flop sweat with an Amtrak-branded napkin.

Oakley gets two free reservations with each meal (a perk of her wildly overpriced sleeper car ticket), and when it's time for us to head to dinner, I leave my phone in her room.

I haven't looked at it since I got the text from Alden.

In the dining car, the first people we see are Mike, the Canadian from the scavenger hunt, and Aya's mom. The two of them are chatting and sitting close.

Oakley convinces the waiter to let us sit with them, and she waves to Aya's mom as she slides into the booth.

"Where's Aya?" Oakley asks.

"She's back in our bedroom," Aya's mom says with a smile that looks like it's taking a great deal of effort. "She stayed up too late reading and passed out on the sofa. I tried to wake her up for dinner but she was out cold."

I smile at that, thinking about the spitfire that is Aya being too sleepy for dinner.

"I'm Oakley, and this is Zoe," Oakley says after that. "I don't know if we've properly met."

"I'm Nanami," Aya's mom says. "And trust me, I've heard quite a bit about the two of you."

"I'm sure," Oakley says, so wonderfully un-shy.

I nod to Mike, who's sitting across from me. "What's up?"

At this, his cheeks redden, and Oakley and I exchange a look.

"Nothing much," he says after too long of a pause.

The awkwardness lasts until the waiter comes by with the menu, and though the options are only slightly different from the first leg, they *feel* fancier.

"For all those in sleeper cars, we're offering our three-course menu tonight," he says. "This includes your choice of appetizer, entrée, and dessert."

I order a salad for my appetizer, pasta for my entrée, and a lemon cake for dessert.

"I'll have the same," Oakley says. "But I'll do the chocolate mousse." She turns to me. "That way we can try a little of both—if that's okay with you."

"Of course," I tell her, taken aback.

"If I get a bottle of wine, would you all split with me?" Mike asks.

"Absolutely," Nanami says immediately.

"We're too young," I tell Mike, my dormant "good kid" behavior returning with a vengeance. "But thank you."

126

"I always forget about the drinking age in the US." He clucks his tongue. "You're a bunch of prudes."

"I agree," Oakley says, and though I shouldn't be, I'm surprised by her saying this.

"Well, more for us," Nanami tells Mike, who laughs so loudly that everyone else in the dining car stares at us, including Clint and Virginia, who wave.

"I'd like to propose a toast," Nanami says when the wine arrives and Oakley and I have our water in front of us. "To men who aren't shitty." She raises her glass to Mike, and we all toast with plastic cups.

"Do you have a lot of bad men in your life?" Oakley asks Nanami, who is sipping her wine. .

I nudge Oakley under the table. It's an invasive question, but when Nanami nods, I have to remind myself once again that the rules of etiquette are different on the train.

"Well, only one," Nanami says. "Aya's father." None of us say anything as she sucks air in through her teeth and dabs her cloth napkin at the corners of her eyes. "We're getting a divorce."

Oakley reaches her hand out and Nanami grabs it. "Are you okay?"

Aya's mom shakes her head, and my heart hurts: a little for her and a little for Oakley's kindness. They both sit there for a while, looking at each other. I feel like a third wheel, or a fourth, defective one, along with Mike.

Nanami can't bring herself to speak, and the silence feels endless.

"I know what it's like to leave something behind," Oakley says finally, and I freeze. "Something that's felt like the only truth for your entire life."

I want Oakley to say more—I *always* want her to say more—but she takes her time. When she speaks again, she doesn't seem to be directing her thoughts at Nanami or really at anyone in particular.

"Maybe it's not this way for everyone," Oakley continues, "but it's like you start to understand how your life *could've* been if you hadn't believed all the lies you'd been fed. But there was no way *not* to believe them, so you were trapped in this world of fear and conformity, and you'd heard every Sunday for your entire life that it was the end of times and Jesus's return was imminent, so it was your job to value the truth in everything you did to hasten His return but only if it was *their* truth. And now you know all of that was just meant to scare you into paying your tithing and meeting all the standards of the Church, but you *still* can't let go of the beliefs because if you don't have those then everything else in your life will come crumbling down."

Nanami releases Oakley's hand, and I want to do more than what I'm doing now, which is staring at her.

Even in the silence, I'm drawn to Oakley. I want to be by her side while she recounts this story to anyone who will listen.

It's a familiar feeling: the desire for more than I can have.

Finally, Nanami says, "Now I feel silly for crying about a man."

"Don't," Oakley says fiercely.

"I shouldn't even have brought it up," Nanami says. "All I

wanted was an hour away from all that. I feel bad enough about Aya spending so much time with you two."

"No," I insist, happy to contribute *something*, "Aya's amazing."

"I know." Nanami rubs her temple and Mike rubs her back. "Which is why I feel so bad that I haven't told her."

"Haven't told her what?" Oakley asks.

Nanami takes a breath. "That I'm divorcing her dad. And that we're not going back to New York. We're moving to Seattle."

"Wait," I say. "What?"

Before Nanami can respond, Oakley says, "She's on the train to Seattle and she doesn't know that she's moving there?" Her sharp jaw is set in a hard line, and the intense compassion that shone on her face before is gone.

"I think it's best to let her have this trip," Nanami says. "She's been so excited about it, and I didn't want to take that away from her. It hasn't felt like the right time," she adds, and then takes a sip of wine.

"When's the right time?" Oakley asks, her voice rising. I might've held myself back, but she'll do nothing of the sort. "When the 'trip' is over and you're not heading back to New York? When she has to enroll in an entirely new school? When she finds out she's not going to live with her dad anymore? Are *those* the right times?"

Nanami blinks back tears, and Mike stares daggers at Oakley.

"Stop that," he tells her.

In her rage, Oakley's scooted closer to me, and her shaking body is pressed against mine. I grab the hand she has in her lap,

129

and she squeezes my fingers so tightly I wince.

"You have to let Aya in on this," she tells Nanami, who looks more than a little shell-shocked. "My whole life I've had things hidden from me—and when I discovered everything I didn't know, it was the worst feeling in the world. You have to give Aya agency in her own life."

She looks out the window, and I'm thrust back to the moment I first saw her on the train. When she was a random mean (hot) blond girl.

I couldn't have been more wrong.

"You think you're protecting her," Oakley continues, "but you're only hurting her by hiding the truth."

"I'm not hungry anymore," Nanami says without looking at us. She pushes past Mike, and as she's about to open the door to the next car, she turns to us, her eyes bloodshot. "*Please* don't tell Aya." The desperation in her voice is almost too much to bear.

"We won't," Oakley says, her voice cold. "But at some point, *you* have to."

Before I can fully close the sleeper compartment door, Oakley starts up again.

"I can't believe she'd do that to Aya."

"I know," I say quietly, nodding and sitting in one of the seats by the now-pointless window. It's too dark to see anything outside, so I stare at Oakley's reflection.

"She needs to tell her."

"I agree."

"Aya's going to resent her if she doesn't say anything."

"Totally."

At this, Oakley finally looks at me. "How are you so chill about this?"

"I'm not," I tell her. "I feel horrible for Aya. But I also get where Nanami is coming from."

"You understand hiding something that big from someone you care about?"

"Yes." I'm surprised it comes out so easily and with no qualifications. But it's true.

Of course, I'm thinking of Alden, though Oakley doesn't know that. She doesn't know anything about him, which is increasingly feeling like a lie by omission.

"Maybe I shouldn't be so worked up about this." Oakley sits opposite me and leans forward so that her knees are almost touching mine. "But it feels personal."

At first, I wasn't going to say anything, but I need to know. "Why?"

She sighs. "I've spent the past six months living my life in a way where the only thing I've cared about was knowing the truth. Finding *answers*." She shakes her head, and a strand of hair falls in front of her face. "And because of that, things have sucked, but it's meant that I'm not living a lie. I've now read every single book I was told not to my whole life, all the 'anti-Mormon' literature my parents warned me about. And you know what that 'anti-Mormon' literature has been? History. The *truth*." She blinks hard at this. "So when I see someone who's lying for their own convenience, yeah, it pisses me off."

"What did you find?" I ask, and when Oakley gives me a

confused look, I add, "You said you only cared about finding answers—what were they?"

She closes her eyes. I know now that when she does this, she's formulating a response in her head.

It's funny what you can learn about someone in a couple of days.

"That deconstructing the beliefs you had about the religion you grew up in means losing all the good parts too." She's looking down at her hands. "That it means I don't have a path laid out before me like I once did, or the hope of an eternal family. Nothing is promised to me anymore, because all those promises were tied up in a religion that I now know is racist and homophobic and sexist. And yet I *still* can't make my brain understand that it's for the best."

I don't know what to say. I've never deconstructed a religion. I've never had beliefs that strong about anything.

But when I think back on my life in recent months—or, more specifically, Alden—a part of me understands.

"Was it better than living a lie?" I ask, because I need to know.

Oakley's eyes are still closed. I'm about to repeat myself when she says, "Yes. The knowing is always better." She nods, agreeing with herself. "You can't go back, can't get rid of that knowledge. But at least now you get to find out who you are in the knowing."

The way she said it all in the second person wasn't lost on me. It could've been subconscious or maybe she really was opening the door for me to talk.

"Did you find who you are in the knowing?"

"I'm trying."

"Me too."

If she's surprised by this, she doesn't let on. "What do you know now, then, that you didn't before?"

She asks it so casually that it disarms me. Or maybe it wasn't that question in particular but the past day on the train with her in such close proximity.

Either way, against all odds, I answer half honestly.

"That I might not be who I thought I was," I tell her. "In regard to my gender, I mean."

It's the first time I've said anything like that out loud.

"That's big." She says offhandedly, her tone not matching her words.

"It is."

"How'd you come to that conclusion?" Oakley's expression is curious, and even though my whole body is tense, it's not because of her. She has a way of asking questions that makes me want to answer with the whole truth.

But this whole truth is a hard one, one I'm not even certain I can articulate. So I go with the version of the truth I can give her right now.

"I'm still figuring it out," I tell her. "But part of it was because of someone I knew at school."

It's the world's biggest understatement. Calling Alden "someone I knew at school" is like Juliet calling Romeo "a guy my dad doesn't like."

But Oakley just nods and stretches, accepting my answer for what it is: a start.

Seven Weeks into College

It was a bright, cloudless day at the orchard. We parked in a large open field surrounded by trees whose final leaves of the season were barely hanging on, the last gasps of autumn in every shade of orange, green, and red.

I hadn't wanted to leave my dorm to do anything, let alone go apple picking, but Alden had borrowed his uncle's car for the weekend, and he wanted to put it to use. He planned out a whole day for us, which I would've thought was sweet if I wasn't hyper-focused on my body, and his, and the decidedly non-girlfriend-like ways I was thinking about both.

The farm was packed with couples and families. Everywhere I looked there were tall boyfriends in flannel shirts and Cornell hats who'd been brought to the orchard by their tiny girlfriends in adorable athleisure sets.

And then there was the two of us.

"Should we get a map?" he asked, already grabbing one.

The map showed the different areas of the orchard, along with the variety of apples located in each.

I pointed to a section labeled "SnapDragon."

"Cornell developed those," I said. Randall had told me this once when I should've been in class. There weren't any apple trees in the greenhouse, but he was proud of all of Cornell's plant-based achievements, and I was his best audience.

"That's amazing," Alden said, looking at me like I'd just told him I'd found a cure for cancer. "Let's start there."

I continued to tell him all the apple facts I'd picked up in the greenhouse, and he continued to be impressed. I liked being the knowledgeable one; it gave me a modicum of control over the situation. Sure, maybe he'd planned the day and he'd driven me here and he was the only person who wanted to spend time with me, but at least I was the apple expert.

"Wanna bet I can get that apple?" Alden asked, pointing to a lone, bright red SnapDragon at the top of a tree. It must've been nine feet in the air.

This was the part of hanging out with him that I loved: doing stupid shit together.

I shoved my hands in my pockets. "What do I get when you lose?"

"Not gonna happen," he told me, jumping a little to warm up. "I've got a huge vertical leap."

I laughed incredulously at that, and Alden mimed thrusting a sword through his abdomen, dramatically wounded by my disbelief.

"Should we put it to the test?" I was bouncing on the balls of my feet now too. If someone passed by, they might think we were about to fight, 1950s greaser-style.

Alden grinned. "You're so on, dude."

I still don't know if he said it as a joke or got caught up in the moment. But either way, the word made me feel more affectionately toward him than I had since I'd started panicking about our relationship.

After his first jump, it was clear I would lose.

He *did* have a giant vertical leap, and he easily could've grabbed the apple. As hard as I tried, my jump was much lower.

I felt stuck in my body. I wanted to shed my skin and fly through the clouds.

I conceded, out of breath and frustrated, and he took a victory leap and plucked the apple from the tree.

"I have a question," he said through a bite of the crisp Snap-Dragon as we walked farther into the orchard.

My heart sped up. "Okay?"

"What were you like in high school?"

The relief I felt that it wasn't anything deeper was overshadowed by the horror of having to relive my high school experience.

"Why do you want to know?"

"You never talk about it, and I'm curious. What were your friends like? What clubs did you do? That kind of stuff."

There was a reason I didn't talk about high school. It was another world from this, one where I had no say in my life.

But look at that: now that I finally had a say, I'd ruined everything.

"I did Science Olympiads." It was a safe answer. "What about you?" He hadn't talked much about what he was like in high school either.

We passed by a bucket of mini gourds, and his expression darkened. "I don't think we would've dated back then."

"Why?" I asked, though on my end I knew the answer: I was a mostly out lesbian.

"I wasn't cool," he said, and I couldn't help but laugh. He frowned at this. "I'm being serious."

"What part of me doing Science Olympiads makes you think *I* was cool?"

"Of course you were cool." He said it with a bone-deep

136

certainty. "You're so chill; you have all these other friends. You're just . . . You're awesome, Zoe."

"Thanks," I said. "You're cool too."

I wanted to launch myself into an apple tree.

I'd been having fun. We were jumping. Jumping was fun.

This conversation was not fun.

This was how it went. One moment, we were hanging out, and the next, he would say something slightly terrible, and I'd be reminded that he was my boyfriend, and that he saw me as his girlfriend.

He grabbed my hand, which was too sweaty for the crisp day, and laced his fingers in mine.

A couple walked past us, and the guy nodded to Alden, while the girl gave me a tight smile. They were holding hands too, but neither of them seemed to be on the verge of a panic attack.

They looked like an archetypal straight couple.

What did Alden and I look like?

There were queer people in relationships that appeared straight to the outside world, of course, but those happened with the knowledge of all participants.

I owed Alden more than I was giving him. I knew it then, and I know it now.

With my hand in his, Alden pulled me close, and I let him. His scent—sour and strong—mixed with the smell of rotting apples around us.

I leaned away, but he kept a tight grip on my waist and pushed my hair behind my ears, even though it was already back in a ponytail.

"I'm falling for you, Zoe Tauber." It was one of his romantic statements. He said it in a way where I knew he had a vision of how cinematic it would sound.

I wanted my life to seem majestic and grand and thrilling too. And maybe it did, to an outside observer.

But I was too close.

"You don't have to say anything," he added when I hadn't. "But I thought you should know."

"Thank you," I said, feeling silly.

A group of boys a few years younger than us ran past, and I had a strong desire to run with them, like a domesticated horse who spots a herd of wild ones in the distance and feels a primal pull.

That was how I wanted Alden to see me—like another guy.

The moment I thought it, I knew it was true. It was the only true thing in the entire world.

He was falling for me, and I was falling for the way he looked, the way he acted.

For the body he inhabited.

But if I told him this, if I was somehow able to articulate the mess of thoughts in my head, we'd have to break up. And if we broke up, we couldn't keep hanging out.

Maybe the good of dating Alden outweighed the bad. And the good was so good: card games late into the night, pressed flowers in a dark room, jumping like fools in an apple orchard across the country from the only home I'd ever known.

So I took the path of least resistance: I squeezed his hand, and he did the same in return. We were trying to convey entirely different messages with that simple gesture.

TUESDAY, 10:00 P.M., APPROACHING THE TWIN CITIES, MN

"Folks, we'll have a thirty-minute smoke break in St. Paul," the conductor announces. "That's right, thirty whooooole minutes. I don't care what you do—get drunk, get high, skinny-dip in the Mississippi River—as long as you're back on the train at half past."

The few other passengers in the observation car grumble as they stretch their tired legs and make their way off the train. I've never felt a stronger sense of solidarity with a group of people than I have here, sitting together, watching the view or waiting for it to reappear.

Once Oakley cooled down after dinner, I dragged her back to our usual seats—a little bit because I wanted to hang out in the observation car and a lot because I didn't want to be alone after what I told her. She didn't push me to keep talking about my thoughts on my gender—or lack thereof—and I haven't brought it up since. It was a sleeper-car confession, not fit for public consumption.

When the train pulls into the Twin Cities, I settle into my seat.

"You're not getting off?" Oakley asks.

"I'm perfectly happy here," I tell her, motioning around the observation car. "In my kingdom."

She bounces up from her seat. "Nope. Come on."

And when she walks away, I can't help but follow.

"There's a park by the station I want to check out," she says as we huddle against the cold.

We stopped by the sleeper car to grab her jacket and gloves, but all I have is the same shell I wore in Chicago.

"You have a *park* you want to check out?" I ask. "It's freezing cold."

She looks me up and down. "You didn't bring enough layers."

"Who are you, my dad?"

"Just a concerned citizen." She removes her overlayer and hands it to me. It's a puffy coat, under which she's wearing a fleece—she was prepared. I was not. "Take this."

"I'm not wearing your jacket," I say as a huge gust of wind blows past and nearly knocks me over.

"You sure about that?"

I take the jacket. "Fuck you."

She has a shit-eating grin on her face, but it's worth it for the warmth of her coat.

The park follows the Mississippi River and features a cobblestone path interspersed with fountains and trellises.

Oakley stops us in front of a fountain that's illuminated from below. Her skin twinkles along with the lights as they blink on, off, on, off. Then she pulls off her gloves, reaches into the fountain and flicks her fingers at me.

I scream at a volume I didn't know I could produce.

"I'm not having a water fight in negative-one-thousand-degree weather," I tell her, wiping the freezing fountain water off my cheeks. "You're on your own."

"Fine," she says, pouting. "I guess I'll skinny-dip in the Mississippi River by myself, too."

I cross my arms. "Have fun getting an incurable fungal infection."

"I will."

She's smiling now, and there's some part of me that's ridiculously happy that I'm the cause of her happiness. This doesn't feel like those glimmering moments with Alden when I could see a different path for us, one where we were two dudes goofing off.

When I'm around Oakley, I don't feel self-conscious about who I am or how I'm perceived. With her, I'm just an underdressed person with a bad haircut, standing in an empty park.

"Back in New York I went on a date with a girl who would swim in the ocean off Coney Island every day."

I didn't think I would be jealous, hearing about a date Oakley went on with someone else, but I am. I hate this open-water swimmer. She probably has great shoulders.

"We didn't go on a second date," Oakley says after a moment. "She ghosted me."

"Sorry," I say, though inside I'm perversely delighted.

"I *never* went on a second date," she adds, looking out onto the river.

"Was it because you won't drink coffee or because you're a know-it-all?" I joke, but her face is deadly serious. I stand up straighter and speak softer. "How is that even possible? You're . . ." I trail off. There are many ways I could finish that sentence, such as "gorgeous" or "stunningly gorgeous" or "a stunningly gorgeous

141

genius." But in the end, I use the only words that encompass all that. "You're Oakley."

She shrugs. "No one ever asked."

"*You* could've asked *them*."

"I wasn't used to that," she says. "I was used to being pursued. I went on, like, a thousand dates in high school, once I turned sixteen. But that was with Mormon boys who my parents approved of."

"It's hard," I say after a beat, like I know anything at all about her life, "to be the pursuer."

I'm not sure if what I did with Alden counts as pursuit, and I've never dated a girl; I've never done *anything* with one.

"It is," she agrees. "But I thought, I don't know . . . that maybe being in New York would be easier. That there would be *rules* to this kind of thing. But it wasn't, and there weren't."

The more Oakley tells me about her time in New York, the sadder I feel. She ate pizza alone. She never went on a second date.

"But was it easier than Ritzville?" I don't want her to stop talking.

"Of course." She laughs humorlessly. "But there's no comparison. In Ritzville I couldn't be out at all. And I used to imagine New York as this queer utopia with lesbians running around topless through Central Park."

"And was it?"

"Honestly? Kind of."

I laugh at that. Oakley doesn't.

"That doesn't mean *I* did any of that, mind you," she says. "I felt like a bird who got pushed out of the nest too soon."

"That makes sense."

"Does it?"

"Sure," I say. "I mean, I grew up in a city known for being super queer and with liberal Jewish parents and it was *still* hard."

I don't know fully what I mean by "hard," and Oakley doesn't rush me to finish my thought.

"I never felt like I had to hide who I was," I tell her. "But that didn't make it any easier. Maybe it made it even *harder* because it felt like everyone else had it figured out and I didn't."

"Exactly!" Oakley looks at me then, and her face is alight with what I now know is her *this idea is exciting to me and I want to talk about it more* expression.

She steps closer, moving into the glow of a streetlight; she's radiant. "I've known I was queer since I was a little kid. I knew it from the moment my bishop's wife first smiled at me once her husband accepted his calling. So I thought that when I went to New York I could quickly put those feelings into action. I thought I'd be able to prove to myself and my family and my ward, my community, that none of it was a blip, that I was who I'd always said I was."

She's huddled close to me now; the cold caught up to her after relinquishing her jacket. I pull my arm out from where she's pinned it-to my side and wrap it hesitantly around her. As I do, she leans in so that she's curled against me, the way the tiny girl from the orchard might've curled into her giant boyfriend.

Hopefully there are enough layers to keep her from hearing how fast my heart is beating.

"When I got to New York, all that confidence I had in my identity went away. To everyone else, being queer wasn't a big deal. But for me, I needed it to be everything, or it couldn't be anything." She shakes her head, frustrated. "What I mean is, if being queer can't be a core part of who I am, then what's the point?"

"It's—" I start, but she cuts me off.

"I know what the point is. But I didn't know how to exist in this new life, and no one else knew what to do with me either. I was like a baby. An ignorant baby."

There was so much else to say, but I settle on, "Babies aren't ignorant." It was silly, but I had a point. "They're just new to the world. Sometimes a baby has to touch a hot stove before they find out it'll burn them."

"Are you speaking from experience?"

Now we're back to familiar territory. The conversation before was too intense—I don't want to think about Oakley floundering at anything. She's so competent.

After another minute, I convince her to get back onto the train and not jump in the river (she threatened it a second time).

It's now nearly lights-out, which the conductor reminds us by shouting over the intercom.

"So, I have bunk beds," Oakley says when the conductor's done. "And you could sleep in the top bunk. If you didn't want to stay in coach."

"Yeah," I say, trying not to look surprised or scared or a combination of the two. "I mean, sure. That sounds good. But what if one of the conductors sees?"

"Does it matter?" Oakley asks. "If they say anything about you being in the wrong section, I'll fight them."

"You're ready to fight anyone on this train, though."

"Correct," she says. "I'd do it in a heartbeat."

"Like with Guy Fieri."

She looks confused. "Who?"

"Guy Fieri, the creepy man."

"No, Guy Fieri's amazing. He's officiated hundreds of queer weddings."

I shake my head. "First of all, how do you know—Actually, don't answer that. Second of all, not the *real* Guy Fieri. I mean the man from Chicago who kind of looked like him."

She gets a serious look on her face then. "Well, he was being weird to you. Obviously, I was going to step in."

It's the word *obviously* that gets me. If Alden had said that, I would've felt uncomfortable. But coming from Oakley, I feel warm, protected.

"So, are you going to stay in my room or not? The top bunk is all yours."

"Um, yeah." I nod. "That would be nice. Thank you."

"You're more than welcome."

Ten

Tuesday, 12:00 a.m., Somewhere in MN

"Nope, nope, nope. I'm not sleeping up there." I'm staring at the newly unfolded beds in Oakley's sleeper room. The attendant came by to set them up, and I tried to look like I wasn't going to spend the night, though all that did was make me seem guiltier. "That top bunk's a coffin."

"Why do you think I offered it to you?"

I give her what I hope is my most withering look, and she smiles in return.

The distance between the mattress and the ceiling can't be more than a couple of feet. I would barely be able to prop myself on my elbow, let alone sit up.

"You get what you get and you don't get upset," Oakley says, smug. "Do you want it or not?"

I pretend to consider the offer. My alternative is going back to my rightful place in coach, bundling my jacket behind my neck in a futile attempt to find a comfortable sleeping position. Or I could go to the observation car and practice my T-spins.

"I want it," I grumble.

We take turns getting changed in the cramped bathroom—nothing falls into the toilet—and when I'm done, I climb into the top bunk.

"If I suffocate here it's your fault," I tell her. "And if I get a concussion from slamming my head on the ceiling, you're paying my medical bills."

"Sounds good," she says, crawling into the safety of the bottom bunk.

Then, it's silent, save for the sounds of the train making its way out west.

After a minute: "Are you asleep?"

"No," I tell Oakley, laughing a little. The train blanket is thin, but in the stale air of the room I barely need it. "Of course not."

"Me neither." She takes a breath.

I wait.

"Can I tell you something?" she asks.

I nod, then I remember she can't see me. "Anything."

Finally, she says, "I'm not going back to New York after Thanksgiving."

"Oh yeah?" I ask, trying not to sound too interested.

"Yeah," she says. "I'm going to stay in Washington. In Ritzville, I mean."

"Okay."

We're silent for another moment, and then she adds, "I miss it. I miss the community I had there. I didn't have that in New York. I might not agree with everything my family believes in, but I love them, and they love me."

147

I make a noncommittal *hm* sound, neither an agreement nor a rebuke.

"I dreamed of having this queer community in New York," Oakley says, and I have to flip on my side to hear her over the train.

"I know," I say quietly. "You said—"

"I was sleeping in hostels every night until my money ran out."

I freeze, and even the train quiets, waiting on Oakley's next words.

"There are places to stay if you're a queer person who needs housing, but I couldn't do that. My family has money, and I didn't want to take those spots away from people who really needed them."

It sounds like *she* really needed them, like she's exactly who those places are for—a queer person fleeing a high-demand religion—but I don't say that.

"So I stayed with backpackers from all over the world in dirty sixteen-person dorms. I went on dates during the day and I slept where I could at night." She breathes deeply. "I thought I'd start in New York, then go to Europe. I wanted to see the cities I'd only read about in books. But I never made it out there."

"That sounds hard," I whisper.

"I'm sure Europe isn't all that good, anyway," she says. Then: "Can I tell you what I miss about it? About home? About the Church?" When I don't speak, she tells me anyway. "I always think about what Joseph Smith preached."

I settle in. I know she's about to talk for a while. And I know I'll hang on to her every word.

"He was a terrible person. He was a liar and a narcissist with multiple underage wives—but I agree with him on this: he said that salvation can only be achieved through community, not individual actions." She shifts in bed, and the creaks join in with the cacophony of train sounds. "That's what an eternal family is: an interconnected web of people reuniting in the afterlife."

"That sounds nice," I tell her. Because, put that way, it does.

"It's beautiful," she agrees. "I don't know if it's a real quote, but apparently Joseph Smith once said something like, 'I would rather go to hell with my friends than heaven alone.'"

"I love that," I tell her. "It's a little queer?"

"Exactly!" She sounds excited now. "It's an extremely queer idea."

"But that was Joseph Smith," I say, staring up at the beige train ceiling that's too close to my face. "That was hundreds of years ago."

"I know," she says. "Trust me, I know."

We're both quiet for another minute.

"Are you asleep *now*?" she asks.

I exhale. "No."

"When I go back to Washington, I'm staying."

"I know, you said."

"And I'm rejoining the Church."

Eight Weeks into College

My hair was an afterthought.

I admired the way some girls could spend hours curling, oiling, massaging, straightening, preening. It seemed relaxing.

But I'd never had it in me to do anything of the sort. My hair was long and thick, and had broken nearly every brush that had ever touched it.

It had to go.

Alden had asked if I'd wanted to hang out, but I'd told him I wasn't feeling well. Which was true, even if I couldn't have described my symptoms. The closest was probably existential dread, and a deep and abiding sense that something was intrinsically wrong with me.

But those weren't chill things you could tell your boyfriend.

He said he'd bring me dinner and we could watch a movie or play cards, but I was running on no sleep and a manic desire to cut my hair.

I'd spent the past three hours watching tutorial after tutorial from hairstylists. It had started with the query "DIY short haircut" and had spiraled into an entire playlist on proper self-haircut technique.

When I was confident—or delusional—enough in my strategy, I headed to the dorm bathroom with fabric scissors and a comb.

No one could've stopped me from what I was about to do. I had to test the theory that if I gave myself a similar haircut to Alden's, I would know once and for all if I wanted to be with him or if I wanted to *be* him.

After he told me he was falling for me at the orchard, I'd spent nearly every waking hour contemplating those two options.

But I didn't have to contemplate anymore; I could take action.

I hid in a stall until the coast was clear, then parked myself in front of the bathroom mirror.

The first step was to put my hair back in a ponytail, then cut the bulk off. I wrapped the hair tie around my hair once, twice, three times. I pulled it taut, then took a breath.

Ten minutes and about a million snips later, the majority of my hair was separated from my body. I thought I'd feel *something*, but I didn't even recognize the heavy, knotted mess. It looked like a dead rodent.

From there, I kept cutting, until there was nothing sticking off the back of my head. I'd saved a bit at the front for bangs, but that didn't feel right anymore—I needed it all gone.

The scissors were dull, but the sound echoed throughout the empty bathroom.

Some time later, I looked into the sink to find a dark mass of hair clogging the drain.

And then I chanced a look at myself. My hair was sticking up at odd angles—there wasn't any discernable style, and it certainly didn't look like Alden's.

It was mine, and I loved it. I kept rubbing my hands over my spiky head. It was punk, almost purposefully disheveled.

I took a million selfies, posing at different angles. My screen was now covered in dark brown strands of hair, warping the photos.

The problem was that I wanted to send the pictures to someone, but I couldn't do that. The Tees might've liked the haircut, but they were out of the question. I didn't want Alden to know what I'd done, and my parents would've keeled over.

So the photos were just for me.

Back in my room, I played with my hair as I watched YouTube videos of these six guys who did ill-advised extreme sports. They constructed waves in rivers to surf, they kite-boarded canals in Amsterdam.

One of them, the baby of the group, had a haircut similar to the one I'd given myself. It was a careless style, his blond hair sticking up when he pulled off his helmet.

The kid was my age, but instead of going to college, he traveled the world with his buddies in order to jump off shit and give his number to random girls he met on mountains and at skate parks.

I was clearly doing something wrong.

Alden texted me good night, but I didn't respond. I was imagining my life with these boys, being a little daring and a little blockheaded and so, *so* cool.

With my short hair, I could almost taste that life, one entirely different from my own.

To Randall's credit, he didn't comment on my hair when I arrived at the greenhouse the next day.

All he did was walk me around the arid plant room and tell me about a cactus that looked like it grew out of a turtle's shell, called *Dioscorea elephantipes*. He said the scientific names of the plants with a level of confidence I didn't have about anything.

As he gave his spiel, I noticed things about Randall I hadn't before: the thick muscle of his forearms covered in graying black hair, his pants sitting low on his narrow hips.

I was noticing boys, noticing *men*, in a way I never had. At first, it had only been Alden, but now it was any man I came across.

It wasn't an attraction, it was more a study. My findings were inconclusive with bouncing-leg-girl, but maybe, if I looked at these men closely enough, I could better understand how they moved through the world.

When I observed them, I could see easily what I lacked, which was more essential than physical. They existed in a way that didn't offer a preplanned apology.

When I met up with Alden after work, I tried to hide my hair under a baseball cap, but he noticed, of course. If I was his observer, then he was mine.

"What's under there, Zo?" He laughed a little as he pulled my hat off, but when he did, his smile fell and he blinked a few times. "That's new."

I couldn't tell if he was mad or disappointed or confused. But suddenly, my excitement for my new hair faded, and was replaced by shame.

The outfit I'd chosen today was too girly or not enough. My hands were too big but smaller than I'd like. I was all wrong.

I excused myself to go to the bathroom, then sat on the toilet in the women's room and cried.

There was no reason for me to be sad. The room technically labeled me properly; I was a woman. But if that was true, why did it feel like I was playing a part?

Everything I'd imagined about myself for eighteen years was crumbling. I wasn't the perfect daughter or the perfect girlfriend.

Because I wasn't perfect, and I didn't even know if I was a girl. I was just a mess.

WEDNESDAY, 12:45 A.M., NEAR ST. CLOUD, MN

"You're *what*?" I ask, leaning over the bed so I can peer down into her bunk. This is no longer a conversation I can have without looking at her.

"I want to go back," she repeats.

I sit up then, and of course, whack my head on the train ceiling and yell every expletive I know in the process.

"Are you okay?" Oakley asks, her voice soft yet frantic.

"I'm fine," I tell her. "My head's not the most pressing thing here."

I lie back down and rub my skull as Oakley nervously adds, "Well, they might not have me back. But if they do, I could be a success story." She laughs awkwardly, her words lacking her usual confidence.

I climb down from my bunk to stand in front of her. "But you won't be able to marry a woman." I know it sounds pathetic even as I say it, but she had told me, hours before, how much she wanted love. How much of a hopeless romantic she is.

She hasn't even been on a second date with a girl.

Oakley doesn't look me in the eye as she says, "Maybe that's not the worst thing. I'll have everything else: my family, my community."

I shiver, the air colder down here than on the top bunk. She pats the mattress and I hesitantly join her. Then she swivels so she's sitting cross-legged on the bed, looking out the dark window. I do the same. It's like being in a fort, enclosed on three sides.

I wait for her to explain herself, but when she doesn't, I say, "Can I tell you something too?"

She nods, twirling her hair between her fingers.

And then I immediately want to chicken out. Because I haven't told anyone this. Not my parents, not Alden. I've barely admitted it to myself.

"I'm not going back either," I tell her.

She turns to look at me. "But the semester's not over."

"Correct," I say, nodding. "I'm dropping out."

And there it is.

Because the truth is that I can't handle being at school for one second longer. Sure, there are only three weeks left of the semester, but I can't do it.

"So, here's the thing," I say after a beat, needing to fill the silence. "I've always thought I knew who I was. For my whole life, I've had a plan laid out for me by my parents. I had to get good grades in high school, then apply to the right colleges, then choose the right major. But the other week I thought—what happens if I keep focusing ahead, ahead, ahead? I'll be looking in front of me and never have any idea who I am right now." I take a deep breath. "That's the scariest part."

Oakley reaches out a hand so it's sitting in the spot between us. I place mine close to hers, and she bridges the gap.

"I'm afraid too," she whispers. "I'm scared that eternal life isn't real. That even if I rejoin the Church, I won't get to be with my family forever just because I'm a lesbian, even though I've never acted on it."

My whole body is jittery, but its movements are concealed by the starts and stops of the train.

"I don't have an eternal life," I say quietly, tears forming at the corners of my eyes. "No one ever promised me that."

She picks herself up so she's facing me entirely, and I do the same. We're sitting cross-legged with our knees touching, using the limited space of the bottom bunk as an excuse.

"Sometimes I think—or maybe hope—that eternal life is just having someone who remembers you," she whispers. "That it's having an impact on the world, no matter how small."

"I don't think anyone will remember me." I tell her, honestly. "I haven't done jack shit."

"I will," she insists. "I'll always remember this trip." She leans forward to put a hand on my thigh. "I'll always remember you here, like this."

I want to tell Oakley that she's starting to feel like someone important to me, that I don't want her to rejoin the Church, but I can't reasonably say either of those things, and especially not the latter.

We both stare at each other, until it's too much. Until the potential energy turns kinetic.

I lean forward, and she meets me halfway. When I press my lips against hers—warm and soft and delicate—everything else quiets.

We kiss like that, bent at the waist over our crossed knees, for a long time.

I reach forward and push her hair behind her ear, and she presses her hand to mine, holding me there. When my legs start hurting from sitting cross-legged, I help her lie down, a tentative hand on her waist, then slip next to her. We're both facing the top bunk, the one I was supposed to be sleeping in tonight.

"Huh," she says, nodding and breathing hard.

"Mhm," I confirm.

Oakley leans over and kisses me again, harder this time. She holds the nape of my neck, and I press a flat palm to her back, and *this* is how it's supposed to feel. My body fits perfectly into hers, pressed against her waist and her stomach and her chest. Even our legs match, puzzle pieces clicking into place.

We kiss until the train lurches, and our noses bump.

"Oh my god, I'm so sorry." I press my fingertip against her beautiful nose at the spot where I hit it.

She's laughing as she wraps her hand around the finger I offered her. "It's fine, Zoe."

I smile at that; my name fits perfectly in her mouth. I want her to say it again and again and again.

We fall against the pillow, our sides touching.

"Maybe you can sleep in the lower bunk tonight?" she says. "You know how cold it gets in the sleeper car."

"Of course," I say, nodding with mock seriousness. "We'll need to cuddle for warmth."

"But I'm the big spoon."

"Fine," I tell her, rolling my eyes. But really, it's more than fine: I want to be held.

I turn on my side, and she burrows her face into the back of my neck.

"I'm glad you're down here," she says.

I grin, and she kisses my shoulder, and we fall asleep wrapped together in the bottom bunk of her sleeper car, in a part of the country I've never seen in the light of day.

With no mention of what we'd just revealed to each other.

Eleven

WEDNESDAY, 4 A.M., NEAR FARGO, ND

Neither of us have slept much since we kissed earlier. Oakley keeps stirring and pulling me closer, as if I might return to coach if she lessens her grip.

"I've never been to North Dakota," I whisper as the conductor wakes the sleeping train to announce that we're pulling into Fargo.

Oakley laughs, and the puff of air tickles my neck. "Somehow that doesn't surprise me."

"Okay, but have *you*?"

She's silent for a moment. "Well, no."

I flip over so that we're facing each other, bodies pressed close under the thin Amtrak-supplied blanket. "Know-it-all."

She shoves me, and we're both laughing, and then we're kissing again, more gently than we were a few hours ago.

When we're touching like this, my brain is blissfully quiet. I'm not thinking about who I am, or who I'm *not*, or the string of bad decisions I made to wind up here.

The only thing in the world is Oakley's hand on my waist,

mine in her hair, our legs twisted like snakes.

My body feels like my own when it's pressed against hers.

"When I booked a room in a sleeper car, I knew I'd get *some* perks, but nothing like this," she says, grinning with puffy lips. "I'll have to leave a good review so Amtrak knows to continue this service."

"What can I say?" I try and fail to keep a straight face. "We offer only the best to our Empire Builder clientele."

I know it's a joke, but it makes me think about how I *haven't* offered my best to many other people.

I turn to the other side so that Oakley can spoon me again. I don't want her to see the look on my face as my thoughts turn sour.

My parents have no idea there's anything wrong because I've hidden it from them. They think I'll be heading back to college after Thanksgiving break, a premed student following the path that's been placed before me.

Their good little girl.

I don't know how to tell them that I'm dropping out. Maybe they'll make it easy and will kick me out when I tell them; at least then I won't have to face the shame of living under their roof.

"You okay?" Oakley asks.

"Yeah," I tell her. "Just a little restless."

"We could go out to the observation car?" she suggests. "Look at the beautiful sights." She points to the pitch blackness out of the lower-bunk window.

"Sounds good," I tell her, and we put on our shoes—she wears her slippers and I throw on the same sneakers I've worn for the entire trip—and make our way to the observation car.

"Hi!" Aya says, sitting with her legs crossed in one of the chairs.

Oakley glances at me, and I try not to make my face too obvious. Our dinner with Nanami was only a few hours ago, but it feels like an eternity has passed since then.

It's the first time we've seen Aya since we were instructed to lie to her.

Oakley checks the time on her phone. "Dude, it's four a.m. What are you doing here?"

"I know what time it is," Aya says, pointing to her bright pink watch. She holds the Percy Jackson book she's reading out for Oakley to see. "I made it to the fourth one, and my mom didn't want to keep the light on for me to read so she told me I could come out here."

I can't speak. If I do, I'll tell Aya everything.

But I don't have to say anything because Oakley takes charge.

"What part are you up to?" she asks as she sits next to Aya.

"They found out there's an entrance to the labyrinth at camp!" Aya tells her, eyes lighting up.

Oakley gasps. "Just wait; it gets *so* good."

"You said that yesterday!" she tells Oakley. "That's why I'm reading it so fast, because I want to be able to talk about it with you!"

Oakley was pissed about Nanami lying, but none of that anger was ever directed at Aya. Maybe the best thing we can do is show her a good time while she's not yet burdened by the truth.

Oakley turns to me, and I hope she's thinking the same thing.

It's apparently common train knowledge that if you book a ticket in coach, you can sleep on the dirty floor of the observation car instead of in your seat, and some people are doing that now. They all seem to be deeply asleep—or they could be dead; we can figure that out in the morning—so no one's bothered by the noise of our conversation.

Oakley asks Aya to read to us, then pats the seat next to her so I can join the two of them.

I settle in, closing my eyes and getting into the story. Aya's great at reading aloud, and when she stumbles over a word, Oakley has her sound it out and then corrects her if she's too far off. ("It's ancient Greek, you get a pass here," she tells Aya a number of times.)

After a few minutes, Oakley reaches back and grabs my hand in the space between our chairs, rubbing her thumb against the skin of my palm. This girl who made out with me and spooned me and laughed into my ear is here, helping an elementary schooler sound out the big words in a book they both love.

And I can't *help* but feel . . . things.

She's so good with Aya; she's kind when she wants to be and protective when she *needs* to be. She's so much more than I could've known when I met her on Monday. (How was that only *Monday*?)

"Are you even listening?" Aya asks.

I open my eyes and spring to attention. "What? Yes, of course," I say, even though I have a sneaking suspicion that I've been asleep for a while.

"Good," she says, then continues reading.

Oakley must've fallen asleep too because she doesn't stir as I half listen to Aya's words.

A few chapters later, the conductor announces the next stop in North Dakota, bringing us closer to sunrise on day three of this trip.

A trip that will end tomorrow, whether I want it to or not.

TWO MONTHS AND CHANGE INTO COLLEGE

I hadn't been to class in a week. In high school I would have stress dreams about showing up fifteen minutes late. I'd cry into my pillow with relief when I realized I'd been asleep, that I still had hours before school started.

Not anymore.

That dream became real, and nothing happened. Professors kept lecturing; they continued administering tests and assigning readings. School went on without me, and no one cared.

The only place I felt like going during the day was the greenhouse. If Randall suspected something was wrong, he didn't show it. He'd greet me with a kind smile and give me updates on the plants and what needed tending. I tried not to think too much about how this was a position for student workers only. That if I stopped going to class entirely and someone figured it out, I couldn't keep coming here.

I spent most of my time with the *Amorphophallus*, though it looked no different than it had a few weeks earlier. Still, I watched over it as if the simple act of my observation could make it flower.

163

Being in the greenhouse was a tactile experience; it was the only thing in my life that felt real. When Randall wasn't looking, I whispered comforting words to the plant or touched it gently.

"Take all the time you need," I told it. "I believe in you."

They were words I could've stood to hear.

At that point, I was back to seeing Alden only at night, though it was by my choice, not his. The roles were reversed—he wanted to spend time with me in the daylight, and I couldn't handle it.

The autumn sun felt like a thousand surgical lamps that illuminated the parts of myself that I could no longer stand.

If I wasn't with him, though, I had to be alone with my thoughts. So, going to his dorm felt like the path of least resistance, like water carving and shaping millions of years' worth of rock to form a canyon.

"Hi," Alden said one night, legs splayed out on his bed.

"Hi," I said. I could barely look him in the eyes anymore.

It was 1:54 in the morning, six minutes before the first of two repeating hours. We were about to enter Daylight Saving Time.

He had a deck of cards in his palm, though after a minute he put it down.

But I wanted him distracted, so I said, "Let's play."

He shuffled, and I closed my eyes to listen. I loved the crisp sounds of cards sliding past each other, swapping places and then neatly realigning.

When the shuffling stopped, he laughed a little, breathing sharply out of his nose. "Are you awake?"

I opened my eyes, and Alden was smiling, his face soft. He only brought out his playing cards when he wanted to *talk*.

"Deal the cards," I told him. I didn't want to talk.

He dealt us each ten cards, which meant we were playing gin rummy. I'd never once beat him, which used to feel like a joke between us but was now another reminder of the ways I couldn't compare to him.

Alden's watch beeped.

"Happy two a.m. number one," he said.

"Happy two a.m. number one," I repeated.

The cards lay untouched in front of us.

"Hey," he said, an unfinished thought.

"You go first," I told him quickly, motioning to the cards.

Our conversations used to flow smoothly, but since my haircut, that had changed.

"The person who didn't deal goes first," he said.

I pulled the ten of diamonds off the discard pile. I didn't need a ten of diamonds, but I absorbed it into my hand. It felt better to make an active choice rather than take my chances with the next random card off the top of the deck.

It was his turn, then, and he was beautiful, sitting there with his cards. My hair was now shorter than his, though it was hardly a competition as he hadn't gotten a haircut yet this semester. His bangs were long enough to tie back in a bun; he probably would've let me braid them if I'd asked politely.

After about ten minutes, Alden said, "Gin," and the game was over. We played three more rounds, and I lost them all.

"Good game."

"It wasn't." I folded my arms over my stomach, and Alden sighed and leaned back against the chipped stucco of his dorm wall.

He nudged my leg with his foot and frowned. "Are you upset about something?"

Other than asking if I was only dating him because I envied his gender, this was the scariest thing he could've said.

Because it meant that he noticed me, and correctly at that.

"No," I told him.

It was the truth. I was upset about *everything*, so I couldn't narrow it down to any one complaint.

"Is it because I said . . . ," Alden began.

"No," I repeated.

He was speaking, of course, about when he said he was falling for me.

A minute went by. Someone stumbled past his open window, shouting incoherently.

"Then have you thought about it?"

Alden was a smart boy; he knew the answer.

So all I said was, "I'll deal us in this time."

It was the worst possible response, and the only one I could give.

We played in silence until his watch beeped a second time.

"Okay, now I get a redo."

"A what?"

"We get to repeat this hour," he said, showing me his watch, which once again read two a.m. "Do you know what that means?" I shook my head. "It means we get a second chance."

He was offering me something very few people ever got, and I wanted to take it. I wanted this one inconvenient form of time travel to change my life, however slightly.

"So what are you going to do?" I asked, knowing full well what the answer would be.

He leaned in and kissed me. Maybe for this second two a.m. I could be the girl who would've told him she was falling too.

WEDNESDAY, 4:45 A.M., APPROACHING GRAND FORKS, ND

Aya throws her book into her lap. "Oakley, you're not even awake," she whines. "And we're getting to the good part."

Oakley mutters in her sleep, and Aya rolls her eyes.

"Sorry about her," I tell Aya. "She's just tired."

I wonder why.

"I'll read more when she's awake," she says, yawning.

I tell Aya that it's time to head back to her room, insisting that she should at least try to get some rest. Then I come back for Oakley.

She leans on me as we walk to the sleeper car.

"Thank you," she whispers.

"Of course."

"No." She leans her head against my shoulder and mutters into my sweatshirt. "For everything."

"Any time."

I ease her into the lower bunk, then sit next to her as she falls asleep. She looks like how I imagine a fairy-tale princess might, lying in her tower, hidden from the world.

She's more peaceful than I've ever seen her.

I head back out to the observation car, and there's a surprise visitor.

"Edward?"

He turns from where he's sitting to wave me over. "Hey, Zoe," he says, peppy as ever.

"What are you doing up here?" I ask.

"I don't live in the snack car, silly."

"I know that," I tell him. "But wouldn't you rather be in the employee quarters?"

"Not right now," he says. "Sometimes I like to remind myself what it feels like to take the train as a regular citizen."

"Of course," I say. "Glad you're hanging out with the plebs."

He laughs and puts his book down, patting the seat next to him. "Let's chat. I like getting to know the people of the train."

I comply. "Happy to be of service."

"So," he says, "tell me about yourself."

"Is this a first date?"

He laughs at that. "You're funny."

"I'm really not."

His face turns serious. "And I'm not kidding. I want to know about you. Let's hear it."

"But we're all getting off the train tomorrow," I say. "Why would you want to know more about me when you're about to meet a whole new batch of people?"

He's taken aback by this, which: fair. Maybe it's a silly question.

For anyone other than me, the answer would be simple. Just *because*.

"Because every single person who takes the train is fascinating to me," he says. "I get to talk to people from all over the world. I've spoken to bankers from Japan and singers from Croatia. I might not see you again, but at least I'll have met you."

His words stir a feeling in me that I don't want to have stirred. I wanted to fade into the background on this train ride—I didn't want to think about who I was or who I had to be.

But Edward sees everyone, regardless of whether they want him to or not. I don't know *how* he sees me; I just know that he does.

My thoughts spiral from there until Edward waves a hand over my face. "Are you okay?"

I nod, and the movement shakes the worst of the anxiety out of me. "I'm fine."

"Come on," he says. "Spill. There has to be a reason you're on the train."

After a moment's hesitation, I do. Not everything, but parts of it—disappointing my parents, how I can't for the life of me figure out who I am now that I'm not going to be a doctor, how it's been hanging out with Oakley. How I'm worried I've messed up what I worked so hard for in high school.

"How old are you?" he asks when I'm done.

"Eighteen."

"I'm thirty-six."

"That's twice my age." It's the same thing I said to Aya on the first day, but in reverse.

"Thank you for making me feel elderly," Edward says, "but that's not the point. The point is, back in my twenties, I started my life essentially from scratch every single year, claiming it was because some planet or another was in retrograde. And you're not even twenty. You're a baby."

"I feel ancient," I tell him.

"That may be so, but you have time to figure out who you are. Honestly, it'll be okay if you never figure it out." I must give him a horrified look because he adds, "Not everything you do has to have lasting, life-altering consequences. Sometimes you can do things just for the sake of it. I went to law school when I was twenty-four—it wasn't for me. I just wanted to be able to say, 'I object.'"

I laugh at that, and he adds, "This doesn't have to be your whole life, forever. You can always change tracks." At this, he stands up. "Speaking of which, I have to set up the snack car."

"Already?" I check my phone. "It's barely five."

The café opens at six, when quiet hours are over and everyone's joints are creaky from a night of train-sleep.

"I don't just stand there and look pretty," he says. "I have coffee to brew, food to unpack, inventory to check and restock. People *need* their snacks."

"I'm sorry," I say, because he's right; he's the one who keeps the train running and the passengers from losing their minds.

He's so easily satisfied with his life; providing travelers snacks and coffee is enough for him.

And yet nothing is ever enough for me.

Twelve

WEDNESDAY, 7 A.M., NEAR DEVIL'S LAKE, ND

The sun is just starting to rise, but the train is already awake, alive.

"Good morning, sleepyhead," I say to Oakley as she zombie-walks into the observation car, her hair in a messy bun. She sits next to me, then flops forward and rests her head in my lap.

I feel like I coaxed a finicky cat onto me: one wrong move and she'll go skittering under the nearest piece of furniture.

"I'm so tired," she groans.

"Coffee?" I suggest.

She sits up. "Not happening."

"Just a little sip?"

"No," she says. "I'd feel too guilty."

"Ooh," I say, feigning shock. "I thought that was just a thing for Jews and Catholics. Nice to know that Mormons experience religious guilt too."

"Not a Mormon," she tells me, then she realizes what she said and backtracks. "Or, not currently, anyway. Not on the train. Not yet."

I let her words hang in the air.

"And you don't own guilt," she says, filling the gap in conversation. "My whole life is guilt. It's literally built into the Church. Every Sunday, they pass around the sacrament, which you can only take if you're 'worthy.'" She rolls her eyes. "So if I knew I was 'unworthy' that week, I had to abstain. And if I hadn't confessed my sins beforehand to my bishop—who was usually a friend's dad asking me if I'd masturbated, mind you—then I'd have to choose between either lying to God and taking the sacrament (because I was never perfect) or passing it along to the next person in my row when it came to me."

"Then there's no reason why you shouldn't try a little coffee," I tell her. "You've tried a little lesbianism."

She coughs, choking on saliva, and I stand and pat her back until I'm sure her airways are clear.

"Nothing to see here, people," I say, making a big show of turning to everyone in the observation car, even though no one's paying attention to us.

Oakley drags me back to her sleeper car after that. Sometime between when I left last night and now, the attendant put away the beds so that the room is back to its two-seats-facing-each-other setup.

"Why did we have to leave the observation car for this?" I ask once we're settled.

She worries at her necklace. "Remember how I said I had never, um, *acted* on anything that went against the rules of the Church?"

I nod, but she keeps staring at me. "Oh my god," I say, realizing what she means. "Oh, fuck." I put my head in my hands. "I'm so sorry," I tell her. "I shouldn't have—"

"Don't be," she says, reaching out to steady my bouncing leg. "*Please*, don't be. This is . . . It was . . . nice."

"But I led you astray," I groan.

"You didn't 'lead me astray,'" she says. "You're not, like, a biblical concubine."

I dig my fingernails into my palm. "You're right," I say, whining. "I'm worse."

Oakley knew the whole time we've been on this train that she'd be returning to the Church when we made it to Washington. She knew and she let me kiss her.

And she liked it.

"You're not worse," she says after a moment. "Please, don't think that."

I close my eyes, hoping that when I open them, I won't have made out with a girl who's about to rejoin the Mormon Church.

I wonder what they would think of me in Ritzville.

But that's not a productive thought, because they'll never know about me. Maybe Oakley's family will hear about me as a secondary character in the story of her cross-country train trip, but I'll never be the main character.

I won't be the love interest.

"What happened last night," Oakley starts again, "it was . . . so good."

It was. It *really* was.

Oakley leans forward and puts her hand on my knee, and I close my eyes.

173

We stare at the flat, amber landscape for a minute, and Oakley doesn't move her hand. When she leans back, I want to pull her toward me.

But I don't, and she sighs.

Yesterday, I would've been happy to fade into the background, to be a side character in Oakley's story. But now, the thought sends a chill down my spine that I can't shake.

NEARLY THREE MONTHS INTO COLLEGE

Alden texted me that one of the kids from his English seminar was throwing a party. The boy was a sophomore, he said, and lived off campus. Would I be interested in going?

No.

Yes.

I didn't know.

I'd been in college for months and had gone to only one disastrous party.

Before I could respond, Alden texted me the address, along with a heart emoji that felt like a threat. He was reaching out, and I was slipping further away.

You should come, he told me. *I'd love for you to be there*, he said.

I'd shoved most of the clothes in which I didn't want Alden to see me to the bottom of my drawers, but I didn't have the energy to dress like the version of Zoe he thought he was dating, not that night and maybe not ever again.

I chose a black beanie, baggy black jeans, and an oversized white T-shirt that I cuffed at the sleeves. I pulled my binder on.

I'd never worn it in front of Alden, but . . . fuck it. It made me not entirely hate myself.

Actually, for the first time in a while, I *liked* the person I saw in the mirror, especially with my short hair.

When I got to the party, Alden was tipsy, which was a state in which I'd never seen him. He handed me a beer in a tall glass bottle, and I felt good holding it, like I had at the other party.

I felt even better after drinking it. I hadn't had anything to drink at all this semester, but here, it felt right.

The apartment was dingier than Mischa's, with a college student–inhabited charm that made it tolerable. People were spread over the floor, lying on top of each other, smoking weed and drinking from various cups and bottles. It was more adult than I'd imagined.

I went to the kitchen to grab another beer even though I hadn't finished my first, and when I did, Alden came up behind me and kissed my neck. He smelled like a mixture of alcohol and body spray, unfamiliar scents.

I opened the beer by leveraging the cap against the counter—my hottest skill, and one that felt extremely queer—then I put a hand on his waist and directed his around my neck. I wasn't doing it to placate him. I *wanted* to kiss him.

I was wearing black boots with a small thick heel, and for the first time, I was taller than him.

I don't know what came over me—maybe one beer and a lack of caring. The kiss was nice. When we broke apart, he was grinning.

"Let's dance," he said, taking my hand.

So we did. We stepped over everyone who had taken up residence on the carpet and joined the small group of people dancing in the living room.

I pulled him closer, and someone whistled. I didn't know what they saw, but it felt like being perceived on my own terms.

We made out a little on the dance floor, and I held on to his hips, leading the movement.

It felt—and there's no other word for it—queer.

"Come back to my dorm," Alden whispered to me after a few songs. He had to crane his neck slightly to reach my ear, which, more than his words, is what sent a shiver through my body.

I nodded. "Okay."

We didn't hold hands on the way back to campus. It was a cold, early November day that foretold winter. I stayed a few steps ahead and held the door open for him when we got to his dorm.

All we did was make out, but it was better than anything we'd done before. I had woken up feeling especially masculine that day, and I wanted him to understand that. I wanted to transmit this feeling to him through the way I kissed, the way I bit his lip, the way I tugged at his shirt but kept mine on.

I don't know if he knew what changed or if he felt it, but he was *definitely* into it.

After we'd kissed for a while, I pulled away. "I'm going back to my dorm," I told him.

I liked what we'd done, but it still didn't feel *right*.

Feeling in control and feeling right were two different things, I'd learned.

"Why?" he asked, pouting. He was sitting with a pillow in his lap, shirtless, small. I leaned down and kissed him. I imagined that he was a girl. I imagined that he was queer, that I was queer in the same way as him.

Maybe this was how queer boys felt, the desire, the hunger.

It was the first time I was pulled to him in this way.

"Stay," he said. He begged.

I shook my head, opened his door, and left.

In the morning, I had no idea what had happened. I remembered everything perfectly; that wasn't where the confusion came from.

I didn't know what had possessed me, what had allowed me to feel so comfortable in my skin for one night.

When I woke up the morning after, I didn't feel as masculine. I washed my face, put on a real bra. It felt right for that day; it was what my brain was telling me I wanted to look like at that moment.

But if I had been feeling this way the night before, I knew I wouldn't have wanted to hook up with Alden. It would've felt too . . . straight.

That's what he was, though, wasn't he? Straight?

Even if I wasn't a girl, he didn't know that.

I didn't know what I was or who I wanted to be.

I didn't know anything.

WEDNESDAY, 8:30 A.M., OUTSIDE OF RUGBY, ND

We've been playing Spit with Oakley's deck of cards for the past half hour. She is, of course, extremely good at it. Maybe better than Alden.

"So," I say, my palms almost too sweaty to move the cards to the spit pile. Oakley doesn't look up.

I need to tell her how I'm feeling, even if I don't know completely myself. "You know how I told you I was having thoughts about my gender?"

She freezes midstack, then collects all the cards into a pile, putting them away and giving me her full attention.

"Yes," she says calmly, as if she might scare me away. "I remember."

"Can I tell you some of the thoughts?"

"Of course," she says.

I take a few deep breaths.

"It's like this: sometimes I feel fine. I'll wake up and I'll feel good about the body I'm in and the way people perceive me. But other times . . ."

I've never had to put this into words before.

I try again. "Then there are other times where I want to be a boy, full stop, and it feels bone-deep wrong for anyone to suggest I'm something else." I swallow the bile in my throat. "But when we, um, kissed last night," I start up again. "That was really good. I felt right in my body then. But maybe I won't tomorrow. Or later today." I shrug. "I don't know. I think my gender is partially being a lesbian. I like you. I like all girls." My face gets hot. "But, yeah. I . . . Yeah."

A beat, then: "Thank you for telling me." I look up, and Oakley's reaching out her hand for me to take. "I need you to know that I didn't kiss you because I was rebelling." She squeezes my palm. "I kissed you because I wanted to."

"Yeah?"

"Yeah." She leans back in her chair. "I think I'm a lesbian, but I've never only been attracted to girls. It's more that I'm attracted to alternative forms of masculinity."

"That's a good way of putting it," I tell her.

"What can I say?" Oakley asks. "I'm extremely smart."

I reach my leg out to gently kick her shin, and she kicks me back, and soon we're playing footsie.

I said something aloud I hadn't told anyone before. Maybe not the full truth, but part of it. For now, that's enough.

"So, pronoun check?" Oakley asks after a minute. "I can experiment, if you want, like if I'm talking about you to someone, I can mix it up."

"Anything is fine," I tell her honestly. "But who are you having conversations about me with?"

She laughs. "Maybe I'm gossiping with Edward; you don't know."

"Edward would have only good things to say about me," I tell her. "We're like this." I twist my middle and index finger together to prove it.

"Folks, next stop is Rugby, North Dakota," the conductor says through the static of the loudspeaker. "It'll be our first smoke break since last night, so get out, stretch your legs, and be back in thirty minutes or—"

"The train leaves without you," I say, mimicking the conductor's serious voice, which makes Oakley laugh.

"There's something I want to do at this stop," Oakley says.

"No." I cross my arms. "I refuse. There's no way you know of an attraction in *Rugby, North Dakota.*"

"That's where you're wrong," she says with a smug smile. "Rugby has designated itself the unofficial geographic center of North America, and there's a little stone monument we can take a picture with."

"You're unbelievable," I tell her. "Let's do it."

"Okay, but here's the thing," she tells me, biting her lip. "The monument is about a mile away, so we have to move fast. We can probably get there in fifteen minutes if we rush."

"I mean, of course," I tell her. "Because we'll be walking on gay time. I always get where I'm going at least two minutes faster than the estimate."

So, when the train pulls into the station, we jump onto the platform, fast-walking like we're in a race.

We make it there in twelve minutes.

The monument is tall and made of stone, and next to it stand the US, Mexican, and Canadian flags.

"Apparently the real center of the continent is about one hundred miles away," Oakley says as we stare at it. "But, you know, close enough."

I have her stand in front of the monument and take her picture on my phone, which I turned on while we were running over here. (There's no service, thankfully.) The sun is still low in the sky, and she's soaking in the early-morning half-light. She's beautiful.

180

"What?" she asks, smiling and covering her face. "Do I look horrible?"

"No." I shake my head. "I want to get it right."

I take the picture and promise to send it to her. Then I covertly tap the heart to add it to my favorites.

"All right, now let me take one of you."

I reluctantly walk over, then strike a series of ridiculous poses.

"Can you do a normal one?" she asks, cocking her hip. "I want to remember this."

That takes me by surprise; I pause my posing and stare at her, half-smiling, half-bemused.

"There," she says. "Perfect."

I flip her off.

"Let's get one together."

I agree and pull out my phone, leaning it against a rock and setting the self-timer. She puts her hand around my waist and I hold her there.

My heart feels pulled in a million directions, out to every city in North America, from here in its beating heart center.

Then, Oakley breaks the spell. "We have to get back," she says, checking her phone. "We have ten minutes before the conductor abandons us in Rugby."

While we're sprinting back to the train, I try not to freak out about the fact that this trip ends tomorrow and I'm having the best time I've had in weeks, months, years. I'm with someone I like who likes me back and it's all going to be over soon.

The thoughts of future sadness are too much—even if right

now is so, so good, I know there's only one way this will end. That my heart will break more than it already has. That all the good of this trip will be eclipsed by bad, bad, bad.

Even as I'm holding Oakley's hand, as we're running back to the train, I'm separate from myself. I'm watching this scene unfold from some unknown future, grieving the current moment.

Because this is going to end, and if my past is any indication, it won't end well.

Thirteen

WEDNESDAY, 10 A.M., SOMEWHERE IN NORTH DAKOTA

We made it back to the train but just barely. The conductor gave us an admonishing look before closing the doors.

Now we're having a Spit tournament with everyone in the observation car who wants to participate. So far, it's just me, Oakley, Aya, and Jeff, one of the people who's been sleeping on the floor like a dead man.

Aya is putting us all to shame.

"My grandma taught me how to play Spit," she says as she wins yet another round. "Who wants to play me next?"

No one does, but we all want to keep her entertained, so Oakley tries her luck again. Nanami hasn't emerged from the sleeper car, but I saw Mike sneak in that direction when he thought no one was looking.

"I'm not going to let you win this time," Oakley tells her.

"You weren't letting me win," Aya says. "You made a mistake early in the game and it cost you."

Jeff and I *ooooh* at that from seats opposite the two of them.

Oakley puts on her game face, squaring up against a nine-year-old. "Let's do this."

Aya's and Oakley's hands move too fast for any of us to keep track of who's ahead, but they're both in the zone. Aya even stands at one point for a better view.

"SPIT!" Aya calls.

Oakley throws the cards she was holding down on to the tray between them. "You don't have to rub it in my face," she grumbles.

I stand to create a barrier between them, ready to intervene if Oakley tries to fight this small child.

"Why don't we go down to the snack car?" I ask Aya. "I'll get you whatever you want."

"I'm allergic to red dye," she informs me.

"Okay, I'll get you anything you want that *doesn't* have red dye in it."

"Deal."

Aya turns around to stick her tongue out at Oakley, who's cleaning the cards and sulking.

"Snack Conductor Edward!" Aya calls when we get down to the snack car.

She's the only person I've heard use his "official" title, and he seems deeply pleased.

"Snack Assistant Aya!" Edward calls back. "The conductor is at your service. What snacks would you like?"

"Nothing with—" Aya starts.

"Red dye. I know," Edward tells her.

I want to hug him for the way he's treating her, until it hits me that this is how he treats everyone: like they're the only person who has ever needed snacks in the history of the world.

"Hey, Edward," I say, waving.

"You know Edward too?" Aya asks, amazed.

"Yeah, Zoe's cool," Edward says, and Aya nods in agreement. I'm honored.

I buy Aya a banana, chips, apple juice, and a box of nachos that Edward reheats in the microwave. She insists on carrying all of it upstairs by herself.

"We should have a party in here tonight," Aya says as we sit back down in the observation car and she opens the nachos. "And there should be balloons."

"That's a fun idea!" I say, humoring her.

"We can invite everyone on the train!" Aya says excitedly. "And it could also partially be my birthday party! Since I didn't get to have one this year because my mom had to work on planning our trip."

Oakley meets my eyes then and I suspect we're thinking the same thing: we need to give this kid the best fucking birthday party in the entire world. Especially if it's going to be the last one she has before her world is changed forever.

"Let's do it," I tell Aya. "What do you want the theme to be?"

She crosses her arms. "Trains, duh."

"I thought you said that you like other things."

"I do," she says, stomping her foot. "But it's easier to have a train birthday party on a train than a Percy Jackson birthday party. And if we can't have a train theme then we can do dogs because I want a pug one day, like for my tenth birthday."

"Come on, Zoe," Oakley says, holding back laughter. "Get your head in the game."

Oakley and I go back to her room after that to strategize.

"What's Nanami going to think about this?" I ask.

"I honestly don't care," Oakley says. "She's the one who asked us to keep a secret from Aya."

I know more about Oakley than I did when she fought with Nanami, even if it's only been a short while. I know how much the truth means to her—how much *this* means to her.

"So," Oakley continues, clearing her throat. "What should we do for the party?"

"No idea," I tell her. "But at least we already know the guest list."

"That's true," she says. "Makes it easy, no family politics."

"Not like when I had my bat mitzvah and my mom forgot to invite her second cousin," I tell her.

"Same for my baptism," Oakley says.

"Mormons get baptized?" I ask.

"They—we do," she says, and I have to fight to ignore her correction. "Basically you meet with your bishop, say that you believe in all the teachings of the Church, and are told that you're now responsible for your sins, and then your dad dunks you while you wear a see-through white jumpsuit."

"How old were you?"

"Eight," she says. "And I barely remember it, even though I committed to an everlasting covenant."

That's what gets me: the thought of eight-year-old Oakley

walking into some giant bath and coming out capable of sinning. Like a mikvah but instead of emerging cleansed, she emerged with the entire weight of the Church and all the rules she had to follow in perpetuity.

When I think of her childhood, I can't help but imagine all the other things I don't know about her life. I barely know *anything*.

It's not like she knows much about me either. She doesn't know that my bat mitzvah party theme was dogs (Aya's second-choice). She doesn't know about the scar on my wrist from when I fell down the stairs as a kid to try to show my parents that I could "cartwheel downhill."

And why *would* she know any of this? We've known each other for three days, and we're only going to know each other for one more.

"Maybe things will go back to how they were then," Oakley says after a moment, pulling me out of my thoughts. "When I get back to Ritzville."

"Yeah," I say, nodding. "Maybe."

I try to stave off the dread that fills my body. Oakley is going back to the Church. The girl who spooned me all last night is going to re-devote her life to a religion that doesn't think she should be allowed to marry someone she loves.

Even if we wanted to keep talking after this trip, nothing could happen. She can't date girls, or girl-adjacent people, or anyone who's not a Mormon man. She couldn't act on her sexuality.

The room feels too small, and the trip feels too short and too immensely long, and why is this country so wide and why is this planet so small?

"Are you okay?" Oakley asks.

"I need some water," I say, running out of her room.

Because running is always my first instinct.

THREE MONTHS INTO COLLEGE

Alden and I didn't talk about what happened the night of the party. Maybe he didn't notice that anything changed.

I, however, did.

It was harder to be around him. I felt ashamed, like I had used him, had been a different person when we made out and I grabbed his waist and told him what to do.

I absolutely could not tell him that that version of me was more real than the person he'd been dating for months.

"Do you want to come home with me?" Alden asked on the Friday before a three-day weekend. "Just for a couple of days?"

I was sure I'd misheard him, so I kept scrolling mindlessly through Instagram on my computer, a habit that had formed early in the semester and was proving hard to break.

"Zoe," he said, tilting my laptop screen down so I was forced to look at him.

"I have a lot of work to do," I said. It was a lie and he knew it; in the months we'd been dating, he'd almost never seen me do schoolwork. "I think I'd rather stay on campus."

"Of course," he said. "Just thought I'd offer."

The last thing on earth I wanted to do was meet Alden's

parents. He almost never talked about them—all I knew was that his mom was obsessed with dental hygiene.

"I'll miss you," Alden told me.

"Same," I said automatically. "I'll miss you too."

On the first day of the short break, campus was emptier than I'd ever seen it.

I wandered into the library for the first time since I had gone there with Alden at the beginning of the semester, which felt like it had happened in another lifetime. There were some grad students writing papers and librarians tiredly stacking books, but other than that it was blissfully quiet.

I climbed to the sixth floor, the designated silent area, and the stillness rang in my ears. Each step I took reverberated off the walls.

It was the first time I had felt peaceful in a part of campus that wasn't the greenhouse.

I didn't want to go back to my dorm so I stayed there for a while, wandering the stacks and pulling books off the shelves just to look at the illustrations.

When I checked my phone, it was nearly evening, and I had an email from Randall asking if I was still on campus.

Yes, I told him. *I am.*

He asked if I wanted to come to the greenhouse and help him with a project.

Yes, I told him. I did.

When I got there, his face was covered in sweat and soil.

"Thank goodness you're here," he told me. "I'm trying to repot this palm."

He was in the main conservatory, standing over a tarp, a small palm tree sitting naked on the ground. Outside of the pot, there was only a clump of soil around its roots to protect the plant from the outside world.

I had an overwhelming urge to hug the palm, even though I knew that logically that was a bad idea because of its desert adaptations: spikes that wouldn't hesitate to poke me and drought-resistant leaves that would block my path.

Randall and I worked in silence for a while. I helped him create a soil mix for the palm tree's new pot, one that was larger, that would allow it to grow unobstructed.

"Three, two, one," he counted down, and we heaved the tree into its new home and covered it with soil. I watered it in, and we were done.

He lifted the collar of his T-shirt to wipe his face. "Thank you."

"Of course," I told him, walking over to check on the corpse plant.

"You know," Randall said, "you have a knack for this."

I turned to him. He was sweeping the mess we'd made from repotting the tree.

"Yeah?"

He nodded. "I can tell you care about the plants."

Of course I cared about the plants; I cared for their well-being more than my own.

All I said was, "I do."

"I'm teaching a botany lab next semester, if you wanted to take it," he said as he shook out the tarp.

It was when he said that, when he mentioned a future academic season, that I knew once and for all that I wasn't cut out for college. That I didn't have what it took to sit through another lecture or take another test.

If I could've taken that one lab, I would've. Spending time with plants and Randall for college credit seemed . . . not terrible.

But I couldn't *just* take that class.

"That sounds nice," I told him. "I don't know if it'll fit in my schedule, though."

"No pressure." He dusted himself off. "Just think about it."

I nodded. Of course, I *had* thought about it, about what it would be like to be Zoe the botanist.

"I will," I promised.

"Good," he said. "I've really loved having you here."

He left me in the conservatory, and I tried not to cry into the *Amorphophallus*.

I checked my phone then, and there was a message waiting for me. The only person who texted me with any regularity was Alden, so I was about to swipe it away, but it wasn't from him.

It was from Autumn.

Autumn: this is kind of random
but i was wondering if you were on campus ?
if you are I'd love to talk !

WEDNESDAY, 12 P.M., CROSSING INTO MT

I feel better after downing a bottle of water and stretching my legs somewhere in the westernmost part of North Dakota.

It took nearly eight hours to pass through the state, and in that time, everything has changed. I found out Oakley's going back to the Church. She found out I'm not going back to college. We made out.

The last one was the most revelatory.

After I cool off and head back to her sleeper car, Oakley and I finish our planning session for Aya's party.

"I love that we're doing this for her," she says. "It's like a grand gesture."

"Except it's not romantic," I say.

"Grand gestures don't have to be romantic." She pulls a leg up to her chest. "I think it's even more special that we're doing it for some random kid we just met."

I kick my foot out so that my socked toe nudges her leg. "You're some random kid I just met."

We decide that we're going to get off at the next smoke stop and run to the nearest convenience store. There, we'll buy balloons and streamers or, more realistically, whatever shitty party decorations we can find.

The conductor announces that we'll have twenty minutes at the first stop in Montana, and that'll have to be enough.

Oakley gets one bar of service as we approach the station, and she uses it to map our route to a place called "Chuck's Party Store and Smoke Shop."

We sprint off the train the moment the doors open and run over to Chuck's. A man—potentially Chuck—greets us, and we wave as we run past him to the "Kids' Party" section. He doesn't seem to find this bizarre. Maybe we aren't the first people to plan a train party in Montana.

"Should we do the dog theme?" Oakley asks. She grabbed a basket by the door and is indiscriminately shoving things in there.

"I'll do you one better," I say as I hold up paper plates with pugs on them. "We'll do the *pug* theme."

"Big haul," Chuck notes as we drop our basket off at the cash register.

"Yup," Oakley says, tapping her foot.

He rings the items through with care and precision, taking his sweet, sweet time. He comments on each product as he bags it, which is how I learn everything from the fact that some people like the taste of party streamers to how he's picking his daughter up from ballet after his shift.

I pass my debit card over, using what must be some of the last money I'd saved working in the greenhouse. At least it'll be put to good use now that it's not going toward tuition.

"Thanks!" Oakley grabs the bag the second he finishes putting in the last item, and we run out of the store.

"We're gonna be late!" I scream at Oakley. "WHY ARE WE ALWAYS CUTTING IT SO CLOSE?"

"I DON'T KNOW!" she shouts, sounding panicked as well.

The train's going to leave without us and we'll be stranded here in Montana with only Chuck and some party streamers to keep us company.

When we get back to the station, though, the train's still there.

I glance at my phone. "But it's been more than twenty minutes."

Oakley shrugs like, *Don't question it*, and we head to the nearest entrance.

One of the conductors is standing there, hand on her hip, shaking her head at us.

"I thought you didn't wait for anyone," Oakley says to her as we hop on.

The conductor motions to our bags. "Edward told me you were getting supplies for Aya's birthday party."

Oakley and I both nod as the doors close behind us and the train picks up speed. Leave it to Edward to be, like, twelve steps ahead of the game.

"Well, I think that's very nice," the conductor says, pulling out her walkie-talkie. She looks down at her practical, Amtrak-approved shoes. "I like talking to Aya about trains. She's a good kid."

I exchange a look with Oakley. "She is," I say to the conductor. "She really is."

WEDNESDAY, 2 P.M., NEAR MALTA, MT

We're back in Oakley's sleeper car, taking inventory of all the supplies for Aya's party. It feels even more important to get it right now that we know that everyone on the train is into the idea.

And we're the only ones who know the full truth: this will

be her last birthday party before she learns that she's never again going to live in the place she's called home for the entirety of her short life.

I pull a stack of paper napkins out of the bag and add them to the "table decor" pile.

"You know how you were talking about how neither of us is the best spokesperson for our religion?" I ask Oakley, and she nods as she rips a roll of streamers open with her teeth.

"And how you don't seem to agree with a lot of the stuff you talk about in regard to Mormonism?"

"Yeah?"

"Then why are you going back?" I ask, and it comes out like a plea. "If you have these beliefs that so deeply contradict your church's then . . . why?"

"Community," she says automatically. "I already told you."

She's looking down now, picking at a piece of lint on her sock.

I knew that's what she was going to say. It's what she told me before. And maybe that should be answer enough.

I haven't found community anywhere. I barely had any friends in high school except for my Science Olympiad teammates, and I gave up what little community I had in college to be with Alden.

"Community is literally the basis of Mormonism. Joseph Smith wanted to create a holy city on Earth; that was his main goal for a while. He was relentless about it. He wanted it to be walkable, he wanted everyone to live near each other, and to have room for farms and gardens within the grid." She thinks for a moment, then adds, "He wanted people to live communally. And that didn't stop with him. When I got baptized, I pledged to bear others' burdens and to mourn when they mourn. There are parts of it that are beautiful."

It's the closest she's come to proselytizing, but what she described *does* sound beautiful.

"And there are bad parts, of course," Oakley continues. "I know that's what you're thinking right now. But it's not all bad." She picks at a perfectly groomed fingernail. "And it's my home. My ward has always been my family. They're so kind, and we're always there for each other. It's just that the beliefs that guide them are sometimes not exactly what *I* personally believe."

"But aren't the beliefs the biggest part of it?" I ask, not able to let this go. "Those are what supposedly connect all of you, aren't they?"

"Do you follow each of the six hundred thirteen Jewish laws?" she snaps back. "There's one that says not to engage in astrology, but you know your sign. And do you pay a half-shekel temple tax? That's one of the laws as well."

I want to laugh, but I don't. She knows too much, and she's deadly serious. "No," I tell her. "I don't do most of that stuff. But I'm still Jewish. I still *feel* Jewish."

"There you go," she says. "That's how I feel about Mormonism."

"But it's different!" I nearly yell, anger bubbling to the surface.

"How?" she asks, unnervingly calm. "Because my religion is newer?"

"You know that's not why."

This is the first time in my entire life that I've felt happy being who I am, where I am. I don't want to leave. I don't want to escape.

But there's a set end date: tomorrow when the train pulls into King Street Station in Seattle. And I can't even tell Oakley how I feel about all of this because she's hell-bent on going back to Mormonism.

None of what has happened here means anything to her; it's just a blip in her eternal life.

Fourteen

WEDNESDAY, 4 P.M., LEAVING HAVRE, MT

"All right, she's gone," I whisper-yell to the other people in the observation car. We were waiting for Aya to finish her conversation with Oakley about the fourth Percy Jackson book. We wound up waiting a *long* time, but—at least for me—it was worth it to see the joy on their faces as they talked about a series they both love.

The plan was to then have Oakley suggest that Aya rest in her room for anywhere from one to three hours. Nanami was *very* on board with this idea.

Now Aya's reluctantly back in the sleeper car, and Oakley and Floor-Sleeper Jeff and Mike and everyone else who usually hangs out in the observation car and I are in here frantically getting decorations set up.

Oakley tosses Jeff the streamers and he wraps them around every available surface. I distribute party hats throughout the car, then stick one on my head and hand another to Oakley.

"Put it on," I nudge her.

She snaps it under her chin.

I lean into her. "You look very cute."

"I feel like a dunce."

She glances between my eyes and my lips, but after a moment of nothing, she looks away.

We haven't kissed since early this morning, and I'm worried it's because we're getting closer to the final destination. To where she has to get off the train and live a life where she pretends to be straight. Or at least where she can't act on her queerness.

Oakley and I continue to set up for the party, side by side. We hang a poster that says, "Doggonit, it's your birthday," and has a Dalmatian standing on its hind legs and wearing sunglasses.

We talk as we work, but we don't broach the subject of Mormonism. I don't tell her that she doesn't have to go back, that she could go to Seattle or return to New York and be in a place that, for the most part, doesn't believe that queer people are ruining the sanctity of marriage.

"Guys!" Jeff yells from the other end of the car. "Look!"

At first, I'm worried something's wrong, but when I glance out the window, I understand. For most of the day, we've been staring at flat plains, at barren land covered with fresh snow.

But now there's an imposing mountain in the distance, glowing purple in the last gasp of sunlight.

When I'm finally able to turn my gaze from the window and look at Oakley, her eyes are watery.

"It's so beautiful," she says, touching the glass as a tear drips down her perfectly upturned nose and onto the floor. "I'm sorry; this is embarrassing."

"No," I tell her, tentatively reaching out to wipe a rogue tear from the corner of her eye. She doesn't flinch as I do. "It's really not."

She continues staring out the window, and as much as I'm moved by the view, it's more that I'm moved by watching her watch the view. By the awe she has for this scenery that we get to witness together.

Before I can think too much, I rest my hand on her thigh, and she grabs it, holding me steady.

It feels so natural, so right. I want to see how Oakley reacts to every landscape on earth. I want to hear every thought she has, which would take a thousand lifetimes.

But I can't let myself think like that, because it's almost over.

"Oakley," I start, wanting to tell her what's on my mind, to say a million things that I can't because we're in a crowded car on a cross-country journey that's going to end before we know it.

She squeezes my hand, as if she knows what I'm thinking.

"It's almost five o'clock!" someone shouts, ending the moment Oakley and I were having, even if it was just in my head.

Five was the time that Aya told us she'd be done with her "rest" (she insisted it was not a nap, and that she would never fall asleep). I think she knows what we're planning, but we all still try to hide from her as best we can. We duck under chairs, behind the steep staircase leading down to the snack car.

"You ready?" Oakley whispers from where we're crouched next to someone's backpack.

I hold my breath; my heart's beating out of my chest, though

200

whether that's from the anticipation of surprising Aya or Oakley's presence, I'm not sure.

"Not really," I tell her. Now that we're done planning the party, it feels like an ending.

She smiles sadly, then whispers, "We did good," into my ear.

Instead of responding, I lean forward and kiss her, hard. It's cramped, but I manage to wrap a hand around her waist, pulling her into me at an odd angle, hip to hip. When we're done, she leans her forehead against mine.

Finally, the door between the cars opens and there's a collective intake of breath as everyone else jumps up and yells, "SURPRISE!"

Two Days before Thanksgiving Break

"Surprise," Alden said, handing me a small box wrapped in brown paper.

"What's this?"

We were in the student union, and though I'd lost track of the time, it had to have been around two in the morning. That's when the security guard stomped through the building to check student IDs. We presented ours, and he nodded and kept stomping.

There were other places we could've been, but this one felt like ours.

"It's nothing," Alden told me. "I just thought you might . . ."

He didn't finish the sentence, but he didn't have to. I opened the carefully wrapped package, and inside there was a small metal key.

"Is this—?"

"A key to my dorm," he offered, nodding excitedly.

"You're not allowed to replicate keys," I told him.

Even after months of not going to class and doing everything in my power to accomplish as little as possible, there was a part of me that clung to my old goody-two-shoes tendencies.

He shrugged. "If I get caught, it'll have been worth it."

"Thank you," I said, though what I wanted to say was, *Why?*

I had my own dorm, and if I wanted to go to his room, he could let me in. The last time I had been there was after the party, when we had the . . . confusing hookup.

The only answer I could fathom was that he liked what had happened that night and wanted it to happen again. Maybe he understood that our dynamic had shifted. Or maybe he just wanted to have sex with me and this was the smoothest way he could think to bring it up.

Looking in his eyes, it seemed more likely that it was the latter.

"Should we maybe use the key now?" he asked, cupping my kneecap with his palm.

If I'd felt the same power I had the night of the party, I would've said yes with no hesitation. But I was curious nonetheless.

"Yeah." My entire body was clenched. "Sure."

As we snuck through campus, the whole thing felt as illicit as all of our other late-night escapades. We scanned our student IDs to get into Alden's building, then ran up the back stairwell.

The closer we got to his room, though, the less nervous I became. I don't know why. Maybe it was the running, the scheming. It brought me closer to myself, to the version of me that Alden made me actually enjoy.

"Use your key," he whispered as we stood in front of his door.

I pulled the small metal key out of the box and tried to get it to work, but I was shaking and the lock wouldn't turn.

"Here," he said, placing his hand over mine and turning the key for me.

"So," he said, grinning.

"So," I parroted, trying to keep my face neutral.

He leaned in to kiss me, but when he grabbed my waist, I directed his arms up to my neck. We kissed like that, standing up, for a while, neither of us wanting to make the move to the bed.

"I have condoms," he said as he came up for air. "If that's what you're worried about."

It wasn't, but I couldn't have told him that.

"Cool," I said, and he took that as confirmation to pull open his desk drawer and rip one off the pack.

We made our way to the bed, and I briefly closed my eyes, imagining myself as someone else. I tried to think myself into a different body, a boy's body, or maybe just into Alden's. He pulled his socks off, and I pulled mine off too.

One item of clothing down, many more to go.

"I've never been with anyone like you," he told me as I sat on his bed. His expression was open and expectant.

I knew from our late-night conversations that he had a high school girlfriend with whom things had ended terribly. He never told me her last name, but it was easy enough to find her online.

Based on her Instagram presence, she seemed like someone I would've gotten along with. She was shorter than me and more feminine. She had two emotional support rats named Mario and

Luigi and was working to make computer science more inclusive.

There was no evidence of Alden on her page, except in her tagged photos. There were pictures of them sharing plates of food at busy diners, of them sitting shoulder-to-shoulder at high school parties. They looked good together. Definitely better than me and Alden, though we didn't have any photos together that would have proven that.

"I've never been with anyone like *you*," I finally responded after some on-the-bed kissing. It was true but only in that I hadn't been with anyone. But the people I *had* fantasized about weren't anything like him.

Alden had a belt on over his jeans, and once it became clear we had nothing more to say to each other that would forestall the moment, I let him take it off himself. After that, we were off to the races. I helped pull his pants down over his non-existent hips, and he got in my way as I pulled my T-shirt over my head.

The fewer clothes he had on, the more I wanted to pause and admire him. He was a normal-looking guy, which made me all the more jealous. His stomach was hairy, and his boxers sat low on his hips, in a way my pants never could because of how wide my own hips were.

He watched me watching him, smiling. I smiled back, a real one this time.

He never tried to take off my bra—a sports bra that was so tight it nearly cut off my circulation—and for that I was grateful. Other than the night of the party, I had never worn my binder around him, but I still didn't want him seeing my boobs. I didn't even know if *I* wanted to see them.

After that, it was mostly logistics, like getting a condom on and all the things people do to prepare for penetrative sex.

"Are you good with this?" he asked, and I nodded. I wanted to try it, to see what the fuss was all about.

I knew some people who had had sex in high school, and when the topic came up, they were more than happy to offer advice.

"You'll just know what to do," they'd say. "Your *body* knows."

That wasn't the case for me, but what my body *did* know was that I wanted to be on top. I helped Alden apply lube that he'd had in his drawer, then straddled him.

He lasted about ten seconds, and when his face scrunched in pleasure, I stared down at him from above, a scientist looking at a lab rat.

He wanted me to stay and cuddle. I wanted to leave.

It wasn't that I hated what we'd done, but it was just that: done. I had that data point. This is how babies were made. Okay. Great. Fine.

"I'm not feeling so well," I told him, my catchall excuse for getting out of situations I didn't want to be in.

"Are you gonna throw up?" he asked, backing away and looking freaked out.

"Yes," I said after seeing his reaction. "I'm definitely going to throw up."

I pretended to retch for good measure, and he let me go without complaint.

When I made it outside, I really did feel a wave of nausea, and I vomited into a large shrub directly in front of Alden's dorm. It splattered onto the red bricks, and I didn't know what else to do so I walked across campus back to my building, hugging my waist to fend off the cold.

As I walked, a number of things became abundantly clear. I was not attracted to Alden. Or maybe I wasn't attracted to Alden *all the time*. I wanted to like him, to date him, on my terms. But he wanted to date me *all the time*.

The next was that, due to this fact, I needed to break up with him.

The third was that I couldn't do that without breaking his heart, and without breaking mine, just a little.

Because breaking up with him would mean acknowledging to myself and to him and to the world that I wasn't the person I'd been trying to be for the past eighteen years.

But instead of wallowing in this pain, I surprised myself by pulling out my phone.

It rang once, twice. I was ready to shove it back in my pocket until—

"Zoe?"

"Autumn?"

"Yeah," she said, her voice drowsy with sleep.

I immediately regretted calling. I had woken her up. She'd probably only texted me over the long weekend due to boredom or pity, and I'd never even texted her back.

She cleared her throat. "What's going on?"

"Did you ever want to be my friend?" The question came from me without thought.

"Of course," they said, concern evident in their voice. "Where are you?"

Ten minutes later, we were sitting in a restaurant called Jack's Grill just off campus.

Autumn picked up our cheese fries from the counter and slid into the seat across from me. I ate as if I'd been lost in the wilderness for days.

She pushed the basket toward me and ordered a second for herself.

"Of course I wanted to be your friend," Autumn said after both baskets of fries were demolished and all that was left were tiny specs of cheese and pepper. She ran her finger over the oily paper, picking up the crumbs absentmindedly. "I may have wanted to be *more* than that for a minute."

Autumn, at one point, wanted to be more than friends. I'd even thought to myself that they were the kind of person who I would normally have a crush on. But I felt nothing for her then, other than thinking she was beautiful.

It was Alden I had feelings for. Complicated feelings but feelings nonetheless.

So I continued to deflect. "How are Rex and Shelly?"

Autumn's lips thinned into a line. "I haven't been talking to them much."

"Really?"

"My architecture classes have been kicking my ass," they said, not quite a response.

I had a real talent for finding people who were experts at *talking around*.

"We're learning how to do this thing called three-point perspective in my representation class," she began, speaking quickly. "You have to do these calculations and make all these lines so that you can give your drawing depth."

They continued like this for a while, and when they were done, I asked, "Why aren't you talking to Rex and Shelly?"

She brushed a face-framing curl behind her ear. "I didn't like how they talked to you that night."

We both knew the night.

"But I didn't like how you spoke to them either," Autumn continued. "I didn't like anything that went down."

"Then why didn't you say something?" I asked, swirling my finger in the empty fry basket as well. "Why didn't you defend me? Or them? Or *anyone?*"

"I didn't know how," she said. "But I should've. And I'm sorry I didn't."

I nodded and pulled my hand away.

After a moment: "So, how's your boyfriend?"

It was the worst thing she could've said. I'd almost forgotten about what had happened earlier that night. That was why I had called Autumn, after all: to forget.

She was just trying to be supportive, but I didn't want support.

I wanted to be told I'd made a huge mistake. More specifically, what I wanted was for her to read my mind and see that I'd called her because I *didn't* want to talk about him.

"He's not my boyfriend," I said finally.

"I'm sorry to hear that," Autumn said with genuine concern in their voice. "You broke up?"

It was a yes or no question, but both answers felt wrong.

I began to cry.

Blubbering would probably have been the right word. I was making incoherent sounds, and fat, wet drops were falling onto the sticky diner table.

Autumn reached their hand out again, but I pulled away.

"I'm gonna go."

I pushed my seat back and the legs scraped against the floor with a terrible sound that paused most of the other conversations in the room.

None of my actions or thoughts aligned. I had left, but I wanted Autumn to come after me. She didn't, which was more than fair.

I couldn't stop running away—from diners, dorms, and well-meaning people.

It was useless, though, because I was really trying to run away from myself.

Out of habit, or as a distraction, I glanced down at my phone.

I had eleven missed calls from Alden. The most recent one was from thirty minutes ago.

I ignored those in favor of my dad's text, which meant my situation was extremely dire. It was late in Seattle, though not as late as here, and he was asking for my flight information.

209

I didn't have any.

I'd meant to book a flight home for Thanksgiving break, but like with everything else, I'd dropped the ball.

I told him I'd send the information the next day, though I never did.

I walked slowly back to my dorm, fighting the discomfort between my legs. I'd just had sex for the first time.

It was a new identity to add to the growing list of ones that felt wrong in my body.

WEDNESDAY, 6 P.M., NEAR SHELBY, MT

Aya stares at us with her mouth open in a perfect *O*.

"Is this all for me?" she asks, wandering around the observation car and gazing in awe at the—maybe excessive—decorations that Oakley and I had bought.

"It is," Jeff tells her. He nods over to where Oakley and I are still crouched. "Your friends wanted to make your birthday extra-special."

We both stand up, though my thoughts are still on the gross Amtrak floor with Oakley.

Aya smiles even wider when she sees us, and runs to give us a huge hug.

Someone who's staying in the sleeper compartment next to Aya's brought a speaker, and they start the music the moment Aya releases us.

Aya runs around the observation car like she owns the place, talking to Clint and Virginia; to Elaine, who's here with Alberto/

Bert strapped to her chest. They all came here just for her. Well, maybe not *just* for her.

It's also an excuse to stretch our legs, to chat with people on the train who we haven't spoken to before. I have a conversation with someone who's afraid of planes but wants to meet her new grand-baby who lives all the way across the country. I talk to a woman who just quit her job and is finally doing all of the things she's wanted to do but couldn't, like seeing Olympic National Park out in Washington, and someone who doesn't have any form of ID but wants to get to Portland for their childhood best friend's wedding.

All the while, I keep glancing back at Oakley, who's also bouncing around, making conversation. When she meets my eye, she smiles shyly.

I smile back, then turn away. It's a secret that only the two of us know, a language shared through a glance.

"ATTENTION EVERYONE!" Aya shouts after an hour or so of intense partying. She's standing on one of the tables at the far end of the observation car, and we quiet down and turn to her.

"Thank you," she says when the room's attention is on her. "I just wanted to say that this has been the best birthday party I've ever had. I was scared about my last year before I turned double digits, but after talking to you all I know that being nine is actually really fun. Um, yeah. That's it!"

Everyone claps like she just won an Academy Award, and a few people rush forward to help her down from the table.

Aya then requests that the person with the speakers play what she calls her "favorite song," which turns out to be "Vengabus."

It's the song where a bunch of Dutch Eurodance singers repeat the phrase *we like to party* over and over again.

"They played it at Rachel's birthday," Aya informs us. "And everybody danced."

The moment the song starts, the same thing that happened at Rachel's banger of a party happens here, and we all run to the center of the train car, jumping up and down and singing along.

Aya finds me and Oakley and we spin her around. She laughs as the beat aligns with the motion of the train. Clint and Virginia and a few other nondancers are sitting on the sidelines, clapping along in their seats.

Halfway through the song, a new party member comes upstairs.

"EDWARD!" Aya screams in that terrible, high-pitched way that only dolphins and small children can.

He dances his way over to us, then throws bags of snacks out to everyone, which earns him raucous cheers.

"Is this allowed?" I shout into his ear over the music.

"I have an extra stash," he tells me. "For events like this."

I'm once again convinced that Edward is a witch or psychic or just the best snack car operator of all time.

I'll be writing to Amtrak after this trip to tell them that he deserves a raise and a million dollars and a train named after him.

After a few more Aya-approved songs, Nanami comes into the observation car. I had barely noticed that she wasn't here. Mike walks over to her, but neither of them speak. They both look deeply uncomfortable.

"She needs to tell Aya," Oakley whispers in my ear.

"Yeah, but not right *now*," I say.

Oakley frowns at this. "Of course, right now. Why *not* right now?"

It's my turn to frown. "Because it's Aya's birthday party."

"Exactly, and she deserves to know."

"She deserves to have *fun*." I keep my voice low so that Aya doesn't hear. "Please, Oakley?" I take a deep breath, trying to quell the desperation rising in me. "Can you forget about this until tomorrow?"

She sighs, and I think I've won until she wanders over to Nanami and whispers in her ear.

I want to run over there and stop her, but when Nanami's face twists in pain, I know she's already done it.

"No," Nanami says loudly enough that I can hear it.

"No what?" Aya asks, happily bounding up to her mom and Oakley.

I want to shield my eyes from whatever's about to happen.

"No nothing, Aya," Nanami says, at the same time that Oakley says, "Tell her."

I walk over to them and reach for her. "Oakley," I say, hoping it can act as a warning and a balm all in one.

She steps away from me.

Other partiers have begun to notice the change in atmosphere, and someone turns the upbeat music down.

"Not right now," Nanami says to Oakley, her jaw clenched.

"Can't it wait?" I whisper to Oakley. *"Please?"*

We're both trying to reason with her, but from different sides.

"No," she says, her voice shaking.

It's hard for me to believe this is entirely about Aya, who's looking up at us with wide eyes.

"What's going on?" she asks. "Because *something's* up." She directs that to her mom. "You've been acting weird."

Nanami gives Oakley the most withering stare I've ever seen, but she leans down and speaks into her daughter's ear. I pick up fragments like "need to talk" and "private."

Aya nods, and Nanami retreats to the sleeper car. But before Aya leaves, she turns around and beams at everyone as if nothing happened.

"Looks like it's time for me to go," Aya says to the crowd. "But it's okay," she adds, her tone serious. "This has been the best night of my life."

She gives me and Oakley one last hug, then follows Nanami into the sleeper car.

After tonight, she can't go back to not knowing.

I want to confront Oakley, to ask her why she did this, why *now*, at the most inconvenient time.

But some part of me already knows the answer—she values truth and knowledge over everything else, convenience be damned. She's told me this time and time again, and yet I can't square this fact with what she's about to do in one day's time.

The party doesn't die down once Aya leaves; it only gets more chaotic. Some of the adults pass around wine and vodka. I try to grab a bottle, but Clint appears out of nowhere and takes it from me, shaking his head.

I *do* manage to snag a slice of pumpkin pie that someone brought with them on the train.

Oakley and I sit on the sidelines, sharing a fork and eating off the pug-covered paper plates in a silence I don't know how to characterize.

"Did you hear what Aya said?" Oakley asks, not realizing that I don't want to talk about it. "She was telling me that she'd heard her mom and dad fighting for months. She's a perceptive kid."

I nod as I chew a bite of pie. "I know," I say. "But how'd you get all that out of her?"

"You didn't think we were just talking about Percy Jackson, did you?"

"Kind of," I tell her. "Yes."

"I can talk about real things when I want to," Oakley says, though her attention is now focused on the pie and the pie alone.

I'm about to ask her if she can, if she wants to have a *real* conversation. But just then, a slow song comes on.

"This one's for the lovebirds," Virginia announces to the observation car. "A special treat." She has her arms around Clint, and she winks at me.

The song is slow and melancholy, with acoustic guitar over gentle piano notes.

Oakley extends her hand. "Dance with me?"

I don't know if it's a peace offering or a goodbye.

I chew the final bite of pie painfully slowly. When I'm done, she leads me to the dance floor (aka the aisle of the observation car).

She puts her hands around my neck and leans against me, and I tentatively wrap mine around her waist.

It happens so naturally, not like with Alden where I had to guide his hands up to my neck, to try to make him understand that that's how I wanted him to hold me.

I shouldn't be thinking about Alden right now.

"Do you think this is the first dance party that's ever happened in the observation car?" I ask Oakley after a minute of swaying.

"No," she says, her cheek on my shoulder. "I think that other people have probably figured out that this is a good way to waste time."

I tighten my grip on her. "That's not what this is, though," I say. "It's not just a way to waste time, right?"

She has to know I'm not talking about the party. She's the smartest person I've ever met.

"I mean, it is, isn't it?"

We sway for the rest of the song, but my mind is elsewhere. I have a sudden, desperate need to talk to her about what this trip has meant and what's going to happen tomorrow.

"I'm glad we met, Oakley," I whisper into her ear, not wanting to ruin the moment just yet.

She hugs me closer. "I am too."

It's how I imagine prom would've been; I went to a Science Olympiad competition instead.

"This is all going to be over so soon," I say as the song finishes and we break apart.

"It'll be okay," Oakley says, looking down.

"So soon that you could've waited to force Nanami to tell Aya," I mutter, not able to let this go.

"I didn't force her to do anything," Oakley says, and I shrug in response.

Because it kind of felt like she did.

Someone switches the music back to the Vengaboys, and the vibe in the car returns to intense celebration mode.

But I fell out of celebration mode a while ago, so I drag Oakley to the far end of the car, where there's a booth for us to sit.

"Are you going to ask me again why I did what I did?" Oakley's voice is colder than it's ever been with me.

"Obviously, yes," I say. "Don't you see how shitty it is?"

"Seriously?" Oakley asks, incredulous. "You don't think it's crappy that Nanami was hiding this from Aya?"

I almost laugh at Oakley's turn of phrase—I've never heard her curse, and right now, I wish she would.

"Of course I do," I tell her. "But you only added to the shittiness."

She closes her eyes, formulating a response. For once, I don't want to hear what she has to say.

"I *had* to," she tells me finally. "I needed her to know the truth."

I don't know how she can believe this, but then again, the amount of things I don't understand about Oakley is innumerable.

"Okay then," I say, "if the truth is everything to you, can *I* tell you the truth?"

She nods.

"I like you, Oakley."

She smiles, but it doesn't reach her eyes. "I like you too."

"No," I insist, "I *really* like you. I know it's only been a few days but this trip has meant something to me." I lower my voice. "Hasn't it meant something to you?"

"Of course," she whispers.

"Then why are you . . . ?" I'm not brave enough to finish that sentence, but Oakley knows what I mean.

"Why am I rejoining the Church?" she asks, and I nod. "Did you think you could change my mind?"

"No," I say, even though I did, or maybe just hoped. "But I don't understand."

She leans back in the booth and crosses her arms. "You don't have to understand," she tells me. "This is my *life*. This is what I'm going to do with it. You can't expect me to change my plans just because we made out a little. We've known each other for *three days*."

I'm trying not to let her see how much her words are hurting me. But I know she knows. I'm pretty sure that's why she's saying them.

"If that's the case, then why did you make Nanami tell Aya about moving to Seattle? Why do you care about her if you've only known *her* for three days?"

"That's different," Oakley says.

"How?"

"Because it doesn't matter how long I've known Aya. She deserved to know."

"But did you have to ruin her party?"

"*I* ruined her party?" Oakley scoffs.

"Yeah," I tell her. "You did."

"If that's what you think, then I don't know how to help you," Oakley says. "It's like you're incapable of understanding that I might know more about what Aya's going through than you."

"Because you know *everything*, don't you?"

She's clearly hurt by my words, but right now, I don't care.

"I'm going to be back in Ritzville—back in the Church— *tomorrow* whether you think that's best for me or not," she says through gritted teeth. "I thought I'd be able to get, like, *one* queer experience in New York. And it didn't happen." She shakes her head, fighting back tears. "But now, we've made out, so . . ."

"So that's it?" I ask. "Now you can go back to a religion that doesn't give a shit about you?" My chest is tight. "*Why*, Oakley? Why are you doing this?" I sound desperate, but I can't help it. "Why are you rejoining the Church? I don't get it. You can have all the queer experiences you want out here!" I gesture to the observation car, though that doesn't help my point, since we're in an enclosed space, a giant metal train barreling through the dark.

"It's not for you to get!" she shouts as a song ends. Everyone looks over at us. "*It's not for you to get*," she repeats in a whisper. "This is my life. It's none of your business."

"But it *could* be," I whisper back. "Maybe I *want* it to be. I fucking care about you, Oakley."

"You don't even know me!" Oakley whisper-shouts.

The next song plays. It's too upbeat for what's happening here. "You could let me know you," I say quietly.

She shakes her head. "Maybe you thought this was more than it was, but that's on you," she says, and my fragile heart shatters. "We were having fun; that's it."

"Well, if that's what this was, then you should know that you weren't the only one trying to 'have a queer experience,'" I say, mimicking her cruel tone. "I just wanted to make out with a girl, and you were here." I hate the words coming out of my mouth, the *lies*, but that doesn't stop me from saying them.

She scoffs. "You've kissed plenty of girls before."

She's so confident that she's right.

"I haven't. You were the first." I take a breath, and finally say it: "I have a boyfriend."

That gets her attention. "You have a *what*?"

"I was dating a boy at school," I tell her. I don't mention how things ended. "We've been dating for three months. He was my first *everything*. So maybe you weren't the only one trying to live a lie on the train."

Her eyes go wide. "What the fuck, Zoe?"

It's the *first* real curse I've ever heard her say.

She storms through the partygoers, back to her sleeper car. The one we made out in, the one we cuddled in together.

The one I'll likely never see again.

Fifteen

Thursday, 12:30 a.m., Crossing into ID

Coach is worse than I remembered.

My seatmate won't stop coughing, then snoring, then coughing again—a vicious cycle—and I can't find a comfortable position no matter how hard I try.

But this is the best option, because if I go back to the observation car I risk running into Oakley. The only thing to do is stay here, in this dark car with the other coach passengers who I've barely gotten to know at all on this trip.

Maybe they're wonderful people, or creeps like Guy Fieri Lite, but I'll never know one way or the other, because I spent the whole trip getting to know a girl who can never be with me, who never *wanted* to be with me in the first place. She just wanted one last go at being queer, and I was the easiest target.

My whole life up until now has been escaping to find the next best thing—the next best class to take, the next best school, the next best label, the next best identity, the next best *anything*.

But what if there's nothing better? What if Oakley was my best thing, and she never even wanted to be with me in the first place?

Even if she did, nothing could've happened. She's rejoining the Mormon Church.

I pull out my phone and play Tetris for the first time since the beginning of the trip. I try to set up a T-spin, but I don't remember the strategy Oakley showed me. So I do what I've always done: stack the blocks four high until I get a Tetris.

There's only one stop in Idaho, and when we get there, the conductor tells us that we have five minutes. It's not a smoke stop, but I run outside anyway, desperate for fresh air.

The brick station house has its lights on, and I'm tempted to run inside and stay there. I could make a nice life for myself here in Idaho.

But no. The train would *definitely* leave without me this time, and I couldn't blame the conductor for doing it. They only waited because of Aya.

Aya.

Nanami is never going to let me hang out with her in Seattle. And the worst part is, I'd *love* to see her. I want to listen to her talk about trains or whatever else she finds cool that day.

I don't have any siblings, and I thought, perhaps naively, that she could be like a little sister.

But it's not like she has a phone. I can't text her. All I know is her first name and that she has an aunt in Seattle and that her mom hates me, because she hates Oakley.

Oakley and I have been a unit on this trip. Nanami probably thinks I agree with everything Oakley's told her.

So Aya will just be one more casualty of caring about someone on a four-day trip.

I climb back onto the train, where one of the conductors shakes her head at me. I raise a hand in apology, then head back into coach. When I get there, though, I'm more restless than before. I force myself to stay in my seat, but my legs are shaking and my seatmate is coughing and I can't be in here any longer.

Maybe it's a bad idea, but I head back to the observation car, trying not to think about how I've now ruined my life twice in the span of a week.

ONE DAY BEFORE THANKSGIVING BREAK

I stood outside my dorm without going in. My whole body hurt for various reasons, and the best thing for me would be to go to sleep, but I couldn't.

So, I went to the one place that would calm me: the greenhouse.

I had a key, and Randall had told me I could come whenever I liked. I'd never taken him up on this until now.

When I got there, everything was still except for whirring fans. The nearby plants in the main conservatory swayed in the artificial breeze. Leaves rustled against each other, and the systems that kept the plants alive popped and hissed in the background.

I could finally breathe.

I took in huge gulps of humid air, then walked over to the *Amorphophallus*. I didn't have the energy to talk to the plant like I normally would, so I just glanced inside its pot. The shoot was even taller now, growing upward in segments that became progressively narrower.

The tiny sprout of the *Amorphophallus* taunted me.

What good had I done for this plant? Sure, I'd taken care of it nearly every single day for months, but even after all of my hard work and love, I was never going to see it bloom.

Everything I'd done this whole semester was pointless.

I'd spent three months lying to myself about who I was, about my gender, my sexuality, my wants and dreams, and now I was facing the consequences.

I arrived at Cornell with some amount of hope, and I was leaving with nothing.

I wanted to rip the small shoot out of the pot and tear it to shreds. It was a frightening impulse, one that came from somewhere primal and small.

Instead of hurting the plant, I screamed until it felt like my already-raw throat was being ripped to shreds.

The most depressing part—and there were many, many depressing parts—was that all of this could've been solved if I'd stuck with the Tees.

There were two versions of me floating in the ether, two Zoes who would never meet. One of us stayed friends with the Tees. That Zoe spent their whole first semester exploring their gender and sexuality. That Zoe wouldn't have alienated Autumn when she was just trying to be nice.

But I was the Zoe who chose to date Alden.

I paced the greenhouse for hours, wondering why I'd done this to myself.

Randall had taught me that most of the plants in the greenhouse had evolved so that they produce both pollen, which is like plant sperm, and eggs. He had said it as an aside, as an interesting fact to share with visitors if they inquired about plant reproduction.

But all I could think was that the plants were lucky. They didn't have the human defect of needing another organism for the survival of their species.

I went back to my dorm and searched for train schedules. I found this route, which would leave from the city a day and a half later. I bought a coach seat with the money I had made from the greenhouse.

After that, it didn't take long to pack my things.

My whole life fit into a backpack and a large suitcase. I didn't have posters up in my dorm, or mementos of a first semester spent with people I'd been learning to love.

I had textbooks I'd rarely opened, clothes I hated, and bedding that I wanted to burn.

It all fit without protest.

The room was empty, but I still had thirty-six hours of waiting, and only one real thing left to do.

I pulled a piece of paper out of one of my many empty notebooks and grabbed a pen that was still full of ink from my unused pencil case.

On the paper, I wrote a note to Alden. It was a cowardly thing to do, to not text or call, but just then, a coward was the only thing I had it in me to be.

My heart beat frantically as I scratched the letter onto the page.

Dear Alden,

Maybe you don't know this, or maybe you've been kind enough not to mention it, but you're my only friend here. Thank you for showing me parts of campus I never would've seen without you. Thank you for bringing me to the clock tower and the library and the bowling alley.

Do you know what I saw in you that first day, in the Straight? I saw myself. Or who I wanted to be.

You were a window into a life I never knew was possible. I hope I was good for you too, even when I was shitty.

Which is what's making it about a thousand times harder to tell you that I'm a lesbian.

Or maybe I'm not a lesbian exactly, but that's the best word I have for it right now.

I really, really like you, Alden. You're smart and funny and weird, and you're almost scarily good at card games. But as desperately as I wish I could, I can't want you the way you want me.

And for that I'm so, so sorry.

This is the ultimate "It's not you, it's me." It's always been me.

I hope one day we can be friends, which is a cliché thing to say but I'm pretty sure I mean it.

I've included the copy of your key—please throw it away; I don't want you to get expelled.

A little bit yours,

Zoe

It took many hours and a hundred failed letters to get that much onto the page. In earlier drafts I tried to explain to him the complexities of my gender, of how having sex with him wasn't horrible, it just wasn't *right*. But this was what I'd landed on.

I folded the paper in thirds with the key inside and wrote Alden's name on the front, then snuck through campus under the cover of darkness for the second time that night.

I didn't technically have access to his building, so I waited a few minutes for someone to come out, then I slipped inside. I ran up the same staircase that we had climbed just hours before. That must've been a different century or a parallel universe.

When I got to Alden's floor, I held my breath and walked slowly to his room. I pressed my ear against the door. I didn't want him to wake up while I was there; I couldn't handle seeing his face.

After a minute of listening, once I was sure he was sleeping or else not there, I slid the note under the door and bolted. I didn't tread lightly like I had coming up to his room. I ran like I was being chased by a horror-movie villain. The stakes felt higher than that.

I locked myself in my dorm then to wait for the shuttle that would take me down to the city, and turned off my phone.

If Alden tried to contact me, I didn't want to know.

THURSDAY, 1:30 A.M., SOMEWHERE IN ID

Alden has texted me a grand total of thirteen times during this trip, which feels like an omen.

I'm counting them now, forcing myself to read each text, to

take in the words he wrote, even though it feels impossible.

This is why I've had my phone on airplane mode: I couldn't face Alden, the boy who was falling for me.

The messages began innocuously enough. The first: **We should talk.** Then they became more frantic. **Are you okay? Where are you? Why aren't you answering?**

Then, finally, **What the hell, Zoe?**

With these texts, I have to face what I've been running away from this entire trip, which is that, to him, we're not officially broken up. I never said anything to his face. I never even said it explicitly in the letter.

I just told him that I was a lesbian, or close enough to it that I wasn't into dating him. He has to know what that means, but still, I didn't have the common decency to have a conversation.

I just left.

And that's what Oakley's about to do to me. And I'm going to let her, because it's not worth it. I began to care for someone who can never return that care. I am to Oakley what Alden was to me.

Maybe this is my curse, that every time I escape a bad situation, it'll come back to haunt me in a new way, like a ghost wearing a hat and a paste-on mustache in a poor attempt at a disguise.

"Zoe?"

It's Virginia, reading a thick paperback and wearing glasses that have a pink beaded chain attached to them.

I wave but don't say anything.

The remnants of the party are everywhere: decorations and streamers and plates and rogue slices of pie. But the partygoers have left, or are passed out on the floor. Virginia and I are the only conscious people in the observation car.

"Are you okay, dear?" she asks.

I shrug, but tears come to my eyes. Virginia stands from her seat to move closer to mine. She closes her book and lets her glasses hang around her neck by the chain.

"You and Oakley looked quite close at the party," she says carefully.

"We weren't," I tell her petulantly. "We're not. I mean, we never were."

She tuts at that. "I'm sure that's not true. The way you two were acting in the dining car . . . you were peas in a pod; I'll tell you that much."

"We got into a fight."

She nods thoughtfully. "Well, that explains the moping."

"But it's not a fight we can recover from," I say, comforted by Virginia's presence. "It's never going to work out."

"Now, how do you know that?"

Regardless of what happened or what will happen between us, I don't want to divulge Oakley's personal information. So I just say, "She's doing something I don't agree with."

Virginia laughs. "Clint does things I don't agree with every day!"

"But does he do things that go completely against your core beliefs?"

"Well, no."

We're both silent, and I let the train rock me back and forth.

Finally, I say, "Can I ask you a question?"

"Of course, dear."

"What do you do when you're done with your train trips?" I ask, and Virginia looks confused, so I keep talking. "These past few days have been some of the best of my life. And it's all going to be over tomorrow." Virginia smiles sadly, recognition dawning on her face. "What if the best version of myself was here on the train?"

I was able to keep these feelings at bay for a bit, while I had Oakley to hang out with, but not anymore.

Virginia shifts in her chair and pulls the glasses off entirely. "You know what I think?" she asks, and I shake my head. "I think that you'll never know who you'll be, even tomorrow. I'm in my *seventies* and I don't know that. There are going to be incredible and heartbreaking things in my future, if I'm lucky. Probably some of that will happen on this very train." She smooths the front of her sweater. "I had to learn that the hard way, though. I was a people pleaser for most of my life—constantly worried about what everyone thought of me. So I changed myself for them."

"You don't feel that way anymore?" I can't imagine getting out of that headspace. Of not being worried that I'm going to disappoint every person I've ever met or cared about, especially when I've already disappointed most of them.

I bought this train ticket so that I could delay that disappointment, with Alden in the East and my parents in the West. But it was a stopgap measure. I didn't expect to get on the train and find a place full of people I care about.

"Heavens, no!" Virginia says, answering my previous question.

Some of the people who are sleeping on the floor nearby stir. "I live for me and me alone." She leans forward in her seat, pushing a strand of gray hair behind her ear. "Now, that doesn't mean I don't care about people. It just means that on the airplane, I put my oxygen mask on before anyone else's. And I never would've done that before."

The man who stirred on the dirty carpet snores loudly and turns so he's lying face down.

"All you can do is live right now," she continues. "And not worry if it's the best life that you could possibly be living. Maybe it is; maybe it isn't. But the best life you can live is the one you're living right now." She grins. "That's it. That's the secret to happiness. Easy as that."

I don't know how it could *possibly* be as easy as that. But the way Virginia said it, it sounds like it could be.

"But what if my life right now sucks?" I ask after a minute. I failed my first semester of college, I failed my parents, I failed Alden.

I definitely failed Oakley.

"That's the thing," Virginia says. "Sure, Einstein said all this crap about time being relative, but for my money, it's not." I laugh a little at that, and Virginia continues. "There's nothing you can compare your present moment to. You can't go thinking, 'Oh, well, the other year I did this,' or 'Next year Virginia can take care of that.' Right now is all there is."

"But there's the past," I tell her. "There has to be. There are things I did—some really shitty things—that led up to this point."

"Sure," she says simply. "But you can't change them. Not everyone agrees with me," she continues, "but I have an inkling that your brain is a bit like mine. And thinking this way has helped me."

I don't want to dwell on the past, and right now I can't imagine my future, so maybe she's right. It makes my head hurt but in a pleasant, tingly way.

"I'm going to try to get some shut-eye," Virginia tells me. "But knock on my door if you need anything. And don't worry about waking Clint; he'd sleep through a tornado."

Before she leaves the car, I say, "Thank you." It doesn't feel like enough.

"Of course, dear," she says, then waves as the door shuts behind her.

I was living in fear of who I was or who I'd become, but maybe that's been my problem. I'm grieving a version of myself that still exists. I'm moving on before the best part has even *started*.

And this train ride isn't over.

There are still twelve hours or so to figure things out. To live in this moment and not move on to the next one. To not live to please my parents or Alden. And especially not Oakley, now that she doesn't want anything to do with me.

Even if it's just for half a day, I can live my life for me, whoever that is.

THE NIGHT BEFORE THANKSGIVING BREAK

The Cornell shuttle bus was chrome on the outside, reflective and bright. As the driver took my bag, I caught a glimpse of myself, tired and confused. But there was something else—something almost cheerful.

Something like hope.

As the bus traveled south from Ithaca to Manhattan, I felt free. Or, at the very least, I felt disconnected from the version of myself that had brought me to this point.

I could've said it was the campus that had been making me feel so terrible, but that would've been an excuse.

I was at least partially to blame for my own suffering, even if I couldn't admit it at the time.

Either way, I was leaving everything behind, the good and the bad.

I'd been gone from home for only three months, and yet I would've been unrecognizable to the Zoe who walked onto campus in the oppressive humidity of an East Coast August. Part of it was the change in appearance—my hair, my clothes. But it was more than that.

I went to college as a lesbian premed student and left as a drop-out who had a boyfriend. It was ridiculous.

A laugh, loud and sharp, bubbled out of me. I covered my mouth and looked around, but no one was awake enough to have heard me.

I tried to hold it in but the more I attempted to keep the laughter at bay, the more it wanted to erupt out of me.

So I let it.

I had four days on the train to figure out what I was going to do—it wasn't enough, but in that moment, I let the humor of my predicament wash over me. Because it *was* funny, in a sad kind of way.

Once I got to Penn Station, I bought an iced coffee and a bagel, then wandered through the Amtrak waiting area. No one paid me any attention.

Maybe no one was *ever* paying me much attention. It was just me, focused to an unhealthy degree on everything I thought was wrong with my body and my life.

Around Alden, I'd started to dissect my appearance, my mannerisms, the way I walked and talked. He'd become a twisted reflection of everything I wasn't.

I shook the thoughts of him out of my head. I was going to fade into the background on the train, I was going to be a person no one thought twice about.

And maybe then, I'd be okay.

Sixteen

Thursday, 2 a.m., Crossing into Eastern Washington

As it turns out, the first thing I have to do isn't for me. It's an apology months in the making.

I check my phone without holding my breath, without fear that texts will stream in from everyone I've ever cared about, telling me that I failed them.

Because I never failed them. I failed myself.

By some miracle, there's one bar of service holding on for dear life here in Eastern Washington, which I have to hope is enough for what I'm about to do.

I head downstairs to one of the communal bathrooms. I can't have anyone overhearing this conversation.

I squeeze my eyes shut and try to bring Virginia's words to the front of my mind. I can't live my life for other people, and that includes not running away from hard conversations.

"Zoe?" Alden asks when he picks up. He sounds dazed.

"Were you asleep?"

"No." He clears his throat, and there's a second of dead air.

I check my phone to see if the call dropped, but he's still there, his name illuminated on my screen.

"I couldn't," he mumbles finally. "Sleep, I mean."

"Oh," I say. "Sorry about that."

"It's fine."

He's speaking in a tone of voice he never used when we were dating.

"Okay, well," I begin, "did you see my letter?"

"The one you slid under my door in the middle of the night before you vanished?" he asks. "Yeah, Zoe. I saw your letter."

"So did you . . . ?" I don't know how to ask this without making him even more pissed at me, but that ship has sailed. "Did you think that we were still together? All this time that I haven't been answering?"

"What? No," he says, sounding shocked. "I assumed we'd broken up when you wrote me a letter saying you were a lesbian and then disappeared in the middle of the night and stopped answering my texts and calls."

I'm the worst.

This is true for many reasons but mostly due to the fact that I'm deeply relieved. I was worried that because of the way I tried to end things, he'd think there was still a chance for us. That he'd try to rationalize, to bargain with me, to say that what we had was good and we shouldn't give it up because of the small matter of me not being attracted to him the way he was to me.

But obviously he knew our relationship was over. All of this could've been clarified if I'd spoken to him, but I was too cowardly to answer his texts.

At least this solves one of my problems: we've been broken up while things were going down with Oakley. It still wasn't fair of me to not tell her about him, especially when she opened up to me.

But it wasn't anything worse than that.

"Are you done?" Alden asks. "I should try to sleep."

"Well—" I start, but he interrupts me.

"Wait, you know what, *I* actually have something I need to say." He takes a shuddering breath. "Did you know you were gay when we were first dating?"

I nod even though he can't see it over the phone. "Yeah," I tell him. "I did."

"Then why the fuck did you date me?"

Because you spoke so eloquently about Charles Dickens. Because you smiled widely at everything I said. Because you made the world seem big.

But I begin with the simplest explanation: "Because I liked you."

"Oh."

The call is filled with static, with his ragged breaths on the other end.

"Seriously, I thought that I could be bi or pan for a little while," I tell him. "Because of *how much* I liked you."

He makes a *hm* sound, and I take it as a sign to keep talking.

"And I *did* care about you, Alden," I add. "That part of the letter wasn't a lie."

"Okay," he says, his voice unreadable. "Well, thanks."

"Wait," I say, willing him not to hang up. "I need you to know that I'm not coming back to school after break. So you don't have to worry about running into me."

"I wasn't worried about that," he says quietly.

I don't say anything. I let the silence just *be*.

After a moment, he says, "Is it wild that I still want to see you?"

"No," I tell him.

Because he was my best friend, and one day, maybe years from now, I want to spend hours on the phone with him. I want to take him out to coffee and laugh at ourselves, at the people we were when we were young and naive and on the cusp of adulthood but not quite there.

"I really did like you," I say. "Just probably not the way I should've."

"Then in what way?" he asks.

"I'm trying to work that out," I take a deep breath, and the Amtrak bathroom smell fills my nose.

I know I need to tell him the truth. I owe him that much. "I'm figuring things out with my gender. And maybe . . . I don't know. You were a fairly nonthreatening man. It wasn't that much of a leap to think that if I was a little more masculine-presenting I could look like . . . you."

He was an easy escape from the thoughts I was having about my gender, about the way I wanted the world to perceive me. But I don't want to hide from that anymore.

"I don't know whether to be honored or scared." He laughs a little, and this time it's more sad and less cold. "At least you didn't try to wear my skin like a suit."

"That was the next step," I joke, and he laughs genuinely, the way he did during our late-night talks.

We're quiet for a moment. Maybe it's because we both know that this will be the last conversation we have for a while.

"Thank you, Alden," I say finally.

"For what?"

"For helping me figure things out."

He sighs, and it comes out like a crackle over the phone. "I wish I could've been more to you. I really, really liked you, Zoe."

"I know," I tell him, tears falling now.

He takes another breath. "I loved you," he whispers.

"I know," I say again, my voice breaking.

How can two people be dating but have two entirely different ideas of what it means? He thought we had a future, and I thought I was *looking* into my future. Into the person I could be.

"I'm going to go," he says. "Probably not to sleep after this, but I might stare at the ceiling."

I smile a little at that. "Have fun," I tell him. "And Alden, I'm so sorry. Like, I can't even begin to tell you how sorry I am."

"I'm sorry too, Zoe."

With that, he hangs up.

I head back to the observation car and wipe my eyes on the sleeve of my flannel, just as the conductor lets us know that we're leaving the station.

Thursday, 3 a.m., Eastern Washington

The first thing I do is grab my beat-up paperback. I wanted to read on this trip, so I do. Living my life for me and all that.

The book with the war-torn woman facing backward is not bad, and once I've read a few chapters, I check that off my mental to-do list.

And then I'm restless again. Because as much as I want to follow through on living my life for me for the rest of the train ride, the only way I can do that is if I fix things with pretty much everyone.

I get up and stretch, pacing back and forth along the aisle of the observation car until I stumble upon a body and promptly turn around.

Apologizing to Alden was just the beginning. I have a million people I want to speak to, but it's the middle of the night, so I start with a text.

The first is to the Tees.

> **Zoe:** I know this is long overdue, but I just wanted to say you were right when you said I was different around alden. You all were so nice to me, and I only hung out with you when he wasn't available.
> I think part of why I hung out with him so much was because I was working through some gender stuff
> I just wanted to let you know that
> and that I appreciate all of you

I don't expect it, but Shelly responds almost immediately.

240

Shelly: ok we love gender stuff

Then, Rex chimes in too. They were the one who judged me most for my relationship with Alden, or at least that's how I felt. But they also made sure I was included, and drove me to get greasy late-night food more times than I can count.

Rex: that's a lot
agree w shelly about the gender stuff
and I'm sorry about what I said too
like, very sorry
Shelly: I'd love to hang out with you when we get back
from break
Rex: same!

I react with a heart to all their messages. It's a small thing, but I hope the two of them know how much their words mean.

Me: I don't think I'm coming back
Shelly: bummer
Rex: we should keep in touch!
Zoe: we should
Shelly: and if you ever want to talk about gender
stuff . . .
Rex: literally
pretty sure all three of us can help you in that depart-
ment haha
Zoe: thanks friends

I text Autumn separately after that, because even if she's not awake, she deserves her own message.

Zoe: thank you for meeting up with me when I was at a low point
I'm grateful for you

There's so much more I could say, but I leave it at that and return to Tetris.

This is what it could've been like if I'd chosen to stay, or if I had chosen Autumn and the Tees over Alden.

No, I tell myself, and the force of it is enough to jolt me awake.

This is what it *is* like, right now. The relationships I have don't have to remain stagnant. They can change, the same way that I hope I can.

I pick up my book again and read for a while. When I check my phone, it's past three in the morning, which means it's past six on the East Coast.

Randall gave me his number so I could contact him while I was on-shift—"if you have any questions about the plants"—but I never used it.

There's still service, so I steady myself, then tap his contact. I don't bother leaving the observation car for the call, since there's no one in here who's anywhere close to being conscious, and I wouldn't mind if they overheard this one anyway.

The phone rings and rings and rings. I almost hang up; I'm sure that he won't answer.

Finally: "Hello?"

I can hear the greenhouse whirring in the background, its own contained ecosystem.

"Randall?" He has me on speaker, and there's a stream of water that sounds dangerously close to the phone.

"Zoe?"

"Yeah," I tell him. "Hi."

"What's going on?" he asks. "Are you all right?"

He's the first person who's asked me that in a long while, and it takes everything I have not to break down on the phone.

But I owe him so much more than that.

"How's the greenhouse?"

Well, I have to ease into it first.

"Everything's good," he says. "But when you're not here it's obvious how much work you do." A pipe hisses in the background and he curses at it.

"Oh yeah?" I'm smiling now, my face reflected back at me in the dark train window.

"I wanted to talk to you," I say. "If that's all right."

"Of course," he says, though the background noises would suggest otherwise. "Let me get to my office."

I can tell when he's there because he sighs as he sits in his desk chair.

"All right, what did you want to tell me?"

I don't know how to start this conversation. It was almost easier with Alden, since I know that that phase of my life is in the past. But I don't *want* the greenhouse to be in the past. I want to keep

243

taking care of plants, to talk to them, to watch them grow like a proud parent.

"I'm not coming back," I tell him finally. "After the break."

"Hm." He doesn't speak for a moment. "I have to say that I'm surprised. Your work in the greenhouse has been impeccable."

"I'm failing all my classes," I tell him, and try hard to not imagine his face on the other end. "The only time I really left my dorm was to go to the greenhouse."

"So that's why you were available for so many shifts," he says, and I laugh a little.

"Yeah," I tell him. "That's why."

"Do you want to know something?" he asks. "I think the *Amorphophallus* might bloom."

And that's what does it. That's what pushes me over the edge from vague sadness to tears streaming down my face. I've been crying more on this train trip than I have since . . . maybe ever.

Taking care of that plant was the only thing I did with my whole heart all semester, and now he's telling me that it may very well bloom while I'm on the other side of the country.

"That spike you were seeing?" Randall says. "That was the start of the flower. The spathe should appear early next year, and then it'll bloom shortly thereafter."

"I can't believe I'm not going to see it," I say quietly. "I spent every day with that plant."

"Well, exactly," Randall says, like it's obvious. "I don't know if this would've happened if you hadn't been there, giving it special attention all semester."

I frown, though I know he can't see me. "What do you mean?"

"I'm a firm believer that you have to nurture plants. They're living things, after all. They don't just need water and light and soil; they need *love*." He sighs. "I saw the way you were with all the plants," he says, and I can tell there's a smile in his voice. "Everything you did was out of love. The *Amorphophallus* is the healthiest I've ever seen it, and I know that's because of you."

"It is?" I ask quietly.

"Absolutely," he says. "I should've told you more while you were here, but you made quite the impact on our little greenhouse."

"Oh."

"I have to go, Zoe," Randall says. "I left the hose running in one of the tanks, but let's talk after the holidays, okay? I don't want you to give up on botany, even if you're not working in my greenhouse anymore."

"I won't," I tell him, a promise.

When he hangs up, I curl into a ball on my seat and sob.

This time, though, it's happy tears.

Well, mostly.

I fled campus before I could see the result of all my hard work—the corpse plant's bloom. Sure, the bloom is known for smelling like rotting garbage, but it would be *my* rotting garbage.

And even though I'm not going to see it, Randall told me that I helped make it happen. I made an impact on a living organism. I left a mark on the world, even if that mark is only going to bloom for a week and fade away.

Maybe that's what's been missing this whole time, that understanding.

I made myself miserable at school, telling myself that because I didn't know exactly who I was, I couldn't be anything.

I didn't want to be a doctor anymore, so I didn't go to class. I couldn't be a girl anymore, so I hid from the world.

But instead of doing those things, I could've chosen new classes or experimented with how I presented myself.

There were so many solutions I didn't see at the time. I could've just deconstructed the boxes all together, taken them out to be recycled.

And it's possible I've done the same thing with Oakley. We never promised each other forever. We never even promised each other a relationship, just a few days on a train. And I ruined it because I didn't know exactly what we were. I worried that if it wasn't perfect, it couldn't be anything.

Now Oakley's going to get off the train somewhere in the middle of the state near Ritzville, and she's never going to know how much these past few days have meant to me. But I need her to know. I was being so precious about the time we had that I forgot that there was more of it.

We still have a few hours left.

But first, I need to sleep.

So I go back to my coach seat, wrap my jacket around my head to drown out the snoring, and do just that.

Seventeen

Thursday, 5 a.m., outside of Ephrata, WA

Even though I hardly slept for two hours, I'm as close to rested as I've been for days. I stretch out, bending forward at the waist and dangling my arms so they touch the train carpet. It feels good to let my head sway, to hand control over to gravity.

When I walk to the observation car, the middle-of-the-night energy is gone and replaced by people slowly rising from the floor, bones cracking from disuse as they prepare for the day ahead, whatever it may bring.

The train has been slightly delayed this whole time, but now we're chugging along, speeding through my home state. I can't believe this is the last morning of the trip. That in a few hours, whether I like it or not, I'll be back in Seattle.

I'm not as worried as I was before, though. Because I know that when I get there, I'll have plenty to do. The first of which includes explaining everything that happened this past semester to my parents. Maybe I'll even look for a job working in a greenhouse.

The world didn't end when I left college without knowing

exactly who I am, and it won't end in Seattle.

It can be a new beginning.

"Um, Zoe?"

Aya is standing behind me, her hands clasped in front of her. It's the most toned-down I've seen her.

"How's it going?"

She doesn't say anything about the conversation she must've had with her mom the night before, instead, she holds up the fifth and final Percy Jackson book. "I'm on the last one," she tells me. "But I'm reading it *reeeaaaaally* slowly, because I don't want it to be over."

"You can always reread it," I say.

She looks so incredibly sad then. "But it'll never be the same as reading it for the first time."

I remember what she said at her birthday party, about being scared to turn double digits. Maybe Aya and I aren't so different. I had a breakdown when I turned ten because I knew I'd never be single digits again, and that thrust me into an existential crisis about who I'd be in the future.

But I don't want to think that way anymore. I wasted eighteen years of my life worrying over shit like that, when I could've just been . . . living my life. I don't want Aya to feel that way either.

"Okay, how about this?" I ask after a moment. "Do you *want* to read it really fast?"

She shrugs. "Yeah, but I'm not going to."

"If you want to, you should," I tell her. "Don't save the book just because you're worried you're going to be sad when it's over.

Trust me, I've done that a lot, and it never made me happier."

She stills, then bursts into tears. I immediately want to take back everything I said and give her a giant hug or, like, a pile of pugs.

"Oh my god, no, Aya," I say. "I'm so sorry." I look on in horror as she cries.

"My mom told me everything," she says through sobs, the physical, shaky kind I haven't had since I was a little kid. "And she said you and Oakley were the ones who wanted her to tell me."

I have no idea what to do, but I have the unhelpful thought that Oakley would know.

"I'm so, so sorry," I tell Aya. Then, because it's the only thing that comes to mind: "It's okay."

"It's not," she says, frustrated and sniffing back snot and tears.

"You know what?" I say. "You're right."

She wipes her eyes and looks at me, surprised.

I know it's not my place to apologize on Oakley's behalf, but I at least want to let Aya know how sorry I am about what happened during her party.

"It's not okay. Your mom should've told you that you were moving to Seattle before now. You're allowed to be mad. And you're allowed to be sad."

She rubs at her eyes. "If I finish this book fast, that means the train ride will be over," she says through sniffles. "I don't want to leave."

"But you're heading to Seattle, right?"

Aya nods, her face red and blotchy. "I don't even know anything about the city, and I'm gonna live there now."

"Did you know that *I'm* from Seattle?"

Her eyes go wide. "You are?"

"Yup," I tell her. "And I'll be staying there for a while, so . . ."

Though her cheeks are still streaked with tears, she smiles at this. "So we can have sleepovers!"

"Maybe," I say, because not only can't I imagine a situation in which I, an eighteen-year-old, would be having a sleepover with a freshly-nine-year-old, but also because there's very little chance Nanami will let that happen.

Even if I'm not the one who forced her to tell Aya about moving to Seattle, I was still part of it.

"At least you'll know that I'm close by," I tell her.

"That sounds nice," she says, and I agree.

"By the way," Aya says. "My mom told me to tell you thank you. You know, for the party."

I'm surprised by this, but try not to show it. "Well, tell her that it was my pleasure."

"And she said that in the winter we might take the train again and go to Leavenworth!"

"That's awesome," I tell her, though I'm still suspicious of Nanami.

Leavenworth is this little town that's a couple of hours outside of Seattle. It's popular in the winter because it's in the mountains and always gets snow, and it's designed to look like a quaint Bavarian village.

"This train passes through Leavenworth too!" Aya says. "But

we only get to stop for fifteen minutes, and my mom said that's not enough time to see everything, so that's why we're gonna go back."

"Your mom's right," I say, though that gives me an idea.

Because Leavenworth is basically a little European town.

And right before Oakley told me she was rejoining the Church, she told me she had planned to go to Europe. She wanted to see what she'd only read about in books. Instead, she slept in a crowded hostel in New York.

Maybe she'll never get there, and maybe we'll never see each other after this, but we could have this one afternoon.

Thursday, 6 a.m., Chugging through Washington

There are a few things complicating this plan.

The first is that I don't even know if Oakley's still on the train. The second is that, like Aya said, the stop in Leavenworth will only last a few minutes.

But I can work around both of these complications. I have to at least try.

"Goooood morning, my dear old friends," Edward says over the loudspeaker. "This is your final wake-up announcement from yours truly, Snack Conductor Edward. For the last morning of this glorious trip, I have sticky buns, bagels, and of course, coffee. Come on down and say goodbye! I'll miss you folks!"

For the first time, I'm not vaguely annoyed by Edward's morning announcement. In fact, he's exactly who I want to see.

"Assistant Conductor Zoe!" Edward says when I make my way down to the snack car.

"I earned the assistant conductor title?"

"Absolutely," he says, bowing dramatically. "Where's Oakley? I was going to bestow assistant-conductor-ship upon her too."

I stare down at the freshly mopped snack car floor.

"What happened?" he asks. "Did you two get into a fight?" I nod, holding back tears. "Oh, no no no," he says, coming out from behind the snack counter to give me a hug. I lean into him, and—no surprise here—he's an exceptional hugger.

"I don't even know if she's still on the train," I tell him. "She's from Eastern Washington, so she might be getting off soon."

He pulls away from the hug and stares at me, confused. "I saw her in the sleeper car a little while ago as I was passing through. She looked upset, but she was definitely still there." He laughs to himself. "I guess this explains why she was moping around the corridor."

"Edward," I say, pulling him in for another hug. "I've never loved a person more."

"I'm honored," he says, blushing, as he retreats behind his counter. "Coffee?"

I nod. "And a sticky bun."

He grins. "I knew you'd cave eventually."

When I'm back upstairs, the observation car is fuller than I've ever seen it. I can't blame anyone for wanting to soak in the last bits of the ride, but I'm not feeling that way. I've spent this whole trip staring out the window, and now's not the time for that.

Because Oakley's still on the train.

She didn't get off near Ritzville. It could just be because the train doesn't stop there, or that her parents are in Seattle for some reason, or any number of things she never told me. But still.

I have a chance.

After a few minutes of brainstorming without getting anywhere, I decide to take Virginia up on her offer of knocking on her bedroom door at any time. I don't have to do this alone, and Virginia knows more about this train route than I ever will.

I haven't been in the sleeper car since yesterday, when I was there with Oakley. I push the button that allows me to step between cars, then hurry over to Virginia's room, wishing with all my might that I won't run into Oakley.

"Virginia?" I ask. "You in there?"

"Just a sec!" she shouts from the other side.

She opens the door wearing a bathrobe and slippers, her hair in rollers.

"Did I wake you?"

"No no," she tells me. "I don't sleep. Shall we go back to the observation car?"

We do, and once we've sunk into our seats, she adjusts her bathrobe. "So, what can I do you for?"

"I have an idea," I say. "But I need your help."

She smiles. "Let's hear it."

I tell her about Oakley wanting to see Europe and about Leavenworth and the fact that it's my last chance to make things right with her.

"You want me to help you delay the train for everyone on Thanksgiving Day?" she asks. "So that you can run around a fake Bavarian city with a girl you just met?"

"Um . . . yes?"

She grins. "Count me in. It's not like we were going to arrive in Seattle on time anyway."

"Really?"

"Sure, why not?" She says it like I asked her to bring me a cup of coffee, not find a way to stall a cross-country train. "Do you have any ideas for how to do it?"

"Well, no." I lace my fingers together. "I thought maybe . . . you might have some."

She shakes her head. "Your generation is so lazy, with your phones and medias and this and thats. Back in my day when we wanted to stop a train, we did it ourselves."

I raise my eyebrows but don't say anything.

Finally, she sighs. "Okay, but just this once." She leans forward and grins conspiratorially. "I was thinking I could fake a medical emergency."

"You'd do that?"

"Sure, I dabbled in acting back when I was a young woman. How hard could it be? A little chest clutching and moaning and they'll stop the train for sure."

We discuss the logistics of the plan, including where exactly Virginia should pretend to have her emergency for maximum train-stopping time.

"I can only guarantee you forty-five minutes or so," she says.

"Anything beyond that and the conductor will be forced to do a medical evacuation, and I'm not getting in an ambulance this morning."

"That's all I need," I tell her. "Thank you so much."

"Don't thank me yet," she says. "This still has to work."

She's right, especially because I don't even know if Oakley wants to see me. But I need to talk to her. I need to let her know that, even if she's going back to the Church, these past few days meant something to me and always will.

And yeah, maybe I need to know if they meant something to her too.

Virginia gathers her bathrobe and stands, but I don't follow her to the sleeper car. I need to prepare what I'm going to say to Oakley, and what we can do with forty-five minutes in Leavenworth.

I'm struck with the thought that Oakley would know what to do. That she'd be able to plan all of this without a hitch.

Hopefully I can do the same, since I'm doing it for her.

Eighteen

Thursday, 7 a.m., 20 Minutes outside of Leavenworth, WA

I've spent the past hour doing research, and I know enough now to know that we can't waste our time trying to run to the town on foot—if Oakley agrees to go with me, that is. I've already called a cab to take us from the train station into the town proper, which feels very old-fashioned, but maybe that's part of what will make it a true grand gesture, because that's what this is.

Oakley's a hopeless romantic, and even if those feelings aren't directed toward me, she deserves something cinematic.

Now there's only one thing left to do, and it's the scariest part: I have to actually *talk* to her.

I've walked the path to Oakley's sleeper car a dozen times during this trip, but I've never felt this mix of nausea and excitement. My heart is beating out of my chest as I stand in front of her door.

After a minute, I knock.

"It's fine," Oakley shouts from inside. "I can close the beds myself, but thank you."

"It's me," I say.

She doesn't respond for a beat, and I'm worried she never will.

Until the door opens, and there's Oakley. She looks rough, like she hasn't slept at all. Her hair isn't quite as shiny as it usually is, and her pajamas are rumpled. Despite all that, she's ridiculously cute.

"What?" she asks, voice hostile.

I swallow the bile rising in my throat. "I just wanted you to know that we're going to have a surprise forty-five-minute stop in Leavenworth."

"Are you a psychic now?"

"Yes. I can see the future and it looks fucking bleak." It might be my imagination, but I'm pretty sure she smirks. "Can you come with me?" It's not the speech I had prepared, but right now it has to be enough.

"I'd rather not," she says. "I'm just trying to make it off this train."

"I'm not expecting anything," I say quickly, and for the first time, it's true. "But I have something I want to show you. Please?" I take a deep breath and say, softly, "After everything you showed me?"

She sighs. "Give me five minutes."

I wait in the observation car for Oakley, pacing back and forth. The train is already slowing down in preparation for its arrival at Leavenworth.

Virginia's in the observation car too, preparing for her star turn as "sick woman on train." I glance over at her, and she gives me a reassuring thumbs-up.

Oakley comes out a few minutes later, wearing a knee-length wool coat that's open to reveal a long pale blue, satin spaghetti-strap dress with a black turtleneck underneath. She has on pink lipstick that perfectly complements her skin tone, and a thin rose-gold headband she's placed gently onto her freshly brushed hair.

"Hi," she says, and I can only stare. The dress hugs every part of her body so perfectly.

"Hi," I say back. "You look beautiful."

She doesn't reply; she must know it's true.

"All right, folks, we're almost at Icicle Station in Leavenworth. If Leavenworth's your final destination, please have your personal belongings packed and ready, as we're only stopping to let passengers on and off."

The sun's rising now, and there's a soft glow over the Cascade Mountains as we pull into the station.

Oakley doesn't know what Virginia's about to do, and I maneuver both of us to the door so that we can run off the moment we know the plan worked.

"Oh, dearie!" Virginia calls to one of the conductors who's passing through the car and waking people to ask if they're getting off at Leavenworth. "I'm not feeling too well."

The conductor hurries over and bends to check on her.

I try not to look too interested as Virginia clutches her chest and moans convincingly.

When the train stops, the conductor speaks into his walkie-talkie. Then, a voice comes over the loudspeaker: "If there are any medical personnel on the train, please report to the observation car. I repeat, if there are *any* medical personnel, please report to the observation car." Then, the voice adds, "We will be stopped in Leavenworth slightly longer than expected as we attend to this . . . situation. Apologies for the inconvenience."

Chaos descends after that, with everyone craning their necks to try to catch a glimpse of Virginia, who's now rolling around on the floor. She's *delivering*.

I glance at Oakley. She's staring at Virginia, who winks at both of us, and then the train doors open. Oakley turns to me, confused.

But there's no time to explain. I jump off, hoping fervently that Oakley's following me. Thankfully, she is, and I usher us into the cab I called. Once the door is closed the driver speeds us to the center of Leavenworth. Oakley's staring out the window, at the Cascade Mountains in the background and the early-morning light rising over the faux-Bavarian village situated in the middle of Washington State.

"I'll meet you back here in thirty minutes," the cab driver says as he pulls into the center of town, glancing at his phone.

"Thank you," I say gratefully.

I checked my bank account to make sure I had just enough to pay everyone helping with this deeply unhinged plan. I promised him a week's worth of my greenhouse salary in exchange for the ride when I spoke to the dispatcher on the phone earlier.

Leavenworth is just waking up as we get out of the cab; most of the shop windows are dark, and only one or two people are on the street, walking their tired-looking dogs. There are already

Christmas lights everywhere, sparkling on trees and benches and lampposts. Like Oakley, I've never been to Europe, but maybe it's like this, with quaint streets and brick buildings and mountains looming over everything, framing the landscape with their grandeur.

Or maybe it's nothing like this at all. That would be okay too.

I turn to Oakley, who's staring at all of this in awe. She runs her hands along a sign for an old-fashioned candy shop (a "shoppe," of course), then spins to face me. I'm thrilled to see that she doesn't look mad. She looks almost *hopeful*.

Which means that now is the perfect time to enact the final piece of the plan. I need this to work; I need to show her how much this trip has meant to me.

I knock on the door of a nearby café—one that I called earlier along with the taxi driver, just as they were opening—and a barista brings out a basket of chocolates and an accordion. She places the basket on the ground in front of us, then props the accordion onto her legs. She clears her throat, then starts singing a song in German, the notes breaking the stillness.

"I brought Europe to you," I tell Oakley over the music.

Her eyes are reflecting the pinks and blues of the sky as she holds a gloved hand to her cheek.

"You told me yesterday you wanted to go there," I continue. "That you wanted to do so many things in New York that you weren't able to do." I shake my head. "You gave me some of the best days of my life, and I wanted to give you something in return." I rub my hands against my forearms, the friction warming me. "So yes, this is my attempt at a grand gesture. Maybe a romantic one and maybe not. But a grand gesture nonetheless. I want to give you everything, even if it's just for the next hour. That's more than enough for me, Oakley."

I had more of a speech prepared, but looking into her now-teary face, I speak off the cuff. "I'll never understand what it's like for you, to come from somewhere where they won't accept all of you. Where they *can't* accept it. And I should never have questioned your decision to go back. I mean, I'm going home too, back to a city I haven't always loved, with people who haven't always made me feel at home. We'll both be back in a place that feels safe, and if not safe, at least familiar."

"Zoe," she starts.

"No," I tell her, "I have so much more to say."

She laughs at that, wiping her nose with a gloved hand. "Can I tell you something first?"

I want to say no, because I'll lose momentum on my grand, improvised, romantic speech, but more than anything, I need to hear what she has to say.

"Okay."

"I've felt like a failure my entire life," she says plainly.

"What?" I ask. The accordionist has been playing through all of this, and I remind myself to tip her approximately 400 percent for agreeing to my bizarre request.

"At first, I felt like a failure of a Mormon, because I always asked the wrong questions," she tells me. "Then, I felt like a failure in my schooling, because I was never satisfied with what my parents taught me. Then, and maybe most of all, I felt like a failure in New York, because I told myself it's where I would finally fit in, that I would have a place to call my own with people who understood me." She looks over at the accordion player, who has the decency to at least pretend to not be listening. "I felt like I was marked by my religion, that *that's* what stopped people from getting too close to me. That they thought I wasn't actually queer, because I had grown up in a church that wouldn't accept them. But then I came on the train, and I met you, and you didn't discount me just because I talked about Mormonism. You *wanted* to have those conversations. And it didn't hurt that you're also extremely cute."

My face heats, and I'm hanging on to her every word.

"So then," she continues, "when we had that argument about you not understanding why I want to rejoin the church, all of those feelings of failure came back to me. I felt like you were just going to try to change me or talk me out of my decision. I felt like you'd never really understand." I want to interject, but she continues. "I know that that was my own insecurity, but I didn't know what to do about it. Maybe I still don't."

She takes a small step toward me, and I take that as a sign that I can speak again.

"Oakley." I say her name like a prayer. "I *want* to understand you. I want that so, so badly." I take a deep breath. "This trip . . . it's felt so different from everything else in my life. It's been every good thing about the world rolled up into one. *You're* every good thing. You're a smart ass full of random facts and I could listen to you talk for another hundred years. But I know we only have a few hours, and I should never have said what I did. Because it took time away from us, and that's the only thing we don't have."

I'm crying now, and Oakley's crying too, but I have to keep going, especially if this is my last chance. "I just like you, Oakley. I care about you more than I should, and I need you to know that. I know I might not see you again after this, that I probably *can't*, but I need you to know that I'm never going to forget you or this trip or any moment we've spent together."

Oakley blinks, and for a second, I'm worried she's going to turn around and walk back to the cab.

But then she knocks the breath out of me, wrapping her arms around my neck and crying into the exposed skin above my turtleneck.

"This is the nicest thing anyone's ever done for me," she says as she pulls away and rubs at her eyes. "I'm so sorry, Zoe," she says. "I'm sorry for running away."

"You didn't run away," I tell her. "You just went to the next car over."

She laughs at that, and the sound vibrates into my chest.

"Thank you," she whispers.

"Any time," I say into her hair.

She hugs me so tightly that I almost fall back into a snow pile before righting myself.

"Can I tell you something?" she asks, but of course, she already knows the answer. "The first time I saw you in the dining car, I thought you were the hottest person alive, and I had just failed at acting on being queer in New York, and I wanted you to be my last hoorah before going home." She sighs. "But that wasn't fair to you. Because I *do* have real feelings for you. And once I started to feel those feelings, I knew that would make it a thousand times harder to leave you at the end of this."

I step so close to her that our noses are almost touching. What I want to say is *Then don't leave.* Instead, I ask, "Can I kiss you?" Because I know the former is impossible.

Rather than answering, she tilts her head up and holds her hand against the back of my neck. We make out there, with the accordion playing, for a long, long time.

Nineteen

Thursday, 9 a.m., near Scenic, WA

"I'm fine, I'm fine," Virginia tells the paramedic that the conductor called as Oakley and I sneak back onto the train. "There's no use shoving me into an ambulance." She swats at him, and the man jumps back like she's a rabid animal.

Oakley holds in a laugh as we walk past Virginia and Clint and into a seat in the observation car. The cab ride back to the train was uneventful, except that we were getting dirty looks the whole time from the driver, which may or may not have been because we were making out in the back of his car.

"I can't believe that worked," I whisper to Oakley, gesturing to Virginia and the conductor. Now Clint's getting involved too, helping Virginia up and checking her for scratches as he scowls. Either he's as good an actor as his wife, or Virginia didn't tell him what was going on, but either way, they make an excellent pair.

"*I* can believe it," Oakley says. "Virginia was a professional actor for, like, twenty years."

"What?" I ask, too loudly.

"You didn't know? She had a major character arc on *Grey's Anatomy* in one of the early seasons."

My mouth is all the way open, and I stare at Virginia, wondering what else I don't know about her.

But then I shake that thought away, because I don't need to know everything about this woman. That's not what's important; at the very least, we got to spend time together. I got to speak to someone I never would've had the chance to talk to otherwise. I know about her life on the train, and she knows about mine.

And I'm feeling weirdly okay with that.

Oakley and I sit for a minute, side by side. She reaches out to grab my hand. It's a small gesture, but it fills me with so much warmth. I take her hand, and she squeezes.

"Do you want to come back to my sleeper car?" she asks after a minute. The train is up and running again, and people are grumbling about how we're set to arrive in Seattle a few hours late. No one seems genuinely upset, though.

After all, if they wanted to get home on time, they wouldn't have taken the train.

"Definitely," I say quickly, then follow her back to the sleeper car.

My heart speeds up as we walk there. Once we flop into the seats, things feel hesitant again. We watch Washington pass us by.

"It's weird to think that we've lived in the same state our whole lives," I begin, "when we come from entirely different worlds."

"Is it *that* weird?" she asks, and I know what she's about to say

266

will be obnoxiously smart. "There are more than seven million people living in Washington. We were both raised in minority religions that want nothing to do with each other. You lived in the city and I lived in a small town. It's a miracle that we're here at all, together on this train, in this room."

And before she can say anything else, I lean forward and kiss her. She grabs my waist, and I crawl over so that I'm on her seat straddling her. When that position becomes too uncomfortable, she pushes me up so we're both standing.

We kiss like it's the last time we'll ever have the chance, which it very well may be.

The train lurches forward, and Oakley falls into me, pinning me against the wall.

"Should I pull down the bed?" she whispers.

I nod, and we both help transform the space from a living room to a bedroom in record time.

Oakley laughs, and I stare at her.

"What?"

She's still giggling as she asks, "Should we use the top bunk or the bottom one?"

"I'm not going back on top," I tell her, realizing how it sounds right after I say it.

I had sex with Alden less than a week ago, and I'm not ready to go through that again, no matter how much I might want to do it with Oakley.

"Can we try something a little different?" I whisper into her ear, and she nods, pulling me down for a kiss.

267

We both climb into the bottom bunk and hold each other tightly, making out for a long while.

"Can I take off your dress?" I ask her once we're both warm from our shared body heat.

"Please," she tells me, lifting her arms to help me out. She pulls off her turtleneck next, then her bra. She makes a move to take my shirt off, and I let her, but I keep my sports bra on. It's what I'm most comfortable with right now.

She's looking at me like no one has before, like I'm someone special and sacred. I'm looking at her with the same reverence.

Next come my pants; Oakley helps me slide them off, but the bunk is too short for me to stretch out all the way and in the confusion, she ends up knocking her elbow into my face.

"Are you okay?" she asks, stroking my cheek with her thumb while holding in laughter. I shove her back down on the bed until we're both laughing so hard tears are coming out of our eyes for no real reason other than that it's nice to be this close to someone you care about.

She holds me close and kisses my neck as she asks, "What was your idea?"

I bury my face into her shoulder. "Would you maybe want to . . . like . . ." I take a deep breath. The worst part will be asking for it, but then maybe it'll be good.

Maybe it'll be the best thing I've ever done.

"Could we show each other what feels good? Could we . . ." I can't believe I have to say this. That I'm eighteen years old and so afraid to talk about my own body, about what I want. "We could masturbate in front of each other," I finally manage to spit out.

Once I do, I want to spontaneously combust.

When I work up the courage to look at Oakley, she's smiling. "That sounds good," she says, reassuring me.

"Good," I repeat with a hand on my forehead.

It's cramped on the bottom bunk, but it works. Our legs bump into each other and we laugh and we watch each other's hands move and it's entirely different from how it was with Alden because we're both in control of the situation.

When we're done, Oakley grins at me as she lies back on her pillow, and I climb over to her, kissing my way up from her stomach to her neck to her mouth.

"Was that okay for you?" I ask her.

She nods. "It was perfect."

Oakley nuzzles into me, and I hold her, and I feel big and small and soft and strong all at the same time. Masculine and feminine and peaceful. I don't mind that it's only for right now, because right now is so, so good.

"Oakley?" I ask after a minute. She turns to me, her head buried in my neck as she makes a *hm* sound. "I'm not dating that boy anymore. And I wasn't, really, the whole time we've been on the train." She's frozen against my chest, and I'm sure she can feel my heart beating much too fast for its own good. "It was shitty not to tell you before, but I didn't know how to talk about it. It's over anyway. I called him late last night."

She doesn't say anything, just cuddles me closer.

"Zoe?" she says after another minute, using the same tone of voice with which I said her name.

"Yeah?" I ask, my mouth against her hair.

269

"I don't know if I'm going back."

I sit up. "What?" Then, because I can't help it: "Was what we just did that good?"

She snorts, then sniffles, and when I look up at her she's crying. "I don't know what I want to do," she admits, flustered. "I need more time to think about everything."

I rub her back and wait to see if she'll say more. We sit like that for a minute, and then she says, "I know I told you I felt like I failed at being queer, but now I'm not so sure."

"Personally, I think you're very good at it," I say as I trace her spine from her neck down, down, down, to the small of her back, with its peach-fuzz hairs. "There's no way to be *bad* at it."

I say this for myself as much as her. I've been trying to figure out what's going on with my gender for this whole semester, but maybe it's not as urgent as I thought. Maybe I'll figure it out slowly, or not at all.

Thank you, she mouths, and I kiss her while I can, while she's right in front of me. "I'm going home for Thanksgiving, but then . . . I don't know."

I nod, like this isn't the most revelatory thing she could possibly say.

"Are you doing it for me?" I ask quietly.

I don't know if she heard me, and I'm not sure I want her to.

She shakes her head. "Maybe it would make more sense if I was, but I'm not. I'm doing it for *me*."

"I'm glad to hear that," I tell her honestly. I pull her down with me and wrap an arm around her. "I really, really care about you,

Oakley," I say. "But I want you to make whatever decision feels best for you. And if that means never seeing you again, that's okay."

She tilts her chin so that she's staring into my eyes. "But what if that's not okay with me? What if I want to see you after this trip? What if I want to kiss you and cuddle you and tell you fun facts while you're half asleep?"

"If you wanted that, then I'd want it too." I squeeze her. "I'm happy with any amount of time you'll give me."

She nods into my chest and hugs me closer, like she's trying to break through my skin.

"You don't have to know right now," I tell her. "But maybe we can not know together?"

"That'd be nice," she says as the train rocks us back and forth in a familiar rhythm. "And I can use any pronouns you want when I tell everyone about you and this trip, by the way. Because I *will* be talking about you."

I grin at that. Oakley doesn't care that I don't have everything figured out. She wants to *help* me figure it out.

"Do you think things will be different when we're off the train?" she asks after a minute.

"Well, we'd be able to sleep in an actual bed together, for starters," I tell her, but then I look down and see that she's serious.

"I don't know," I say honestly. "But I can't wait to find out."

Twenty

THURSDAY, 10 A.M., ONE HOUR OUTSIDE OF SEATTLE

Oakley and I lay in bed for a while longer, letting Washington pass by outside our window. Whenever the train slows, she snuggles closer to me, and I pull her in.

"We should go back out there," I whisper to her after a while. "Aya's probably wondering where we are."

She groans but stands up, mostly naked. I turn away, and she laughs. "You can watch me get changed," she says. "If you want. I mean, you saw me . . ." Her face reddens, and I continue looking away out of sheer embarrassment for what she might have said next.

When I turn back around, she's wearing her turtleneck and pulling her dress over her head.

I shiver as I step out from under the warm blankets, then throw my clothes back on. Before we emerge into the hallway, Oakley pushes me against the metal door and wraps her arms around me.

"What's this for?" I ask, laughing.

"You're just very cute," she says into my shirt.

I pull her closer before I reluctantly let go, squeezing her hand as we head into the hallway.

It's the last time we'll walk from the sleeper car to the observation car to see what's going on, to spend time with the random, wonderful people we've met on the train. But that thought doesn't fill me with the same dread that it has in the past. We'll get off the train, and maybe, if I'm lucky, I'll still have Oakley. Or at the very least, I'll have the memories, the party, the slow dancing.

And I'll have new things to look forward to as well.

When we step between the cars, someone shouts, "Surprise," and Oakley and I both startle.

I'm sure they must be trying to surprise someone else, but then I look down, and Aya's there, smiling up at us.

"Come on," she says as she guides me and Oakley to the dining car.

The first thing I see is the crowd of people. Then there's the turkey and the pie and the stuffing laid out over all the tables.

"What's going on?" I ask, turning to Aya.

She shrugs as she sits at one of the booths and pats the seat across from her, motioning for me and Oakley to sit as well.

When I look up, Clint and Virginia are standing there, hand in hand.

"Aya came to us a couple of hours ago," Virginia says. "She wanted us all to have a big dinner together, since we'll be apart tonight."

Oakley and I turn to look at Aya.

"You did this?" I ask her.

"I had to do something for you guys since you gave me the best birthday party ever," she says as she pulls a huge slice of pie onto her plate and digs in, despite the early hour. "And I didn't make the turkey, by the way. That was Mike."

I laugh at the fact that Aya had to clarify that she *didn't* cook a turkey on the train, then turn to Mike, who waves awkwardly. Clearly this was going to be used for his Thanksgiving dinner. I have no idea how he's kept a turkey from going bad, and honestly, I don't want to know.

Some things are meant to remain train mysteries.

"You didn't have to repay us for the party," I tell Aya. "It was our pleasure."

Oakley rubs my back, and I lean my head against her shoulder.

"We did," a voice says from behind me.

I shift in the booth so I can turn around, and Aya's mom is standing there, hands in her pockets. "Thank you for everything you've done for my daughter," she says to me and Oakley.

"And you were right." Nanami directs this part to Oakley, though she glances at Aya as she says it. "I should've told Aya everything from the start."

"You should've," Oakley says harshly. When I squeeze her hand, she adds, "But, uh, thank you."

"Aya's the coolest," I say to Nanami. "And if you ever need a babysitter in Seattle . . ."

"Yes!" Aya shouts, bouncing up and down. "Please, please, please, please?"

"I'll get your number before we leave," Nanami says, and Aya squeals.

Some of the conductors are here too, along with the kitchen staff. Everyone's eating and laughing, and it's like Aya's party again, only this time we're also saying goodbye.

But that's okay. The goodbyes might not be for forever, or maybe they will be, but either way, I got to meet dozens of strangers on this trip who I never would've met if it wasn't for the train.

On Monday, all I wanted was to blend into the background, to not be noticed, because I was so uncomfortable with myself. But I think I accidentally became a main character of this trip, and I'm more than okay with that, because it brought me Oakley, and everyone else.

Edward comes by after a minute and slides into the booth next to Aya. "Thank you so much for your help on our voyage, Assistant Conductor Aya," he says to her, and she beams.

"You're welcome, Conductor." She pulls a piece of paper out from under her butt. "I made this for you." She hands him the butt-warmed paper and he takes it like she just gave him a priceless gem. "It's a picture of us!"

For a second, Edward doesn't react, but then his face reddens, and he bursts into tears.

Aya stares at us with her eyes wide until Edward wipes his cheeks and says, "No one's ever made me anything like this." He folds it into quarters and puts it in his front pocket. "It's so beautiful."

"Can we see?" Oakley asks, and Edward hands the picture to us.

275

It's made from colored pencils, and although Aya has many talents, it's clear that drawing is not one of them. The two figures in the foreground are supposed to be her and Edward, and they're holding hands. Then, behind them, are two other figures, standing close.

"Who are these people?" Oakley asks Aya, pointing to the figures in the background.

"That's you and Zoe!" she says. "I wanted to make a drawing of all of my best train friends, and I wanted to show you two together since you're always holding hands and stuff!"

And now it's my turn to cry. The tears come fast and furious, and Edward and I are blubbering messes, and Oakley pulls me close to her and she's tearing up a little too.

"You guys are weird," Aya says as she watches the three of us sob from her shitty artwork.

"All right, folks," the conductor says over the loudspeaker. "This is it. We're making our final stop at King Street Station in Seattle in approximately twenty minutes. The local weather is forty-five degrees and foggy, and the time is eleven a.m." Then she clears her throat and adds, "It's been a pleasure having you on the Empire Builder. We hope you've had an enjoyable experience, and *please*, for the love of all things holy, do not forget your bags on the train. It'll be a bigger pain for you than it'll be for us."

"Well, I guess it's time to dig in," Clint says from the table next to us when the announcement is done.

Oakley grabs a slice of pie, but I just stare around the car, marveling at all of these people who wanted to have one last meal together. There are Elaine and Alberto/Bert. Elaine is laughing and bouncing as she talks to Jeff. There are Virginia and Clint, sharing a slice of pie. There's the conductor who held the train for us, holding hands with one of the waiters. Everyone is glowing, peacefully eating and talking in the soft morning light.

I'm never going to know everything about all of these people. I don't even know half of their names. But they're the main characters of their own lives. They have people they love and people who love them.

Everyone here is *someone*, which sounds silly but feels like a revelation. They are their own worlds, with their own labels and lives and identities that I will never know and never need to.

"Should we go pack up?" Oakley asks when she's done with her slice of pie.

I nod and we both get up, but we don't leave until we've hugged everyone—Edward and Aya and Clint and Virginia.

"Thank you," I whisper to Virginia as she holds me tightly.

"Don't thank me, kid," she says. "This has been one of the best train rides of my life."

"Seriously?"

"Absolutely," she tells me. "Maybe we'll see you on next year's trip?"

When she first told me about doing this ride every year, I couldn't understand it. But now I do. Now I want to come back.

Even if you do the same thing over and over, you can find new people, new places. Even if it's just for a few days, they can change the course of your life.

277

"Maybe," I tell her, smiling.

I hold Oakley's hand as we walk back to her bedroom. But before we get there, she stops me at our regular spot in the observation car, then tilts her head up to kiss me.

Her hands are on my waist, and I smile down at her. "What was that for?"

"I just wanted to kiss you here," she says. "Where it all started."

"Well, technically it started in the dining car of an entirely different train."

"Dang," she says, making a big show of looking angry at herself. "Should we go back there and make out?"

I roll my eyes and wrap her into me and kiss the top of her head. "Absolutely not."

When we're in her room, she sits me down on the bed and then pushes me into the pillow, flattening her body against mine.

"When are we going to get to do this again?" I ask her after a few minutes.

"Soon," she says with so much certainty. "My parents decided they wanted to spend Thanksgiving with my cousins in Tacoma, so they're meeting me here. I'll head back to Ritzville with them after that and stay for a few weeks but then . . . who knows?"

"Yeah," I say, but I'm worried now.

What if she doesn't leave? What if she decides to return to the Church after all?

She must see the panic on my face because she says, "Zoe, I want you to be part of my life."

I wipe my eyes and nod, leaning into her chest. "Are you

scared?" I ask quietly. "That you might not get your eternal family if you leave?"

Oakley pushes me off her and stares at me intensely. "I don't want you to worry about that."

"That train has left the station," I tell her, and she smirks. But then her face gets serious.

"I want you, Zoe," she says. "Maybe not everything has to be eternal. And right now, I want you so badly. It might not be forever, but nothing has to be."

I nod, and Oakley kisses me harder than she has before, biting my lip and leaving me bruised and wanting more.

"This isn't the last time we're going to get to do that." She grins as she starts throwing her clothes into her suitcase.

"Why are you being so chill about this?" I ask her, worried. "You were so set on going back to the church."

She barely looks up at me as she says, "Because I prayed on it yesterday."

I stare at her. "You did?"

"It's what my parents would always tell me to do when I had to make a tough decision as a kid, and it's what I wanted to do yesterday, after our fight."

"So what happened?"

She takes a breath, and I know she's about to tell me a story. I sit back on the bed, ready to listen.

"Mormons believe that we live a premortal life," she says, and I appreciate that she didn't add, *Did you know?* She's learning. "It was a life where we all lived with our Heavenly Father, and it's part of His big plan of happiness for us. Then we get a physical body so that we can have experiences that God wants us to have, that we couldn't have any other way. We're supposed to learn what's right. We're supposed to sin—do things we know are wrong—so that we can repent and understand the proper path and then rejoin Him."

She stops packing and sits next to me, putting her hand on my thigh in a way that now feels familiar and comforting.

"When I prayed yesterday, I waited to hear a voice, a confirmation, anything." She squeezes my leg. "And I did. I don't know if it was my own thoughts or if it was the Spirit or the conductor or someone else entirely. But I heard a voice, clear as day, that said that caring for someone is not a sin. The voice said that what we did wasn't wrong at all. Because a sin is doing something you know is wrong, but Zoe, I *know* this is right. Every part of my body knows it."

It's the nicest thing anyone's ever said to me. That being with me is right, that what we're doing is holy.

"I agree," I tell her, putting my hand on top of hers, then leaning in and kissing her cheek, and her forehead and her other cheek and her nose and her lips.

She laughs at each kiss, then pulls me back down onto the bed. "We have to get off the train soon," she says.

"Or we could just refuse to leave." I hold her against me. "They'll have to drag us out."

"I like that idea," she says.

But just as we start making out again, the train slows to a stop.

"Folks," the conductor says. "Once again, on behalf of the whole crew, I want to thank you for riding with us. It's been a pleasure and an honor."

"MORE than an honor," Edward says, taking over the loudspeaker for the last time. "Thank you to my friends, new and old, for everything you've given me."

I smile at that and silently thank him one more time too.

I throw my stuff into my suitcase and then, when everything is packed, Oakley and I stare around the room.

"I'll miss her," I say, gesturing to the bunk beds.

"I won't," Oakley says. "I want to make out with you on a California King."

My face reddens at that, but I tell her, "I want that too."

As we step off the train, my legs are stiff and my body aches and I need a shower, but I feel better than I have in a long time.

The air is humid on the platform, and it smells like evergreens and mist and home.

"Wait," Oakley says, grabbing me in the middle of the platform and kissing me.

"You'll text me?" I ask as we pull apart. "Keep me updated about your life?"

"About everything," she promises. "I can even update you on my poops if that's what you want."

"You don't have to do that."

"Too bad," she says as she wheels her suitcase down the platform, toward the station house. "It's already happening."

"Fine," I tell her as I catch up.

281

Right before we walk through the doors of the station, she turns to me once more. "We can talk as much or as little as you want," she says seriously. "But I want to text you good morning. And I want to hear your voice at night. And when I come back to Seattle—*when*, not if—I'm going to make *sure* your dreams are sweet."

"Okay," I tell her, because that's all I can say over the beating of my heart.

Finally, we step through the doors. She looks back at me one more time before she runs over to her mom, who, like I expected, is blond and pretty and wraps her in a hug.

At the other end of the station is my dad, who waves as he walks over to me.

"Have a good trip, bubala?" he asks.

"Not bad," I tell him.

We have a lot to discuss, but for now, I want to live in the glow of what Oakley said to me. I want to feel the ghost of her lips against my mouth for as long as possible.

Right before we're about to leave, I turn around to find Oakley looking back at me.

She waves, and I wave back.

"Who's that?" my dad asks.

I think about lying, about bending the truth. But I'm about to come clean about everything, so I might as well start with this.

"Someone important," I say. "We'll talk about her later."

And with that, we leave the station and head toward our car in the light rain of a Seattle morning.

When I look down at my phone, I have a text:

Oakley: miss you already
Me: you can't miss me
because im right here
for as long as you want me to be

Epilogue

Three Months Later, the Cornell Greenhouse

The *Amorphophallus* couldn't hold itself in any longer. It had waited years for this moment. It had started as a seed, and then the person with the lovely words came, and it grew and grew and grew.

That person had left, but they weren't gone forever. They had gotten a job at a different greenhouse across the country. The *Amorphophallus* knew this because it had roots everywhere. It heard tell from the other plants—this person spoke gentle words to them as well; they helped them grow.

And there was someone else too. A girl who made the person with the lovely words happier than they'd ever been. They would go to the greenhouse together and kiss among the plants. They would hold hands as the person with the lovely words explained that *this* was how you water them and *this* is the best soil and *this* is how they like to be spoken to.

The girl did research of her own; she found scientific papers and read them aloud to the plants. The person with the lovely words would roll their eyes at this, but the plants loved to hear about themselves.

The *Amorphophallus* could feel all of this, could sense the stirring of a new generation of plants and caretakers.

Many small actions of countless people had gotten the *Amorphophallus* here, to the edge of something wonderful.

And so, after years of waiting, it bloomed.

Acknowledgments

This book began as an idea on a long meandering walk in the fall of 2020 (as all my walks were at that time). So much has changed in the ensuing years—in the world, in my life, in this book—and I'm beyond ready to thank everyone who has helped me on this journey.

First of all, to Jim McCarthy, for more than half a decade of working together. You have done so much for me and for this book, and I hope you know how truly, truly grateful I am.

Thank you to Stephanie Guerdan, for all your work and care on the early versions of this story, and for everything you've done to make publishing more equitable.

To Tara Weikum—with your guidance, this book has become something I am immensely proud of, and I cannot thank you enough for all the time you've devoted to both me and this story. You gave me the confidence to dive back into this manuscript, and I appreciate your kindness and incisive edits more than you know.

To Christian Vega, for so patiently answering my questions, and for your thoughtful feedback. Thank you so much for all you've done.

Thank you to everyone at HarperCollins who has helped this

book reach its final destination. Thank you to Jon Howard and Gweneth Morton. Thank you to Sean Cavanagh and Vanessa Nuttry. Thank you to designers Chris Kwon and Alison Klapthor for once again creating such a beautiful cover, and thank you to Natalie Shaw for your illustration; your talent inspires me. Thank you to Shannon Cox and Jenny Lu, as well as Patty Rosati and Mimi Rankin. Thank you to Robin Roy for your careful copyediting, and for noticing an astrological error, which would've been embarrassing for me to publish as a lesbian. Additionally, thank you to the Epic Reads digital team and the Harper Sales team for all your hard work.

Thank you to Marisa Urgo for notes on a very early draft that I am honestly embarrassed you read.

To Jina—this time I only stole one thing from your life and it was the name of your childhood friend. I am writing this days before your wedding and devastated that I can't be there, but just know that when I write books for kids, they're always for you, because I can't separate who I was as a child from who I was as your friend.

Thank you to Zareen for cover advice, and to Ana and Arthur for the beautiful and completely functional apartment in Madrid from which I finished my pass pages. To Gruber for book ideas while deciding whether we should jump over waves or dive under them. To Lena for hearing the idea first, and to Sal for the countless hours spent FaceTiming from our respective childhood bedrooms.

To Cam for playing the blurb game with me, and to Rocky, Christina, and Joelle for commiserating and celebrating.

Thank you to the Portland librarians who have been so kind to me even though I live in the other major city of the left coast, including Lori and Linda (you should probably ask your son about this book).

To Nick at the greenhouse: thank you for not firing me even though I never knew exactly how much each plant needed to be watered. And, of course, thank you to all the other student greenhouse workers.

To Mae Martin for *Feel Good*. To Guy Fieri for officiating gay weddings. To David Archuleta for "Hell Together." To Carly Rae Jepsen and boygenius and John Craigie. To Jacob for reminding me of the Vengaboys. To Cheekface for the song "Best Life," and to Dani and Sal for being as obsessed with it as I was.

To all the transit YouTubers I watch, especially the ones who had Empire Builder videos up when I was stuck at home in 2020. Thank you specifically to Miles in Transit, Tom Thorton, CityNerd (and Gruber for his CityNerd impression). Sorry to the foamers—all the Amtrak inaccuracies are mine (and there are quite a few for the sake of the story). And while we're thanking YouTubers, thank you to the Sickos (iykyk).

Thank you to everyone I met on my own trip on the Empire Builder, specifically Jean (hi!!!!) and my drumming queen who hyped me up at a low point. Thank you to Son of Egg in Rensselaer and the snack car operators who were all so good to me.

Thank you to Marchelle and Sedona who so graciously spoke to me all those many years ago about growing up queer and Mormon. Your stories have been integral to the shape of this book.

Thank you to the many YouTubers and podcasters who are so open with their experiences as Ex/post-Mormons, including Jordan and McKay (my loves), Alyssa Grenfell, and Haley Rawle. Thank you as well to Fundie Fridays for everything you do.

Thank you to Mormon Stories, John Dehlin, everyone who works at the Open Stories Foundation, and all the guests on the podcast who have been brave enough to share their stories. You have changed the way I look at religion and life. Thank you to the CES letter, to the Ex-Mormon subreddit, and to all the kind ex-Mormons, progmos, post-Mormons, and questioners I have spoken to.

Now to thank some people from high school, who hopefully know who they are and how much they impacted me: to Riley and Genieva for being the kindest people. And, of course, thank you so much to Laynie for answering all of our many silly questions about your religion back in the day. It could not have been easy moving to a new place and being an outsider in the way you were, but you handled it with so much grace (and always looked the most put together at every standardized test).

Thank you to my parents, who are not like the ones in this book. Thank you to my grandmas, just because.

Thank you to Zaidie and Uncle Lee, who I wish could read this, and who I love dearly.

Thank you to Chridge, Vy, Maire, James, Mia, Rob, and the rest of the second-floor crew for making my first year of college so bizarre and wonderful and magical.

To Fry, for always being there, and for walking across my

keyboard when something looked wrong (you're always right, and you're always perfect).

To Daniela, who has loved me through every change that has come while writing this book. As I write this, I'm with you in the country where you were born, sitting at a coffee shop and staring lovingly at you!!!! I'm being sappy, but you make me that way. Thank you for introducing me to *Before Sunrise* in 2020 (which I watched for the first time *after* coming up with the idea for this book, shockingly). You are my best life.

To anyone who is actively deconstructing something—their religion, their gender—it's better on the other side.

And finally, to Griffin, without whom this book would not exist for a variety of reasons.

Thank you for teaching me how to shuffle a deck of cards ten years ago. Thank you for firsts, and thank you for lasts. You always said you admired how I kept a journal—how about now?

Truly, truly, truly: thank you for being my friend. You deserve the world, and you're on your way to getting it.